CW00693651

MURDER IN RATCLIFFE

Penny Green Mystery Book 10

EMILY ORGAN

THE PENNY GREEN SERIES

CHAPTER 1

"Tiger has more scratches on her nose," I said as I buttered my toast at breakfast. "She's been in another fight. There are too many cats in Henstridge Place."

"I'm sure she was just telling them who's boss," replied James, looking up from his copy of the *Morning Express*.

"I think they're bullying her because she's new to the area. Poor Tiger."

"She looks all right to me." He glanced over at the cat sitting on the hearthrug cleaning her face. "In fact, she seems quite happy."

"I'm worried about her scratches."

"They merely show that she's been standing her ground in an argument. They're a good sign."

"Scratches are a good sign?"

"Would you rather she simply turned tail and ran away from the other cats?"

"Yes, I would. I can't bear the thought of her getting injured."

"I think it admirable that she's been standing up to them."

"I've seen a rather fat black cat prowling about. I think it belongs to your neighbour, Mrs Harrison."

"*Our* neighbour."

"Oh yes, *our* neighbour."

James and I had been married a month, but I still wasn't fully accustomed to considering his house in St John's Wood my home.

"Mrs Harrison's cat may look large and intimidating," said James, "but I think he's fairly harmless. It's always the strays that cause the trouble."

"I don't suppose there's a great deal we can do about strays."

"Especially when Mr Walpole across the road is determined to feed them."

"Perhaps we should ask him to stop doing so."

"But the strays are rather useful, they keep the rat population down. I once saw a cat with a rat the size of a small dog in its jaws."

"Ugh! Perhaps I should keep Tiger in the house!"

"She needs to learn how to handle herself." James drained his cup of tea. "What do you have planned for today?"

"I need to finish my article on the summer hedgerow for *The Ladies' Miscellaneous*."

A mirthful expression appeared on James's face.

"Oh, don't laugh!" I protested.

"I wasn't laughing!"

"I can tell when you're trying not to, you know."

"Really?"

"Yes, it's obvious. Your eyes crease up and your mouth takes on a funny shape."

"You make me sound so very handsome."

"Stop pulling strange faces, then. If you must laugh at me, please don't try to hide it. My work isn't quite what it used to be, is it?"

"No, it isn't. But I'm sure something more interesting will come along soon."

"I can't imagine what. I envy you going out to work, James. Life has changed so much since we got married."

"Should we trade places?"

"Yes! Although I'm not sure your colleagues would be particularly happy about that."

"It would certainly make their day a little more interesting." He wiped his hands on his serviette. "In fact, I think they'd be more than happy to see you turn up in my place."

I glanced up at the clock on the wall. "You'll be late if you're not careful."

"Yes, I will." He got up from his chair and kissed me goodbye. "There'll be more interesting work for you soon, Penny, and in the meantime you have the book about your father to work on. He can give you a helping hand with it now he's returned."

James departed then Mrs Oliver the housekeeper bustled into the dining room and began rearranging things on the sideboard. This was her usual routine once James had left for work, so she was accustomed to tidying up at this time. Although I was perfectly entitled to ask her to return when I had finished my breakfast, I always felt it would be an imposition to do so.

"Oh, don't mind me, Madam," she said once I had drained my tea and got up from my seat. "You take your time."

"Thank you, Mrs Oliver, but I have things to be getting on with."

"Of course." She smiled and swept away the breakfast dishes as soon as I left the table.

I liked Mrs Oliver, even though she seemed a little set in her ways, having been James's housekeeper for eight years.

Her hair was fair, like mine, and she was of a similar build. We weren't unalike in appearance, in fact, although she was a little older than me and didn't have to wear spectacles.

I grabbed the newspaper and went up to my writing room on the first floor, where my old desk sat beside the window. My view no longer displayed the rooftops of east London, but a suburban, tree-lined street. The houses opposite were large, semi-detached villas covered in cream stucco.

James and I lived in a row of smaller terraced houses. Our home was three storeys high but fairly narrow, and the little yard at the back provided just enough space for a small garden. The sweet peas were in flower and I had placed a little vase of them next to my typewriter.

With two large bookcases and a cupboard, my room provided plenty of space for my belongings. There was also an easy chair beside the fire that Tiger liked to curl up on. Whenever she was feeling watchful, she would sit on the windowsill and observe the comings and goings of milkmen, delivery boys and coalmen. In the afternoons she watched the nursemaids out with their charges. The street had a regular, orderly routine to it that felt quite different from the constant noise that had surrounded my previous home. I had become accustomed to the sound of trains from the nearby Moorgate station and vehicles rumbling along the road at all hours. Now I could hear the trees rustling in the breeze just outside my window, and the air felt decidedly fresher without the lingering odours from breweries and factories.

James and I often took walks in nearby Regent's Park, then headed up onto Primrose Hill, where we could look out over London to see the distant dome of St Paul's Cathedral rising above the pointed spires and smoking chimneys. The cranes and wharves of the docks were just visible to the east. But much as I loved to admire this view, it also left me with a twinge of sadness; a sense that I had taken a step back from all the excitement of London town.

There was no doubt that the neighbourhood was a pleasant one, but perhaps it was a little *too* pleasant; not a great deal happened here as a result. It all felt rather quiet, especially when James was out of the house all day. Sometimes work would take up his evenings and weekends. Having worked with him on a number of cases, I accepted this was the demand his profession placed on him. I had anticipated it and bore him no grudge. However, the excitement of working as a news reporter on a daily newspaper was something I missed greatly. I had enjoyed having my mind occupied, but now I found myself worrying about much more trivial matters, such as how my beloved Tiger was getting on with the neighbourhood cats.

I tried not to feel too downhearted that my days had become a little dull. Although I loved my husband deeply and was delighted to be his wife, day-to-day married life was much as I had feared it would be. I had received a few commissions from various periodicals but being a lady writer, the subject matter usually pertained to fashion or household matters. Requests for articles on the natural world were also quite common. Although not averse to nature, I struggled to find myself becoming overly enthralled by the subject.

I sat at my writing desk and flicked through the *Morning Express*. As I browsed the reports, I envied my former colleagues who were able to write about important worldly matters, such as the British occupation of Egypt and the death of Victor Hugo. Although it wasn't long since I had left the paper, I fondly recalled my visits to the British Library's reading room where I had researched most of my articles. I even missed the short deadlines and the gruffness of my former editor, Mr Sherman.

I folded up the newspaper and set it aside. Then I

retrieved my notes on the summer hedgerow and rolled a sheet of paper into my typewriter.

Tiger strolled into the room, jumped onto the windowsill and began to mew at the birds in the tree.

I hadn't been working for long when a faint acrid smell reached my nose. I wouldn't have paid it much heed in my previous home, but this wasn't the usual smell I associated with St John's Wood. Tiger also noticed it and started sniffing intently at a gap in the window frame. Deeming it offensive to her nose, she jumped down and retreated to her chair.

I got up from my seat and peered out of the window. As I did so, the smell intensified and a great cloud of thick grey smoke billowed over the rooftop.

Something was alight.

CHAPTER 2

I instinctively picked up my notebook and pencil before dashing down the stairs to the front door. Mrs Oliver was presumably out on an errand, there was no sign of her.

As soon as I stepped out into the street, the smell of the fire hit the back of my throat. It wasn't merely the burning of timber or coal; the odour was distinctive. As I looked east, I saw plumes of black smoke rising above the rooftops. It appeared to be coming from Avenue Road, a busy thoroughfare that ran from north-west London down to Regent's Park. I followed behind a couple of maids who also seemed interested in identifying its source. As we walked, more smoke billowed overhead as if being fuelled by a huge pair of bellows. A sickening sensation lurched in my stomach as it occurred to me that somebody might be trapped in the fire.

A short walk brought me to Avenue Road and the view of a house completely ablaze. I could feel the heat of the flames from my position some distance away. It was a large three-storey home on the east side of the street, which backed onto parkland. Black rafters were all that remained of the roof and a chimney teetered dangerously beside them. Bright orange flames flowed out of the upper-storey windows, fuelled by the midsummer breeze.

A steam fire engine painted in red and gold sat in the middle of the road, hissing and clicking as firemen directed two powerful jets of water toward the top of the burning building. Close by, a manual fire engine with several firemen working its pumping levers jettisoned water into the lower storeys. Despite their joint efforts, the water appeared to be having little effect on the flames.

I found myself standing among a sizeable crowd of people. Specks of ash floated toward us, and I had to keep wiping them from my spectacles. The heat was too intense for any onlookers to get close to the house, although some of the gathered children occasionally ran toward it – as if taking part in a dare – only to receive a sharp ticking off from a mother or nursemaid for their trouble.

"That there's one o' them new fire engines," commented a woman standing to my left. She was a broad-shouldered lady of about fifty. Judging by her bonnet and apron, she worked in service at one of the nearby houses. "Powered by steam. Fat lot o' good that's gonna do. Fire's too strong for it."

"Do you know who lives in that house?" I asked her.

"No one. Been standin' empty for months, it 'as."

"That's a relief. Let's hope no one was caught up in the fire."

"Old Steinway died back in March."

"Had he been living there alone?"

She nodded. "'Cept for 'is 'ousekeeper and a maid."

"I wonder how it started."

"Search me, 'though a tramp's been seen round 'ere. He might've 'ad summat to do with it."

"I hope he wasn't in the house when the fire started. Presumably, the place was waiting to be sold."

"I think it were, yeah. But there's been some dispute 'mong the fam'ly. Couldn't agree on 'ow it should be shared out, or somethin' or other. Terrible shame, really. It were a lovely place and now they'll 'ave to pull it all down... if the fire don't completely raze it to the ground first, that is. Then again, I s'pose it were bound to 'appen."

"Why do you say that?"

"Nothin' ever went right for that fam'ly after Mrs Steinway died."

"When was that?"

"Must be over twenty year ago now. Twenty-five, proberly."

As I watched the fireman shovelling coal into the steam engine, I wondered how one family could have endured such a long period of misfortune.

"What went wrong?" I asked.

"Oh, all sorts o' things. The worst of it were Mary, I reckon."

"Who's Mary?"

"Mary Steinway. One o' the daughters. Murdered, she was."

"How awful!"

"That must've been twenty year ago. I remember it, 'cause it 'appened just after that Staple'urst railway accident. D'you remember that?" She surveyed me for a moment before answering her own question. "I don't s'pose you would. You'd only've been a babe back then."

"Not quite, but it's very kind of you to say so."

She laughed. "That's the accident the writer fella Charles Dickens was in. Shook 'im up bad, it did." She suddenly whipped around, her attention diverted elsewhere.

I had a vague recollection of Charles Dickens being involved in a train accident but was unable to recall any of the details.

"That's Mrs Grosvenor callin' me," said the woman, turning back to face me. "I'm the cook at number twenty-four, see," she grinned. "I'm s'posed to be preparin' lunch."

"What happened to Mary Steinway?" I asked.

"She were murdered, like I said. Terrible shame, it were, and they've never caught the killer. I've gotta go. I'll be in trouble now for comin' out 'ere."

I made a few more enquiries about the house once the cook had hurried away. I discovered it was number thirty, and that Mr Steinway had been a retired solicitor. There was no clue as to how the fire had started, although several people repeated the cook's claim that tramps had been seen in the area.

After jotting down a few notes, I walked to the post office on the corner of Townshend Road and St Edmund's Terrace to send a telegram to Mr Sherman at the *Morning Express*. Although I was no longer employed by the newspaper, my former editor had hinted that there was still a possibility I could contribute on an ad hoc basis if I found something newsworthy to write about. I felt sure that Mr Sherman would be interested in publishing a first-hand account of the fire.

I hoped to see Mrs Oliver on my return home so I could find out what she knew about the Steinway family. Unfortunately, she was still out of the house. Before long, a messenger boy arrived with a reply from Mr Sherman informing me that a report on the fire would be most welcome. I hurriedly typed up my article and headed off to catch a train into town.

My walk took me past the long brick wall of Lord's Cricket Ground. A match was being played and I could hear the enthusiastic hum of the crowd. I glanced to the east, where a cloud of smoke was still rising high into the sky. I imagined the cricket spectators watching it drift overhead and wondering where it was coming from.

The train journey from St John's Wood Road train station to Farringdon Street took a quarter of an hour. I travelled in second class and re-read my short report on the fire to pass the time. As I did so, my thoughts returned to Mary Steinway. *What had happened to her? And why had her murderer never been caught?* I realised it was impossible for the police to catch every killer, but I wondered why no one had been apprehended in Mary's case. I felt sure that Scotland Yard would have been involved in the investigation, although it had happened long before James joined the police. I wondered if he had heard anything about the case. *How old had Mary been when she died? And what had the motive for her murder been?*

CHAPTER 3

From Farringdon Street station I caught another train to complete the short journey to Ludgate Hill, which stood at the eastern end of Fleet Street. I reached the *Morning Express* offices an hour after my journey had begun.

"Miss Green!" my former colleague, Edgar Fish, said with a beaming smile. "How are you?"

"It's *Mrs Blakely* now, you fool," Frederick Potter corrected him.

"Oh gosh, I am sorry," replied Edgar. He was a young man with heavy features and small, glinting eyes. "I almost forgot you'd married that schoolboy inspector, Mrs Blakely. Have you been missing us?"

"Of course I have."

"Keeping busy?"

"To a point. Today's been particularly busy, given that a fire broke out just a few streets away from our house."

"And the reporter in you couldn't resist putting pen to paper, eh, Mrs Blakely?"

The door swung open and Mr Sherman marched in,

leaving it to slam behind him, as usual. His shirt sleeves were rolled up and his oiled hair was parted to one side. "Fish! Where are you up to with that report on the cholera in Spain? Oh, good afternoon, Mrs Blakely. How are you keeping?" He greeted me with a smile, which would have been unusual had I still been working for him.

"I'm very well, thank you, sir. Here's my report on the fire, as promised." I handed it to him.

"Thank you very much. Finally, a bit of drama in St John's Wood."

"Fortunately, no one appears to have been caught up in it. The house had been empty for some time, apparently. It belonged to a family by the name of Steinway."

"What was the cause of the fire?"

"There has been no official line on that yet, though there are various reports of vagrants and tramps in the area."

"Let's hope the firemen don't come across any unpleasant surprises as they clear the rubble," he said with a grimace.

"I wondered whether you happened to recall the murder of Miss Mary Steinway, sir?" I asked. "It happened twenty years ago."

"I'd need more detail about the circumstances to jog my memory."

"I'm afraid I don't know anything more than her name and the fact that she was murdered."

"The family name sounds familiar somehow, but perhaps I'm just thinking about pianos."

"Oh, yes. Steinway pianos! That's where I've heard the name," interjected Edgar.

"Do you remember anything about Mary Steinway's murder, Edgar?" I asked.

He shook his head in reply.

"Can't say that I do either," added Frederick. "Twenty years is a long time. I would only have been three."

"What utter nonsense, Potter!" laughed Edgar. "*Twenty-*three, I'd say!"

"I was *not* twenty-three!"

"Her father, George Steinway, died recently," I said to Mr Sherman, choosing to ignore Edgar and Frederick's jokes. "He was a solicitor. I mention Mary Steinway because someone I spoke to today told me her killer was never caught."

"How very sad."

"I'm wondering why, though."

"You seem very interested in the poor woman, Mrs Blakely," observed Mr Sherman.

"I think it rather awful that the circumstances of her death were never uncovered."

"It is indeed. Not terribly unusual, of course, but quite unfair all the same. You're not for a minute entertaining the idea of looking into the case yourself, are you? You have that familiar expression on your face, which I must say worries me somewhat."

"Would you be interested in publishing a report on Mary Steinway's murder if I managed to find out any new information, sir?"

"It would depend on what that new information was. It would have to be something our readers would be interested in, of course. I'm very happy to accept submissions from you on an informal basis, Mrs Blakely, but you'd need to be extremely careful dealing with a murder case. You're not a police officer, remember. You may be married to one, but you can't go about naming suspects and so on. That sort of thing is a matter for the police."

"I realise that, sir."

"I clearly have no way of influencing your decision as to whether you look into the case or not. I shouldn't think anyone has; not even that husband of yours. Neither can I promise to publish any information you find. It might not be newsworthy enough, or we may land ourselves in hot water by writing about a case the police have failed to crack." He paused, then added: "But don't be disheartened. If you do discover something, by all means bring your report in and I'll take a look at it." He checked his watch. "I must go and speak to the compositors about an error in the layout for this morning's edition. Thank you for your report on the fire, Mrs Blakely. It'll appear in tomorrow's edition." He peered over my shoulder at Frederick. "Where have you got to with that story about the Liberals' meeting in Newton Abbot, Potter?"

"Almost done, sir."

"Just make sure it's more interesting than your last report. I know these meetings are inexorably dull, but it's the reporter's role to make them sound interesting." He turned back to me. "Good luck, Mrs Blakely. And you'll be very careful if you do decide to look into Mary Steinway's case, won't you?"

"I will, sir."

As the editor left the room with another slam of the door, Edgar put down his pencil and gave a knowing laugh. "Not content with married life, then, Mrs Blakely?"

"Of course I am."

"Only you're so bored that you've found yourself a twenty-year-old murder case to report on!"

"It's not *boredom*," I retorted. "I simply can't abide the injustice of someone escaping punishment for such a heinous crime."

"That's life, I'm afraid," replied Frederick with a sigh. "It's incredibly unjust."

"It certainly can be, but there's no need to sit back and accept injustice."

"Oh, I don't accept it. I complain about it enough."

"But do you actually *do* anything about it?"

"Sometimes."

"How do you plan to investigate something that happened twenty years ago, Mrs Blakely?" asked Edgar.

"I'll begin by reading through any newspaper reports I can find."

"It happened in 1865, did it? Historical copies of the *Morning Express* might have been able to help you if it had been founded before 1872."

"I suppose I shall have to rely on other newspapers, in that case."

"Other newspapers? You're not permitted to use such a phrase in the newsroom of the *Morning Express*, Mrs Blakely!"

⚜

"I hear there was some drama on Avenue Road today," said James as we sat down to dinner that evening.

Mrs Oliver stood at the sideboard, spooning out our tomato soup.

"I walked over to take a look," he added. "The house has collapsed in on itself and smoke continues to rise from the embers. The fire brigade is still in attendance. I spoke with a few of the firemen and, by all accounts, they've had quite a job to do. The house has been sitting empty for some months, apparently."

"Since March," I said. "When Mr Steinway died."

He gave an impressed nod, then smiled. "You've already started investigating."

"I wrote a brief report on the fire for the *Morning Express*."

"You *have* been busy!"

"Of course. I like to be busy. Did the fire brigade know how the fire was started?"

"There was a broken window in the basement of the building, which suggests someone may have gained entry that way. That said, the window may simply have broken in response to the heat from the fire."

"Several people mentioned seeing tramps in the area."

"Yes, I heard that, too. Perhaps they broke into the building and started the fire accidentally. I don't see why anyone should have wished to do so deliberately."

"I hope anyone who might have been in there managed to get out."

"So do I. Time will tell, I suppose."

"What do you know of the Steinway family?" I asked.

"I'd never heard of them before."

"But they live so close by."

"As do many people, Penny. I couldn't possibly remember the names of all my neighbours!"

"I wasn't sure whether the family was well-known or not. The house was quite large."

"Perhaps they were, but not to me."

"Mr Steinway was a solicitor. Did you hear what happened to his daughter, Mary?"

"No. Should I have?"

"She was murdered."

"Really?"

"And apparently the killer was never caught."

"When was this?"

"Twenty years ago. Around the time of that train accident Charles Dickens was involved in."

Mrs Oliver brought our soup bowls over to the table. "It was in June 1865," she blurted out. "Do please excuse my manners for interrupting, sir, madam, but I remember that train accident happened early in June that year. It was the boat train that picked arrivals up off the boat from France, and it'd been travelling from Folkestone to London. They'd lifted up the line on a viaduct in Kent and were supposed to put it back before the train arrived. But there must have been some mistake, and the train arrived when they weren't expecting it. There'd been a man in place with a red flag to warn the driver, but it turned out he was too close to the bridge and the driver couldn't stop in time. A fair few were injured, and ten poor souls lost their lives that day. Dickens helped tend to them with brandy, along with some water he'd scooped out the river in his hat. Shaken up pretty badly, he was."

"And lucky to escape with his life, by the sound of things," said James. "Do you happen to know anything about the Steinway family, Mrs Oliver?"

"I can only tell you what I've heard, sir, seeing as I didn't move to the area till twelve years ago. I'd heard rumours about the daughter... how she died in east London."

"Do you know what happened to her, exactly?" I asked.

"No. Her mother had died a few years before, and then Mr Steinway married again. I never encountered him myself, but I've heard he lived in that house with the second Mrs Steinway till her death a few years ago. Then he lived in that house on his own, and it's sat there empty since he died. He worked in the law."

"The cook from number twenty-four told me there had been a family dispute over the property."

"Yes, I've heard that too, madam, but I wouldn't know what it was about exactly."

"Have you heard anyone mention tramps in the area?" James asked her.

"Foreigners, apparently. Yes, they've been seen about. I haven't seen any myself, but I've heard about them. They've been known to make themselves at home in empty houses. It never does for a house to stand there, forgotten about. I bet those foreigners started that fire. Enjoy your soup, sir, madam."

Once Mrs Oliver had left the dining room, I shared my

plan to find out more about the case. "I could write about it for the *Morning Express* if I manage to uncover new information," I said, stirring my soup.

James's brow furrowed. "What sort of information?"

"I don't know yet. That's why I'd like to look into it."

He sighed. "I'm sure there's a very good reason why the police were unable to identify the culprit at the time. I don't know what you'd be able to do differently, Penny, especially twenty years later."

"Perhaps a simple fact was overlooked."

"It's possible, I suppose."

"I'll pay the reading room a visit tomorrow and look at the reports from the inquest. That should give me a better idea of what may have happened."

"It might be interesting to find out some of the facts of the case, but I really don't see why you'd want to spend any time on this, Penny. It was so long ago."

"I don't like the fact that the person responsible for Mary's death has gone unpunished all this time."

"I shouldn't think anyone would like that fact. However, it's worth considering that the culprit may have committed murder a second time and been hanged for it. Or he could be in prison for another offence. I should think it quite likely that he continued his life of criminality and was eventually caught."

"But that's just speculation. Don't you at least think it would be interesting to find out?"

"I imagine it'd be rather difficult." He buttered a slice of bread. "And even if you did discover something, you'd need to be careful, Penny. Mary Steinway was murdered. You might unwittingly stir up trouble if you delve too deep. Someone out there is capable of committing murder and has already got away with it for twenty years. How do you think he'd react if he found out you were trying to track him down?"

"Didn't you just tell me the culprit was likely either to have been hanged or to be in prison?"

"Yes, but he may have associates. Oh, I don't know." He sat back in his chair, still holding the butter knife. "If you're determined to find out more about this, Penny, then why not? But do please be careful."

CHAPTER 4

A smile spread across my face as I stepped inside the circular reading room at the British Library the following day. Its familiarity served as an immediate comfort to me, having spent many hours working beneath its domed ceiling in the not-so-distant past. Summer sunlight filtered through the windows in the dome, giving readers at their desks plenty of light by which to work. I envied their study, wishing I, too, had interesting topics to research. I secretly felt pleased that I had found a reason to return.

I glanced around for my friend Francis Edwards and eventually spotted him in the upper gallery, which encircled the room. I waved my hand and it wasn't long before the movement caught his eye.

He descended the staircase and walked over to meet me with a grin on his face. "Penny," he whispered, pushing a flop of sandy hair away from his spectacles. His face was still a little sunburned from his recent South American expedition to find my father, who had been missing for many years. "How are you?"

"I'm very well, thank you, Francis, and pleased to be back

here again. I was wondering whether you could give me a hand in the newspaper reading room."

"Of course."

Our whispers caught the attention of a man sitting close by, who glared at us. Francis and I swiftly headed toward the newspaper reading room.

"What is it you're looking for?" he asked as we surveyed the shelves of heavy leather-bound volumes.

"Newspapers from 1865. June 1865, to be precise. I would have started with the *Morning Express*, but it didn't exist back then."

"Will *The Times* do?"

"It's not as good as the *Morning Express*," I replied with a smile, "but it'll have to do."

Francis humoured me with a chuckle as he pulled over a nearby footstool, clambered onto it and lifted the relevant volume down. "Will you be all right with this?" he asked, carrying it over to a nearby table. "It's rather heavy."

"I'll be fine. Thank you, Francis."

We exchanged a smile.

I wanted to ask whether he had seen my sister, Eliza, of late. Since our father's return from Colombia, she and I had different opinions of him. Whereas she felt resentful about his failure to contact us, I had wanted to understand what he had been through. Therefore, the hushed environment of the British Library was no place for me to mention Eliza, though I knew that she and Francis had been growing closer. I merely thanked him again for his assistance and began my work.

"I can't bring myself to speak to Father yet," Eliza had said during our last conversation. "I greeted him at your wedding, Penelope, and that's all I've been able to do. I struggle to look at him; to think about him, even. He allowed us to believe he was dead for ten years!"

We had been strolling alongside the Serpentine in Hyde Park, a short walk from Eliza's Bayswater home. The trees were in full leaf, and laughter had drifted across the water as people paddled about in their boats.

"Perhaps it would help if you were to hear Father's side of the story," I suggested.

"Has it helped you?"

"A little."

"You seem to have forgotten what he did rather swiftly, Penelope. You even offered him your old room in Milton Street."

"I happened to think it a sensible offer, given that he had nowhere else to stay."

"But that was entirely his fault. He turned up in London completely unannounced. And at your wedding, of all places. He completely upstaged you on your special day!"

"I didn't feel upstaged, Ellie. Besides, offering him my room made sense. I was moving into James's home and Mrs Garnett needed a new tenant. She's over the moon to have Father staying under her roof."

"I can't think why."

"Because he was so well-known before he went missing, and he has many interesting tales to tell."

"It's quite clear to me that you've already forgiven him."

"Not completely; it isn't that simple. There's still a lot to understand about the past ten years. But it makes sense to spend a bit of time getting to know him, don't you think?"

"We already know him. He's our father."

"He's not the father we once knew. I don't know whether his fall down the ravine had something to do with it or whether the tribal life he's led for the past ten years has changed him. I suspect a bit of both. Can't you at least visit to hear his version of events?"

"Does it vary a great deal from what Francis has already told us?"

"Not a great deal, no."

"Then that's all I need to know."

"But he can fill in the gaps for you."

"I feel as though I know enough at the present time. And I can't help but remember the fact that he has behaved abominably. He's caused us untold suffering, not to mention Mother. He can't simply turn up uninvited and expect us all to forgive him."

"That wasn't the reason he travelled here."

"What was the reason?"

"To see us."

"But he's had ten years to do that! He only returned because he was discovered by Francis and felt it would look bad if he didn't make some sort of effort to see us. And now he thinks I'm about to accept his request to meet when he didn't even bother to write all those years! I have no interest in making him feel better about what he's done."

"I don't think he'll ever feel better about it. There's no doubt that it weighs heavily on his mind."

"And so it should!"

"But don't you at least want to hear directly from him? I know it's difficult and uncomfortable, but sometimes we have to face these things."

"I know what it's like to deal with difficult and uncomfortable emotions, Penelope. My husband is in the process of divorcing me! And quite honestly, I need all the energy I have for that rather than wasting my time listening to Father's pitiful excuses."

"He wasn't making excuses when I spoke to him, Ellie, and he wasn't pitiful either. He was quite rational, in fact." I followed this last statement with a sigh and looked out over the lake, where the sunlight dazzled in the ripples of water. I understood why Eliza was so upset, but I didn't share her anger. I had sensed that Father was filled with sorrow and regret when he turned up at my wedding. Perhaps a cynic would suggest that his demeanour had been carefully orchestrated to convey such an impression, but I felt his manner had been genuine. Besides, I hadn't seen the sense in remaining angry with him; it wouldn't have achieved anything. In fact, there was a danger it would have driven him away again, and then we would have lost him forever. At least we finally had an opportunity to build a relationship with him again. What divided me and Eliza was the degree to which we were willing to overlook his flaws.

"Has he asked you to persuade me to visit him?" she asked.

"No. He understands why you're upset with him."

"Good. That's something, I suppose."

"He isn't expecting you to forgive him. He's merely hoping to see you again before he returns to Colombia."

"He's going back, then?"

"So he says. He has a wife and children there, after all."

"*Wife?* They're not married in the eyes of the law."

"He's told me quite a bit about her."

"That's another reason I don't want to see him. I don't want to hear a thing about her! I have no interest in that at all. He chose *her* over *us*. That tells me everything I need to know."

"He was going through a very difficult time, Ellie."

"Weren't we all? I see you've received quite the sob story from him, Penelope."

"It wasn't a sob story. He has certainly treated us badly, but he's still our father, and I felt we should at least give him the opportunity to explain himself. But I can see that you're quite determined not to have anything to do with him, so I shall respect your decision."

"You think I should meet him? That I have an obligation to do so?"

"We only have one father, Ellie."

She wiped a tear from her eye. "He has six children now. Why should he even care about us?"

"He cares about all his children."

"Enough to allow his eldest two to believe him dead. I'm quite sure James agrees that you're making a mistake in meeting with Father. I haven't heard that husband of yours impart any warm words about him."

"He's angry with him, just as you are."

"It seems you're the only one who is capable of showing him any generosity, Penelope. Doesn't that make you wonder whether you're doing the right thing after all?"

CHAPTER 5

James returned home late that evening. Mrs Oliver had prepared some supper, which he ate at a small table in the front room while I told him what I had learned about Mary Steinway from the reading room newspaper reports.

"I know a lot more today than I did yesterday," I said.

"And you've written a lot more, too, judging by all those pages of notes."

I glanced down at the pile of papers that lay on the settee next to me. "Yes, I have written rather a lot, but then it's quite a fascinating case."

"Any idea why the police didn't catch the culprit?"

"Let me tell you the facts I've gleaned first."

"Ah, here it comes," he grinned. "You're going to see if I can solve it while I sit here eating my mutton chops, are you?"

"It's worth a try, don't you think?"

"Although I have a fair idea that you're joking with me, I can never be too sure with you, Penny."

"She wasn't known as Mary Steinway when she died," I said. "She called herself Jane Stroud."

"Had she married?"

"No."

"Interesting. People who change their names often have something to hide."

"She died in east London, as Mrs Oliver told us, aged just twenty-two. She died at her lodgings on Harris Terrace, just off St George Street."

James paused with his fork raised halfway to his mouth. "That's not the St George Street I'm thinking of, is it?"

"If you mean the street once known as the Ratcliffe Highway, then yes, it is."

"Good grief! How did a girl from a nice family in St John's Wood end up *there*?"

Ratcliffe Highway was well-known for its bawdy alehouses and dancing halls, where sailors from the docks went to meet women generally described as 'unfortunate'. The area had gained greater notoriety in 1811, when seven people were murdered in separate attacks against two families, the suspect had then committed suicide in jail before the case went to trial. Recent attempts to improve the street had met with moderate success, but it had failed to lose its seedy reputation.

"The newspaper reports didn't explain how she ended up there," I said. "That's something I'll need to find out."

"Why's that?"

"Because I think the solution to this mystery must lie in Mary's tragic story."

"I'm sure it must. No doubt the police looked into it all at the time, though. What did the inquest report say?"

"That Jane Stroud, as she was then known, passed away on the evening of Saturday the tenth of June 1865 after being taken ill at the White Swan public house."

James gave a groan. "Otherwise known as Paddy's Goose; possibly the worst alehouse on the worst street in the whole of London! Did it suggest that seamen were in the habit of paying for her company?"

"There was no suggestion from the inquest report that she was an unfortunate. She appears to have made her money from thieving."

"Oh dear. Her solicitor father wouldn't have taken kindly to that."

"He didn't. By the time of her death, she had become estranged from most of her family. When she was taken ill in the public house, it was first thought that she was suffering from the effects of drink. She was known to be quite a drinker. Her lodgings were located in the courtyard behind the alehouse, so her landlady's daughter, Miss Sally Walcot, helped her home. By the time she got there she was too insensible to climb the stairs to her room, so Sally and Mrs Walcot had to put her in Mrs Walcot's room on the ground floor. At that point, Jane was gripped by violent convulsions, and her landlady grew so concerned that she asked Sally to fetch a doctor.

"At the inquest, Mrs Walcot said the convulsions came and went, but that each time they returned it was with a new ferocity. She said Jane's eyes were fixed wide open and her face was forced into a wide grimace. As the convulsions reached their very worst point, Jane's body became rigid and her back arched. It must have been horribly distressing for Jane, as well as for the people attending to her."

"How awful. Was it poison?"

"Yes."

"Strychnine?"

"How did you guess?"

"Various types of poison can cause convulsions, but the arched back is quite a distinctive symptom of strychnine poisoning, as is the fixed grimace. Both are caused by strong muscle spasms."

I smiled. "You should be a police doctor."

"No, thank you."

"The doctor who attended to Jane Stroud believed her symptoms could either have been caused by poisoning or tetanus," I continued. "But having determined that the onset had been extremely sudden, he correctly deduced she had been poisoned and tried to feed her a charcoal biscuit. Apparently, charcoal can reverse the effects of strychnine poisoning, but in this case the poison had already taken too much of a hold. The doctor ordered that Jane be taken to the London Hospital in Whitechapel. A cab was summoned, but her condition rapidly worsened and it was then that she sadly died."

"What a horrible way to go," said James. His mutton chop remained half-eaten. "I take it strychnine poisoning was confirmed at the post-mortem?"

"Yes, and it was suggested that the strychnine may have been placed in Jane's drink at the alehouse."

"And in such a rowdy, chaotic place as the White Swan, I imagine it was impossible to find out who had put it there."

"There was a suspect, but never a clear motive."

"Who was the suspect?"

"A friend of Jane's, Miss Molly Gardstein. She was about the same age."

"What became of her?"

"She was nowhere to be found after Jane's death."

"You mean to say that she implicated herself by running off somewhere?"

"Yes. No one could prove that she had anything to do with the murder, but it seemed rather suspicious when she suddenly vanished."

"And you said there was no obvious motive."

"There were rumours the two women had fallen out, but

apparently that was a fairly common occurrence for the sorry pair."

"Then the jury presumably returned a verdict of murder by person or persons unknown, and the police were left to get on with their investigation."

"Except they didn't appear to do a great deal more after that."

"I'm sure they must have done."

"They didn't even manage to find Molly Gardstein."

"She had presumably hidden herself rather well. Was she ever found, I wonder? She could be just about anywhere by now, I suppose, if she's still alive."

"If she were the same age as Jane, she'd be forty-two by now. It's fairly likely she's still alive."

"And you're going to look for her, are you?"

"I don't know yet, but someone must know what became of her."

"If she's kept herself hidden for twenty years, I'd say she must be rather good at it."

"But no one's really been looking for her for twenty years, have they? The police would have searched for a little while after Jane's death, but for how long do you think they would have done so? No longer than six months, I'd say."

"I'm sure they wouldn't have lost interest in the case after a mere six months."

"I'm not suggesting they lost interest, but I'm sure they would only have searched for a limited amount of time. No doubt they had other work to be getting on with, and perhaps they hoped someone would eventually contact them with information on Molly's whereabouts."

James sighed. "Yes, I suppose that sounds plausible. Much as I'd like to think they did their very best, they could only have continued searching for one person for so long."

"I wonder if they looked for any other suspects."

"I'm sure they did."

"I imagine it would be quite easy to find that out."

"Why are you looking at me in that way? Are you insinu-ating that it would be quite easy for an inspector at Scotland Yard to ask H Division about their old investigation?"

"Wouldn't it?"

"No, Penny, it wouldn't! Certainly not in an official capac-ity, that's for sure. Doing so would suggest that they hadn't done a thorough job and that I wished to meddle in their case. It wouldn't look right at all."

"How about in an unofficial capacity?"

"I don't think there is such a thing. I must be very careful about the way I conduct myself, Penny, especially now. I can't be seen to be using my influence to carry out investigations based on the whims of my new wife."

"Oh."

"Well, don't you agree?"

"Not entirely. I'm sure there must be something you could do to assist me."

"This murder happened twenty years ago. There's very little that I or anyone from H Division can do about it now. Besides, we're rather busy with the cases we're currently working on. What do you think we could possibly do that hasn't already been done?"

"You could find someone who felt unable to speak up at the time."

"Such as who? That would be like trying to find a needle in a haystack."

"There's quite a lot of information in the inquest report."

"If the news reporters reported their findings accurately, that is. They don't always get their facts right."

"Some may not, but others are very good indeed!"

He smiled. "Maybe so, but I think the chances of you being able to solve this case now are very slim."

"I could go and speak to H Division myself."

"I suppose you could, but I'm not sure how much time they'd be prepared to offer you, especially considering the age of this case."

I felt my enthusiasm beginning to wane. "I think you're just trying to put me off, James."

"Why would I want to do that?"

"You think I'm only interested in looking into it because I'm bored."

"I didn't say that. But if you were as busy now as you were at the *Morning Express,* I don't believe you would have the time to look into a twenty-year-old murder case. *Are* you bored?"

"No, not at all! I'm very happy with our life here." I went over and gave him a kiss. Then I sat on the arm of his chair with my arms around his shoulders and stared at his half-consumed supper. "But there's only so much time I can spend writing about summer hedgerows," I said eventually. "Perhaps I am bored. I certainly miss my old work... the work we used to do together. I'd like something more interesting to focus on, and if I were able to make some progress with this, maybe I could sell the articles to a newspaper or periodical and make a bit of money at the same time. I could make a start, at least. Perhaps I'll pay a visit to St George Street. I know where Jane Stroud's lodgings were, and where the White Swan is."

"Yes, and very pleasant places they must be, too." James turned his face toward mine. "It's not the sort of place you want to go walking around asking questions, Penny."

"You're forgetting the work I recently did in St Giles's Rookery."

"No, I certainly haven't forgotten that."

"And the cases in Bermondsey and Shoreditch."

"I remember them all. But there's no need for you to go to those sorts of places any more."

"I know that."

"But you want to, don't you?"

"I want to find out what happened to Mary Steinway. Not just in terms of her death, but her life as well. How did she end up on Ratcliffe Highway? And why did she call herself Jane Stroud?"

James shrugged. "If anyone's able to find that out it'll be you, Penny."

CHAPTER 6

The heavy grey clouds threatened rain as I descended the steps from Leman Street train station, just a short journey east from the centre of London. I looked in my carpet bag to check for my umbrella. Disappointed to find that I had forgotten it, I began to make my way toward the street that had once been known as Ratcliffe Highway.

My route took me through Wellhouse Square, where the sickly odour of refining sugar hung in the air. Most of the sugar bakers were German, and I caught glimpses of them, shirtless due to the heat of their work, through the windows of the tall, brick-built refineries.

A great number of Jews lived in this area, the most recent inhabitants having recently fled from Russia and the eastern states of Europe. Little oblong mezuzahs had been attached to the doorposts of coffee shops, kosher butchers' shops, Hebrew bookshops, confectioners' stands and clothing wholesalers. Part of me wished I could read Hebrew so I could work out what they said.

Pleasant scents drifted over from the fried fish shops and

bakeries, tempting me to indulge, but I continued on my way, resolving not to partake until I had completed my search for Mary Steinway's landlady.

It wasn't long before I reached St George Street; a busy place that I imagined was more pleasant to visit during the day, as I was doing, than at night. The large warehouses of Western Dock loomed to the south, while the street itself was lined with little shops, many offering useful services to visiting sailors. I noticed a number of tattoo parlours, laundries, boot repairer stores, tailors' shops, tobacconists and hairdressing salons packed in among the many public houses. People of various skin colours, speaking languages I could never hope to understand, were busy milling around about me. It seemed as though the ships beyond the dockyard wall had rounded up every race from around the globe and brought them ashore to this tiny piece of London.

I looked out for the White Swan alehouse, which backed on to Harris Terrace, where Mary Steinway had lived before she died. Three men were rolling barrels off a wagon outside the Jolly Sailor alehouse and lowering them through a trap-door in the pavement to the cellar. Beyond the alehouse sat the premises of famous animal importer Charles Jamrach. The door stood open and an acrid animal odour wafted through it, accompanied by the chatter of exotic birds. A famous event had occurred on this street thirty years previously, when a boy had been snatched up by a tiger that had escaped from Jamrach's shop. Fortunately, the boy had been rescued unharmed and the tiger was sold to a circus.

Continuing my search for Harris Terrace, I soon reached the junction with Betts Street. Glancing across the road, I spotted an inconspicuous chandler's shop. The building had been a linen draper's shop back in 1811, when it became the scene of the first Ratcliffe Highway murders. The poor Marr family had lost their lives there one dark December evening.

I paused for a moment to acknowledge the tragedy before continuing on my way.

I refused an invitation to purchase lucky heather, ignored several coarse remarks from a group of sailors outside the Royal Crown and eventually began to wonder whether I had walked past the White Swan without noticing. I was almost ready to turn back when I reached a narrow three-storey building with a timbered facade at street level and four large sash windows above it. Filthy velvet curtains hung at the windows, and the stale smell of beer and tobacco smoke lingered in the doorway. Sitting on top of the building was the statue of a swan, its long, elegant neck silhouetted against the foreboding grey clouds. I passed the alehouse and a small shopfront before reaching a squalid alleyway marked Harris Terrace.

I was compelled to hold my breath in the alleyway as it smelled like a latrine. It opened up into a dismal courtyard lined with cramped, wooden-fronted lodging houses. The inquest reports stated that Mary Steinway had lived at number four prior to her death. I walked on, unable to spot any numbers on the doors. Two women who had previously been engaged in animated conversation paused to stare at me. Their heavily rouged faces and colourful clothing gave me an indication of their profession.

"Can I 'elp yer, madam?" one of the women asked. Her face was gaunt and her hair looked unnaturally thick and shiny, as though it were a wig.

"I'm looking for number four," I replied. "In fact, I'm looking for Mrs Walcot, if she still lives here."

"Yeah, she's still 'ere." The woman used the clay pipe she was holding to point to the far end of the courtyard. "It's that one wi' the laundry outside."

I thanked her before approaching the building she had

pointed out. Various bedraggled items of clothing dangled from a pole that protruded from above a rickety window.

I hadn't expected it to be so easy to find Mrs Walcot twenty years after Mary Steinway's death, and I felt a smile appear on my face when she answered the door.

"You ain't after a room, are yer?" she asked, the heavy lines on her forehead sunk into a scowl. Her sharp eyes looked me up and down, no doubt noting my smart skirt and jacket. "I ain't int'rested in followin' Jesus, if that's why yer 'ere. Far too late to be savin' the likes o' me!" Her thin mouth broke into a wide grin and she gave a loud cackle. The few teeth she still had were stained black.

"I'm a writer," I explained. "A journalist. I write for newspapers. My name is Mrs Blakely."

Her face became sullen and she folded her arms. "What d'yer want wi' me, then?"

"I'd like to speak to you about Mary Steinway... or Jane Stroud, as she called herself at the time of her death." I held my breath, unsure how my mentioning the poor girl's name would be received.

Mrs Walcot sniffed, then smoothed down her thin, silvery hair as she gave this some thought.

"We 'ad lots o' them noospapers 'ere when she died. You're twenny years too late, miss!" She laughed again.

I smiled, hoping she would warm to me.

"What d'yer wanna know abaht 'er, anyway?"

"I'm interested in the case because her murderer was never caught."

"No, she weren't."

"*She?*"

"It were that Molly Gardstein."

"You believe she murdered Jane Stroud, do you?"

"Either that or she jus' 'appened to take 'erself off ter get a bit o' sea air. Took a little 'oliday, like we all does when a good friend's jus' died."

"She went to the coast?"

"'Ow should I know? No one knows where she's went. Jane were dead and Molly Gardstein weren't nowhere ter be seen. Make of it what yer will."

"Would you mind telling me what happened that evening?"

"I can't tell you nothin' I ain't told other folks before."

"My hope is that if I can write an article about the sad incident, it might encourage someone who knows what happened to speak to the police."

"What? After twenny years?"

"There may be someone who was too afraid to speak up back then, but life has no doubt changed for them now, so they might be willing to share some important information."

She laughed. "'Opin' for quite a lot, ain't yer, Mrs Blakely? A miracle, I'd say." She stepped back into her hallway and hollered "Sally!" up a flight of narrow wooden stairs.

"Do you think she can help?" I asked her.

"Dunno. She's me daughter, but I'll let you decide if she's any 'elp or not. Yer'd better come in."

CHAPTER 7

A short while later I found myself seated on a wooden chair beside a little iron stove in Mrs Walcot's small kitchen. The floorboards were covered in oilcloth, and the faded wallpaper was curled and torn at the edges. A single window, set high in the wall, allowed a small amount of dim, grey light to filter in. Despite the stricken appearance of the place, there was a faint scent of carbolic soap, suggesting that Mrs Walcot tried to keep it as clean as she could. She laid a fresh tablecloth over an old but well-polished table and poured tea from a teapot with a chipped spout.

"How long have you lived here?" I asked.

"Thir'y years. Ma and pa left me this 'ouse."

"You own it, then?"

"Yeah. I'm lucky enough ter be a lady o' property!" She laughed. "I wouldn't never entertain the idea o' leavin' this place. I knows a lot o' people ain't got much ter say about it, but I reckin it's got a lot better over the years. Int'restin' people passin' through, mind. Yer never knows who yer gonna meet next."

"We don't often get visits from gentlewimmin like

yerself," commented Sally Walcot, a broad-shouldered woman who had slumped herself in one of the wooden chairs. She had the same sharp eyes and thin lips as her mother, but a heavier jaw. There was something about her that reminded me of a pugilist, with her thick forearms and large hands. I guessed she was about forty years of age.

"I don't consider myself a gentlewoman," I replied.

"We get them ones off'rin' chari'y, don't we, Sal?" said Mrs Walcot as she handed me a tin cup filled with tea. "But they're the ones what want you ter start worshippin' Jesus in return fer it."

"Jesus ain't done nothin' for the likes of us," said her daughter.

"That's 'cause we ain't been followin' 'im," responded her mother. "If we did, we'd 'ave one o' them big 'ouses up the West End. We'd be livin' up Mayfair way, Sal!" She gave another of her cackles and settled herself in a chair opposite me, which shifted a little as she moved. "Oh, I got the wobbly one," she commented. "Give up on me one o' these days, it will. I'm gonna live longer'n this chair, I'm certain of it. Don't yer reckon I'll outlive it, Sal?"

"I 'ope not."

"She's only teasin'," Mrs Walcot explained when she noticed my surprised expression. "She'd miss her old ma if I died tomorra."

"Says who?" replied her daughter.

"Says me. Now, mind yer manners, Sal. We gotta tell Mrs Blakely all what's 'appened wi' Jane Stroud. Remember 'er?"

"'Ow could I forget?"

"Mrs Blakely wants to know all about 'er. She's writin' summat in the noospaper and she's 'opin' someone's gonna tell the police what they know abaht it. Reckons they might even track dahn that Molly Gardstein after all them years."

Miss Walcot huffed derisively.

"Watch it, Sal! Yer don't want Mrs Blakely writin' all abaht yer bad manners in the noospaper, do yer? Sit up straight like I've always taught yer. Yer'll get an 'ump in yer back sittin' like that."

It took me a while to steer the conversation around to the evening of Mary Steinway's death, but I eventually managed to obtain a reasonable account from Mrs Walcot and her daughter.

"Taken ill dahn Paddy's Goose, she were," said the landlady.

"That's the White Swan, isn't it?"

"Yeah. Jus' over there, it is." She gestured in the direction of the courtyard. "Sal was there an' all."

"It were a normal night," said Miss Walcot. "Busy like it always was, an' a lot o' dancin'. Jane liked dancin', but she weren't feelin' right that night. She got ter swayin' about, and then she went asittin' on the floor. I tried to get 'er up and told her not ter go sittin' there, case she got trod on. That's when she asked me to 'elp 'er."

Mrs Walcot continued the narrative. "First thing I know, Sal's hammerin' on me door sayin' as we gotta get 'er in, 'cause she's had too much ter drink. Well, I seen plenty o' people what's had too much to drink in my time, and they dint none of 'em look like Jane did that night. Cryin' out, she were, like she's in pain. Sal 'ad two sailors 'elpin' 'er, and there still weren't no chance of us gettin' Jane up them stairs to 'er room, so we put 'er in mine, just by the door. We got her on the bed but she were senseless by that point. Foamin' at the mouth, she was. I told Sal to fetch the doctor, then I tried gettin' Jane ter take some water. Her jaw was all locked up stiff, so I couldn't get no water or nothin' in her mouth. I ain't never seen anythin' so awful in all me days. She was cryin'; said she dint know what was wrong wiv 'er. Then them terrible spasms took ahold. So strong, they was, that she bent right back on 'erself. She 'ad this 'orrible grin fixed right across her face. Her cheeks was all red and her eyes was bulgin' out their sockets."

Mrs Walcot shuddered and took a large gulp of tea. "The cries o' the poor woman," she continued with a shake of her head. "I figured as she might be birthin' a baby, even though she never looked like she was wi' child. Then I reckoned the devil'd possessed her. I made the sign o' the cross, but that dint do nothin'. When the doctor arrived, I told 'im we needed a priest. I said, 'The devil's 'ad ahold of her.' He's told me it weren't nothin' ter do with the devil, but he dint like the look of 'er one bit.

"Then the doctor asked me 'ow she'd been earlier that day, and I've told 'im she's been right as rain, or as right as she ever were. She weren't the 'appiest o' sorts, and she'd taken to drinkin' a lot. But I told him 'ow the sickness 'ad come on all of a sudden, like, and 'e said it could be the lockjaw or some kinda poison. He got to askin' me what she'd ate and drank, like I knew! I weren't able ter tell him much, and there weren't nothin' else I could do neither. Them fits and spasms kept comin' all the while. Ev'ry time they stopped I 'oped that were the last of 'em, but then another one'd come, worse than the last." She shook her head sadly. "Doctor said 'e would give 'er some charcoal on the off-chance it were poison. Biscuits, weren't it, Sal?"

Her daughter nodded. "Charcoal biscuits. But he couldn't get 'em in 'er mouth of account of her jaw bein' all locked shut."

"Doctor told us we 'ad to get 'er to the London 'ospital," continued Mrs Walcot, "so Sal's went out ter fetch a cab. By then, Jane's in such a bad way we couldn't lift 'er up from the bed, let alone get 'er in a cab. The doctor got all sorrowful then. Said there probably weren't nothin' they could do for 'er dahn the 'ospital. Too far gone, she was.

Then everythin' went quiet. 'Er eyes rolled up and she were gone."

The room fell silent for a while. Sally stared into the bottom of her tea cup, while her mother absent-mindedly smoothed down her apron in her lap.

"I think of 'er often," said Mrs Walcot eventually. "It weren't right for 'er to suffer that way. She weren't no angel, but there ain't no one deserves that. Not no one at all."

"What did the police do about it?" I asked.

"Kept me up all night askin' questions and turnin' over the 'ouse, top ter bottom. That's what they done. Treated me and my Sal like criminals, they did! Accused me o' puttin' poison in a pie or a loaf o' bread, then asked if I'd served 'er up any mushrooms! I told 'em I 'adn't done nothin' o' the sort. They was questionin' me other lodgers, an' all. I get all sorts stayin' 'ere: sailors and men what work in the docks, an' a lotta foreigners, too. I 'ad a Swedish lodger at the time, and 'e 'ad no idea what the coppers was sayin' to 'im. Then they took away all me medicines and rat poison, and they took me cups and bowls, too. Said they was gonna look at 'em for traces o' poison. Good luck wi' that, I told 'em!"

"They dint find nothin'," added Miss Walcot. "We done our best to save 'er, and we was the first ones they tried ter blame."

"If Molly Gardstein 'adn't run off we'd proberly of swung for it," added Mrs Walcot. "Disgraceful to be treated like that, ain't it?"

"You couldn't have been convicted if there was no evidence to suggest that you had poisoned Jane," I said.

She gave a snort in reply. "That's what you fink, miss. They'd of found a way, I'm sure of it. I told 'em whatever 'appened to Jane must of 'appened dahn Paddy's Goose. Weren't nothin' ter do wi' me. I dint 'ave no reason ter do it, did I? No reason at all. Anyways, they worked out it was strychnine what poisoned 'er, and that's abaht all they found out. They dunno 'ow or even why. If they'd got ahold o' Molly Gardstein they'd of found out. She'd sooner o' told 'em what she done than suffer an 'angin' fer it. But in all that time they was in 'ere, searchin' my house, Molly got 'erself away! They ain't got no one ter blame but theirselves, I reckon."

"What can you remember about Jane?"

"Pretty little thing, she were. Stood no taller'n me. Brown 'air, brown eyes. She weren't the 'appiest sort, were she, Sal? Kept 'erself to 'erself, but that ain't unusual round 'ere. There's a lotta folk who's got pasts they'd rather not speak abaht. She dint say a lot, but when she 'ad summat ter say she sounded like a lass wiv a proper education. More'n what I ever 'ad, 'any'ow. But her clothes was jus' like mine. She 'ad ter patch 'em up and mend 'em. An' she sewed things to earn a bit o' money. Shirts, overcoats, that sort o' thing. She weren't no good at it, truth be told, and some jobs she dint get paid for. She'd pick up the pieces to be sewn, then bring 'em back 'ere and work on 'em all day long. Ten or twelve hours and there still weren't a lot o' money in it. Some days she dint even bovver."

"She did a bit o' thievin' instead," added Miss Walcot.

"Well, yeah, she did do a bit o' that. That's 'ow she knowed Molly. They done their thievin' together."

"What sort of thieving?"

"From shops. They got nicked a few times, but they was too good at sellin' on whatever they pinched. Them coppers never found no evidence they'd stolen anyfink. I never even knew 'er name was Mary 'til the inquest. I figured she must've come from a decent family. Turns out she were born into money. Dunno where it all went, mind."

"She liked a drink," said Miss Walcot.

"She did," confirmed her mother. "She were a quiet drunk most o' the time."

"Did her drinking cause any problems for either of you?"

"Not as a rule, no. I'd 'ear 'er stumblin' abaht in 'er room now and then, droppin' stuff or bangin' into summat. But she weren't never angry wiv it, and she never called no one any bad names. A few times I told her it weren't safe fer a girl ter go wanderin' abaht when she's the worse for drink. I told 'er there's men what takes advantage. She dint pay much attention ter that, and I was always worried summat would 'appen to 'er. She weren't as used to the streets as some girls. Some of 'em 'ave to learn it from young, but she'd never 'ad to. They said as she'd been married at the inquest, which were news to me."

"Married?" I didn't recall seeing anything about a marriage in the newspaper reports.

"Yeah. They wanted the 'usband to speak at the inquest, but 'e refused. Dint even turn up. It was 'er sister what come to identify her, and she spoke abaht 'er, too. Family used ter live up near Marylebone, I reckon. Somewhere near Regent's Park, any'ow. Jane's ma and pa weren't there, neither. They'd 'ad some sort o' fallin' out, 'adn't they, Sal?"

Her daughter nodded.

"Did you find out anything else about her marriage?" I asked.

The landlady shrugged. "All I know is the p'lice wanted the 'usband there and 'e dint turn up. Jane never mentioned no 'usband to me."

"And what of Molly?"

"I knowed her since she were so 'igh." She held her hand about three feet above the floor. "Always trouble, that gal, but likeable wiv it. Big family, they was, the Gardsteins. Lived just off of Cable Street."

"Do you know where?"

"Not exactly where, no. D'yer reckon Molly might of went back there?"

"It's a possibility, don't you think? She might have changed her name and returned many years later."

Mrs Walcot shook her head in response to this suggestion. "The 'ole family was chased outta there. Coppers wouldn't leave 'em alone after Molly run off. Ain't none o' them Gardsteins around no more. Dunno where they went, mind, but you ain't got no chance o' findin' 'er now."

"Was the only evidence pointing to Molly Gardstein's guilt the fact that she ran away?"

"There was talk of 'ow they'd argued over money, too. I never 'eard nothin' abaht it meself, and Jane never said a word. Molly's long gone, if yer ask me."

"Dead, you mean?"

"Dead, livin' abroad... Who knows?" She shrugged. "Enough people's tried lookin' for 'er over the years, but they ain't never got nowhere wiv it. We ain't seen 'er since that night when Jane died, and I don't think none of us'll ever see 'er again."

CHAPTER 8

The worn floorboards at the White Swan alehouse were sticky with dried beer. Gas lamps flickered on the walls and a cloud of tobacco smoke hung around a group of noisy sailors. Aside from this, the establishment was reasonably quiet at this hour of the morning, and from the dingy depths of the pub I could hear a piano being tuned.

I approached the bar, where a hard-faced barmaid was pulling at a beer tap. She shot me a quizzical look but waited until she had passed a full tankard to an old, sallow-faced man leaning against the bar before she addressed me.

"'Ow can I 'elp yer, miss?" she asked, wiping her hands on her apron. She wore a plain grey dress, but her hair had been carefully pinned into an elaborate cascade of curls.

I told her who I was, and that I was interested in discovering the whereabouts of Molly Gardstein. My explanation was greeted with a peal of laughter.

"A lotta people'd like to know that!"

"Do you know anyone who was particularly friendly with her?" I asked. "Or any family members she was close to?"

She shook her head. "No one ever wants to talk about 'er. The ones what knew 'er wish they never 'ad. No one got left alone after she run off."

"You've never heard a whisper about where she might have gone?"

"Not me; I never knew 'er. All I knows is what folks told me after I come 'ere. I'm from the country meself, so I dunno anyfink about what 'appened back then."

"Perhaps *he* might?" I suggested, gesturing toward the old man leaning against the bar. His eyes were closed and his head was nodding gently, as if he were taking a nap standing up.

"Alf," she barked at him. "Alf!"

There was no response from the man until she prodded his elbow, at which point his eyes opened and he gave an irritable grunt.

"This gen'lewomin wants ter know what 'appened ter Molly Gardstein," she said to him. "D'you remember 'er?"

The man's fixed his gaze on the wall behind the bar. He mumbled Molly's name, appearing to mull it over. Then he frowned and turned to the barmaid. "Did you say Molly Gardstein?"

"Yeah. D'you know where she got ter?"

He shook his head and pushed himself a little more upright, attempting to stand without the support of the bar. His eyes focused on me for a moment and he took a deep breath, giving me the impression that he was about to speak. But nothing came out of his mouth, and he slumped down again, his head bent over his tankard.

The barmaid gave an apologetic shake of her head.

"Is he all right?" I asked.

"What, Alf? Oh, 'e's always like that."

I thanked her and turned to leave. As I did so, a narrow-eyed man with rough whiskers and a broken nose strode past me. I followed him through the door and out onto the street. Despite the overcast day, my eyes took a moment to accustom themselves to the light following the dingy interior of the alehouse. I looked up and down the street, wondering if there was anywhere else I could go to enquire about Molly Gardstein. I was beginning to wonder whether it would be possible to find anyone who could help after such a long period of time.

I began to walk west, in the direction of the city. The man with the broken nose was still walking ahead of me. He was short, but his shoulders were broad and his head was held high. He paused to light his pipe, and as I stepped past him he grabbed my arm. I startled as he brought his face close to mine.

"Get off me!" I cried out, trying to pull away.

"Molly Gardstein," he said gruffly, looking me directly in the eye.

I stopped struggling, wondering whether this aggressive approach might lead to something helpful after all.

"Yer ain't doin' yerself no favours goin' around askin' about 'er," he continued. "Folks round 'ere don't wanna know. Yer'll take yerself back off west if yer know what's good for yer."

"Did you know her?" I ventured.

"No more questions!" he snarled, his grip tightening on my arm. "Now get goin'!" He gave me a rough shove as he released my arm. "Get away from 'ere!"

I turned around and walked away as quickly as I could, almost knocking into a watercress seller. Tears pricked the backs of my eyes as I began to wonder whether I had been foolish and naive for having dared set foot in this part of town.

CHAPTER 9

I told James about my visit to St George Street that evening, choosing to omit the threat I had received from the man with the broken nose. I knew it would cause him concern. We were sitting on the settee together with Tiger asleep on my lap.

"What a stroke of luck that the landlady and her daughter still live there," he commented. "You've managed to find out quite a bit."

"Much of what they told me was recorded at the inquest," I replied, "apart from the fact that Mary Steinway married. That wasn't mentioned in any of the newspaper reports, for some reason."

James tutted. "That's unreliable news reporters for you," he said with a smile.

"*Some* are very unreliable," I responded.

"And her estranged husband refused to speak at the inquest, you say?"

"Apparently, yes. Mrs Walcot and her daughter couldn't recall his name."

"You couldn't really expect them to, given the amount of

time that's passed since then. You'll need a lot of patience if you're to investigate events that occurred so long ago."

"I realise that."

"You'd have been rather stuck if Mrs Walcot had no longer been living there. Perhaps Detective Sergeant Nicol would be able to tell you more about the case."

"Who's he?"

"A friend of my father's. He's retired now, but I recall him spending some time with H Division a number of years ago. I sent him a telegram about the case and he promptly replied."

I felt a flip of excitement. "Is he willing to speak to me about the case?"

James nodded.

"Thank you!" I leaned in and kissed him.

"Perhaps I should arrange meetings with retired detectives more often!"

◌◈◌

We visited the former detective at his home the following weekend. The train journey took us through north London, and we were greeted with pleasant views of green fields shortly after crossing the River Lea. The construction of countless new houses was very much in evidence as the train slowed on the approach to Walthamstow, however.

Mr Nicol lived in one of these new houses. It was a small, neat, terraced home with large sash windows and a neatly trimmed privet hedge. The door was answered by Mrs Nicol, who greeted us both warmly.

"You look more like your father every time I see you," she said to James. "And how lovely to meet your new bride! We were delighted to hear the news."

Mrs Nicol was short and grey-haired, and she wore a patterned, plum-coloured dress beneath a starched apron.

She showed us into the parlour, where Mr Nicol was standing beside the fireplace. A tall man with a large stomach, he wore a dark blue woollen suit.

He made perfunctory enquiries about the health of James's family while Mrs Nicol prepared tea, sandwiches and cake. She laid everything out on a large table at the centre of the room.

The conversation eventually moved on to the topic I was most interested in, at which point Mrs Nicol excused herself.

"I have some mending to be getting on with," she explained. "I tend to make myself scarce whenever he talks about his work." She gave me a wink and left the room.

"I recall the case," said Mr Nicol, his head resting back against the embroidered antimacassar draped across his easy chair. "An unpleasant business." He turned to me. "I suggest you join my wife in the kitchen, Mrs Blakely. The tale I'm about to tell isn't fit for ladies' ears."

"Mrs Blakely is a news reporter," explained James. "Her ears are well accustomed to such tales."

Mr Nicol raised an eyebrow. "I see. Come to think of it, I recall hearing that your new wife had a profession. A news reporter, eh? Whatever prompted you to pursue such an unprincipled profession, Mrs Blakely?"

I gave a polite laugh. "I don't consider myself to be unprincipled, Mr Nicol."

"Oh, I wouldn't wish you to think I was accusing you of being unprincipled in the slightest! I certainly didn't mean it that way." He appealed to James. "I'm terribly sorry, Blakely, if I've caused your wife any offence."

James smiled. "I'm sure Penny has heard far worse, Mr Nicol. In fact, my wife is the reason we've come to discuss the case with you. She recently heard about it and wondered why Miss Steinway's killer was never caught."

"Ah, yes." Mr Nicol crossed one leg over the other. "I've wondered about that, too."

"What can you tell us about the case?" James asked.

"I worked on it directly, so I can tell you everything I know. As I recall, Miss Steinway was taken ill at the White Swan, or Paddy's Goose as we called it back then. Being taken ill in that place wasn't unusual then, and it still isn't now!" He gave a dry laugh. "I remember her lodgings were just behind the alehouse. It wasn't a pretty sight that greeted us there; she was consumed by the most terrible spasms."

He gave me a cursory glance, as if to check that my feminine sensibilities hadn't been too upset by this description.

"It was awful," he continued. "She was terribly unwell. They thought it was the drink, or epilepsy, or even a fit of madness. The doctor thought it might be tetanus, then poison was considered. Died an awful death, she did, and the post-mortem found the cause to be poisoning from strychnine. It's commonly used as a rodent poison, as you probably well know.

"We initially suspected the landlady and her daughter, as they had the best opportunity to put the poison in Miss Steinway's food. We took away every poison we could find in the house, along with all the eating and drinking vessels. Everything was examined, but we found no sign of strychnine at all. Having found no evidence that the landlady and her daughter... I forget the name..."

"Walcot," I said.

"That's it, Walcot." He nodded. "You've clearly read up on the case, Mrs Blakely. Having found no evidence that they had poisoned her and, more importantly, when we could discern no motive, we had to release them. Our attentions then turned to the alehouse, assuming that someone had put strychnine in Miss Steinway's ale."

"Someone put the strychnine in her drink?" I queried.

"It's a possibility, but it wouldn't have been as straightforward as you might think. Strychnine has a bitter taste and can easily be detected in food and drink. Some poisoners get around this by putting it in food with a very strong flavour in an attempt to mask the bitterness. But I imagine it'd be easily discernible in beer. Besides, the poison is a powder and doesn't dissolve quickly in liquid."

"So if someone had put strychnine into her drink, would it most likely have sunk to the bottom of the glass?" I asked.

Mr Nicol nodded. "It would dissolve eventually, after prolonged agitation, but not before the intended victim noticed it."

"And the poison would only be effective if the sediment at the very bottom of the drink was consumed," added James. "Quite unlikely, I'd have thought. If the bitter taste hadn't put her off, the suspicious powder certainly would have."

"Exactly," said Mr Nicol. "Although it's important to remember that Miss Steinway was reportedly intoxicated at the time, which may have impaired her judgement. However, even someone the worse for drink would most likely have noticed it."

"It's not a particularly subtle way of poisoning someone," said James. "There was the case of Christiana Edmunds, of course, who laced a box of chocolate creams with strychnine."

"Around 1870, that was," added the retired detective. "A good number of people were taken ill and one poor young lad lost his life."

"How awful," I said. "I can just about recall that."

"The chocolates masked the flavour of the strychnine to some extent," continued Mr Nicol, "unlike the ale Miss Steinway consumed. I don't think it would have been easy to drop the substance into someone's drink and expect them to consume it without noticing the rancid taste or the powdery sediment. However, we can't overlook the fact that beer is sometimes flavoured with strychnine."

"Really?" I exclaimed.

"Publicans used to add it to their beer to improve the taste. At one time it was commonplace to water it down in a bid to make it go further, but the beer naturally lost some of its flavour. That's when other flavours were added, strychnine being one of them. It was common practice for many years, though it happens much less frequently these days.

"We spoke to the publican at the White Swan and he was initially tight-lipped on the subject. Publicans aren't keen to admit that they water down their beer, you see. He eventually confirmed that he occasionally used a brewers' druggist to flavour his beer, though he denied watering it down. He stated that the druggist had added one or two ingredients to improve the taste. That was how the sailors liked it, apparently."

"Then the brewers' druggist could have added strychnine?" I asked.

"Yes. *Nux vomica*, they sometimes call it. We considered the possibility that the brewers' druggist had accidentally added more strychnine than usual, but that would have affected the whole barrel, and therefore a good number of other people would have been poisoned."

"Were you able to find the tankard or glass Miss Steinway had been drinking from?" asked James.

"Unfortunately, no. We think it was probably gathered up with all the others and washed."

"Was the publican ever considered a suspect?" James queried.

"We spoke to him at great length, as well as the brewers' druggist, and we found no evidence of wrongdoing for either party."

"What did you find out about Molly Gardstein?" I asked.

"The girl who ran away? We knew she was a ne'er-do-well. A *butterfly of the street*, I should add."

"Was Mary Steinway a 'butterfly of the street'?"

"We found no evidence to suggest that she was. We'd arrested her a number of times, but only for minor thieving offences. Molly Gardstein, on the other hand, had been arrested for soliciting as well as for thieving. She was a coarse-mannered woman, but almost a beauty in some ways, which is more than could be said for many women of her ilk. She had terribly loose morals. In fact, it would be fair to say that she had no morals at all!" He gave a hollow laugh.

"Did Miss Gardstein vanish straight after Miss Steinway was poisoned?" asked James.

"That's right. And I don't believe anyone has ever clapped eyes on her since."

CHAPTER 10

"How much time did you spend searching for Molly?" I asked Mr Nicol.

"A month or two, but she was determined to evade us."

"Do you believe Miss Gardstein was the murderer?"

"Why else would she disappear?"

"But what might her motive have been?"

"They must've had a falling out. They worked together; if you can call thieving *work*. It's what a whole load of people on the Ratcliffe Highway do. We'd arrested the pair of them together a few times. I recall arresting them myself once when they were suspected of stealing boots from a shop on Commercial Road. I never caught sight of the boots – they'd got rid of them quickly – and with no evidence available I had to let them go. My theory is, there was a disagreement over stolen goods or money... or both. It must have caused bad blood between them, and Miss Gardstein decided to exact her revenge."

"But how?" I asked. "We've disregarded the idea that

someone could have put strychnine in Miss Steinway's drink at the alehouse."

"We can't completely disregard it, Mrs Blakely. Perhaps that's exactly what Miss Gardstein did, and perhaps Miss Steinway was just too consumed by the effects of drink to notice. Or maybe Miss Gardstein coerced her into drinking it. She had a threatening manner about her on occasion. Miss Steinway was of a milder character, and from a middle-class background, too, as it turned out."

"The daughter of a solicitor," I added. "Do you know how she ended up on Ratcliffe Highway?"

"I think the drink took hold of her," he replied. "Once the drink's taken hold, the demise of the individual is often inevitable."

"What do you know of her husband?"

"Oh, I'd forgotten about him!" He gave a low chuckle. "He wasn't happy when we paid him a visit, that's for sure."

"Who was he?"

"I forget his name now, but he was a curate."

"She was married to a curate?" I asked. Learning that Mary Steinway had once held the respectable position of a clergyman's wife made her lowly death seem even more unusual.

"He'd had nothing to do with her for a good few years," continued Mr Nicol, "and he had no interest in attending the inquest. He refused the summons. He told us he'd washed his hands of her; even in death. He hadn't seen her for a year or two before she died anyway, so it was unlikely he'd have had anything useful to tell the coroner."

"Perhaps his name was Stroud," I said, "and that's why she called herself Jane Stroud."

Mr Nicol shook his head. "I would have remembered if it were Stroud. No, Jane Stroud was a name she invented for herself. She was clearly keen to hide the fact that she had once been married."

"The people of Ratcliffe knew her as Jane Stroud," I said. "How did you discover her true identity?"

"From a locket she wore around her neck, it contained her mother's name, Amelia Steinway, and a lock of her hair. We were able to trace the family from that."

"Did you have any suspects other than Miss Gardstein?" I asked.

"We didn't, no. The fact that she seemingly vanished off the face of the earth incriminated her. Personally, I never completely ruled out the landlady and her daughter, despite the lack of evidence and motive, but there were no other obvious suspects."

"Did anyone witness an altercation or misunderstanding between Mary and another party on the evening she died?" asked James.

"Not that we heard. There was the usual amount of bawdiness, of course, so a minor disagreement could have taken place without anyone noticing among all that noise."

"But no one would have been carrying poison about in case they happened to argue with someone that evening and wished to kill them, would they?" I said. "If someone went to the alehouse that evening with the poison about their person, it was because they intended to use it for a specific purpose. They must have had a specific victim in mind."

"You're right," agreed Mr Nicol. "Poison is certainly associated with a well-planned murder. It's not the sort of thing someone would carry about on the off-chance they might meet someone and decide to use it."

"Perhaps an altercation took place at an earlier point and the culprit went to the alehouse intent on exacting his or her revenge," I suggested.

"Very likely, and I feel sure that's what Miss Gardstein

did. We can't ignore the possibility that Miss Steinway's poisoning could have been accidental, though. Perhaps someone else was the intended target. As you might expect, there had been a number of criminal characters at the White Swan that night. Miss Steinway may have just picked up the wrong drink."

"In which case, I imagine it would be almost impossible to determine who the intended victim was and who the murderer might have been," commented James.

"Quite right," said Mr Nicol. "If anyone wishes to write a list of everyone who was inside the alehouse that evening, I wish them the very best of luck. It was difficult enough to do so a mere day or two after Miss Steinway's death. Attempting it twenty years later would be nigh on impossible, especially when you consider all the seamen and travellers who drink at the place. Within a few weeks of her death, most would have dispersed themselves across the globe. Despite our best intentions, some will never be found.

"Miss Steinway led a complicated life. She was born into a good family but somehow died a pauper's death in a lodging house on Ratcliffe Highway, and she changed her name along the way. Can't say we ever fathomed the reason. These people don't help themselves when they behave like that. Makes it hard for the police to investigate."

"Do you regret not finding her murderer?" I asked.

"Of course! Your husband here will agree with me when I say that there's nothing more galling to a police officer than being unable to solve a case."

"Perhaps the culprit can still be found," I suggested.

Mr Nicol let out a laugh and slapped his palms down on the arms of his chair.

"Why not?" I queried. "Someone who wasn't willing to say something at the time may be happy to do so now."

"Like whom?" he asked incredulously.

I felt irritated by his mocking tone, certain that if I hadn't been James's wife he would have dismissed me completely.

"Obviously, I don't know *whom*," I replied tartly, "but loyalties change over the years and threats diminish. Perhaps someone would be willing to speak out now."

"Good luck to them if they are, but it'd only be one person's word, wouldn't it? I can't imagine any proper evidence being found all these years later. You're not, for one moment, planning to work on this case, are you, Mrs Blakely?"

"I'd like to try."

He sighed and shook his head.

"Miss Steinway's murderer has managed to get away with a terrible crime," I said.

"So have many others!" he snapped. "You think you can do a better job than the Metropolitan Police, do you? You're a lady news reporter, not a police officer. And to attempt to do so twenty years later... When you consider all the men we had working on the case and all the time we put in—"

"I think we should take our leave," interrupted James.

Mr Nicol was clearly riled, with colour in his cheeks and a clenched jaw. It was a look I was accustomed to seeing in people who disliked being questioned in any way.

The retired detective wiped his brow with his handkerchief and slumped forward, as if all the hot air had now seeped out of him. "I do apologise, Blakely," he said, "it's the notion that someone is thinking of looking at the case again, and somehow—"

"I understand," said James. "You put in a lot of work, and to no avail. No one doubts for a minute that everyone did their best at the time."

Mr Nicol wiped his brow again. "And I do apologise to your dear wife. Clearly an intelligent and spirited lady. I see that you have your hands full, Blakely! In the nicest possible way, of course." He gave me a condescending smile, attempting to laugh off his ill-temper.

He stood to his feet as we bade him goodbye. "May I just add that it's really not worth wasting any more time on this," he said to James. "It's really not worth it at all. Some things are best left alone."

"Well, I think we did rather a good job of offending your father's friend," I said to James as we returned home on the train.

"Yes, a good job indeed. I don't know of any retired police officers who enjoy reflecting on the cases that have been left unresolved."

"Then why did he agree to meet with us?"

"I'm not sure. Perhaps he anticipated that the conversation would be a little easier."

"I think he would have been quite rude to me if you hadn't been present."

"Possibly. The police had very little to do with news reporters in his day; they were considered nothing more than a nuisance. The police hadn't recognised the potential benefits of involving the newspapers in their investigations back then."

"Besides which, there were fewer newspapers on sale twenty years ago," I added, "and even fewer people who were able to read them. It's quite different now, of course. The police can use the newspapers to appeal directly to the general public for assistance if they see fit."

"Although I must say that only a handful of police officers have capitalised on that benefit so far. I'm afraid the general opinion continues to be that reporters are an annoyance more than anything else. And I don't think Mr Nicol could quite comprehend the notion of a lady news reporter."

I smiled. "Well, I'm fairly used to that. Do you think he'll complain to your father about our visit?"

"Possibly, but I wouldn't worry about it, Penny. My parents are very fond of you." He gave my hand a reassuring squeeze. "You'd have to do something quite dreadful to change their opinion of you."

"I'll try to think of something."

We both laughed.

I glanced out of the window at the passing fields and considered Mr Nicol's final words to James. *Some things are best left alone.* Then I thought about the man with the broken nose who had accosted me on St George Street. He had said that I was doing myself no favours by making enquiries about Molly Gardstein. *Why were people warning me off?* There had to be an explanation, but for some reason it remained hidden.

"It was interesting to hear Mr Nicol talk about the case, don't you think?" said James.

"Yes. It was certainly useful to hear what he had to say before he got angry. I'd like to find out a little more about Mary Steinway's husband."

"There must have been a lot of bad blood between them. He didn't even want to cooperate with the police after her death!"

"I wonder what happened. It's a shame Mr Nicol couldn't remember his name. I wonder if H Division would allow us to look at the case file. Surely her husband's name would be in there somewhere."

"No doubt it's sitting in storage somewhere, never to be looked at again. And it is police evidence, of course. It's not for members of the public to look at."

"*You'd* be allowed to look at it."

"I've already explained that it wouldn't look at all good if I used my professional status to obtain one of H Division's files. Can you imagine the ructions it would cause?"

"You don't have to *obtain* it, exactly. You could simply look up the name of Mary Steinway's husband and then put it back where you found it."

"I'd need a proper reason for doing so, and carrying out a favour for my wife wouldn't count as a proper reason. I only managed to set up that meeting with Mr Nicol because he's an old family friend."

"Or *was*," I added with a smile.

"I'm sure no lasting damage has been done, but what I mean to say is that I can't do much more than I already have. This murder happened twenty years ago, and the commissioner will take a dim view of any official police time being spent on it now."

"That's a terrible shame."

"The police have enough to be getting on with, and spending time on an old, unsolved case is unlikely to lead anywhere. Are you sure it's what you want to be focusing your attention on, Penny?"

CHAPTER 11

Perhaps I was more accustomed to St John's Wood than I realised, for my former home in Milton Street looked shabbier than I remembered when I returned there. The brickwork was grimy with soot, paint was peeling from the door and window frames, and a stench of filth rose up from the gutter. Despite this, I still felt a deep fondness for the place where I had lived for so long and, as I climbed the steps to Mrs Garnett's house, I felt pleased that I still had a reason to visit.

My former landlady grinned as she answered the door. It wasn't an expression of delight on seeing me again, however, but the fact that she had clearly just been sharing a joke with someone. She wiped her dark eyes with one corner of her apron and chuckled a little as she continued to recover from a seemingly uncontrollable bout of laughter.

"He's in the parlour," she said, gesturing toward the doorway beyond the stairs, as if I might have forgotten where it was.

I smiled to myself as I approached the back room. I

found it quite amusing that my father and Mrs Garnett got along so well; it was a pairing I couldn't have predicted.

"Penny!" My father got up from his seat, his arms open wide. "How nice of you to visit. Come and sit down!"

His grey whiskers were paler than his skin, and I realised that ten years of living in Amazonia had left his face permanently darkened by the sun. Only a few thin curls remained on top of his head, though his hair continued to grow thickly over his ears. Since returning from South America he had discovered that he needed to wear spectacles, a pair of which were sitting, slightly askew, on the end of his nose.

He looked a lot happier than he had at my wedding. Back then he had fiddled nervously with his collar and cuffs, his eyes large and wary. He had been nervous back then, and we had all been extremely surprised by his sudden appearance.

"It would have been better if you'd written to let us know of your plans," I had said to him in our garden after the wedding. "I think everyone would have been a little more welcoming if you had." I remembered glancing back at the house behind us, where Eliza and my mother were waiting. They had just told him in no uncertain terms what they thought of his ten-year silence.

"You might have taken steps to avoid me if I'd written," he replied. "I didn't want that to happen. I so wanted to see you, though I know that I haven't behaved as a father ought."

"And how ought a father to behave?"

"He ought to be a role model for his children. He should be their protector, especially if he has daughters."

"I was twenty-four by the time you left. Hardly a child!"

"A father never stops being a father, Penny. I could never explain the weight of guilt I felt for not writing to you. I always meant to."

"What prevented you from doing so?"

"My fall down the ravine and capture by a tribe inconvenienced me a little." He gave a chuckle at this understatement. "It took some time to recover, but actually I did put pen to paper. In fact, I wrote a letter to your mother informing her of my accident. I also wrote a letter to Kew Gardens, asking for assistance. I told them where I thought I was and explained what had happened to me. The problem was, I had no idea how to get either letter to England. I hid them, worried the tribe would suspect that I was asking for help. If help had arrived, there was a danger the tribespeople would have considered themselves to be under attack. I felt as though I were stuck in a rather tricky situation.

"I suppose I still wasn't very well, and I rather lost the track of time for a while. Each day was a battle to recover my strength. I eventually found the letters among my belongings and realised I needed to write you another. I sat down to do so, but for some reason I struggled to find the words."

He had leaned on his walking stick as he surveyed our little garden. "This is kept very nicely, isn't it? I particularly like that rose bush over there. You can smell the beautiful scent from here, can't you?"

"James looks after it well," I said. "I shall have to learn how from him. I can't say that I inherited any of your knowledge about plants."

"You can't inherit knowledge, you funny girl!" He flashed me a grin. "Although I suppose I could have taught you if I'd been around more..." His voice trailed off and he stared at the rose bush again.

"You were saying that you struggled to find the words to write another letter," I said, keen for a clearer explanation as to why he had remained silent for so long.

"Yes, I did struggle, and I would have been in terrible trouble if they'd caught me writing anything. The womenfolk nursed me back to health but were always suspicious of me. I remember feeling rather confused. They had helped me so much, yet they still regarded me with great caution."

"Because you were a foreigner, I suppose. Perhaps they wanted to be on friendly terms with you but weren't quite sure of your motives."

"I think that may well have been the case. I did my best to charm them. I felt as though my life depended on it, and I didn't want to pose any threat to the tribe. I'd hoped to escape at the first opportunity. They kept me tied to a tree at the beginning. That was a thoroughly miserable time, I can assure you. The children used to come and visit me. I was a curiosity to them, I suppose. With no language to share between us, I decided to entertain them with a few of my old tricks. I used a handkerchief to make stones appear and disappear right in front of their eyes. Just the silly sleight-of-hand tricks I used to do at dinner parties; nothing particularly skilful, but entertaining nonetheless."

"I still remember some of those tricks."

"Do you? I remember you and Eliza being quite entertained by them. You both thought I was a magician back then." He gave me a sad smile.

"You clearly won the tribe's trust in the end," I said.

"Somehow I did, yes. The children were initially urged to stay away from me, but they kept coming back. I suppose they found me rather interesting and different from what they were used to. Eventually, some of the adults stayed to watch my tricks too and found them very amusing. Wonderful, isn't it, how the simple act of laughter can create a bond? I persevered with my magic and presented myself as a silly old fool who had fallen down a ravine. The ropes used to restrain me were finally released for a little while each day, so I had some time to stretch out and wander about a bit. The thought came to me that I could perhaps escape, but my leg was still in a bad way from the fall and I needed a stick to get about. And look, I still need that stick!" He tapped its tip on the ground. "I knew I wouldn't get far with a crippled leg. I'd have died of hunger and thirst before long, or been captured by someone else. There was also a very real danger that my captors would find me again, and most likely kill me."

"Why did you think they would do that?"

"They'd have feared that I would gather a group of people together and return to the camp to attack them. These tribespeople live with a great deal of fear. I imagine that's how we all lived at one time. There are uneasy alliances between some tribes in the region and simple rivalries between others. They wouldn't think twice before extinguishing the life of a perceived enemy; it's a matter of survival. These are primitive, turbulent lands, and each tribe is a law unto itself. It's rather disconcerting when you find yourself on the wrong side of someone, I can assure you. It's very different from here, where you have the police and law courts on your side."

"Depending on who you are, that is."

"I suppose so; to some degree, at least. But I'm confident they would largely have been on the side of a chap like me, whereas just about anything can happen in the jungle, and I must add that it often does. A great deal of my time was spent ingratiating myself with the tribe as my very survival depended on it. My body was in a weakened state and I knew that I wouldn't have lasted long out there all on my own. Prior to the fall I'd been with my guide, of course, but since he had sadly lost his life in the accident I felt very much alone. We recruited various men to help us on our travels, but it had only been the two of us when we fell.

"Awful, it was. I recall plummeting for what felt like forever and feeling certain that I was about to meet my doom. I remember countless thoughts rushing through my mind as I fell helplessly. I saw the foliage rushing up to meet me and thought to myself, 'Ah, so this is the end.' I was quite convinced of it. I thought of you, Eliza and your dear mother, and I remember wondering if you would ever discover what had happened." His voice became choked and he turned away.

I remembered focusing on the wall at the far end of the garden at this point, but from the corner of my eye I had seen my father wiping his eyes with his handkerchief, his head bowed. A lump had risen into my throat and I bit my lip.

After a moment or two he took a step toward me and spoke again. "Oh dear, Penny. What a silly old fool you have for a father."

CHAPTER 12

"Would you care for some coca wine, Mrs Blakely?" Mrs Garnett asked, shaking me out of my reverie. "Your father introduced me to it, and I must say that it's quite delicious."

"And you trust my father's recommendation, do you, Mrs Garnett? I should have given you a stronger warning about him!"

"Vin Mariani coca wine," said my father, "is the very best. Would you mind fetching my daughter a glass, Mrs Garnett?"

"No, thank you," I replied. "I'm quite all right for now. It'll only send me to sleep."

"Nonsense!" he said. "It'll have quite the opposite effect. It's an excitant; perfect for stamina."

"All the same, I won't have any for now, thank you."

"Your father was just telling me that he has been looking to replace his coca leaves with something else," said Mrs Garnett.

"My supply has run out," he added, "and it's not the sort of thing one can buy from the grocer's or druggist's."

"Of course not," said Mrs Garnett. "You don't need to be

chewing on leaves here, anyway, Mr Green. You're not living in the jungle now. Although you might beg to differ if you'd seen the people who recently moved into the house opposite!"

She gave a hearty laugh and my father joined in. I glanced at the bottle of Vin Mariani and saw that it was already half-empty.

"I much prefer drinking the wine to chewing the leaves," continued Mrs Garnett. "Didn't your jaw ache after a while, Mr Green?"

"Not really. One easily becomes accustomed to it."

"And you chew them with a powder of some sort, isn't that right?"

"Yes, a form of calcium carbonate obtained from crushed sea shells, or sometimes burned quinoa or sweet potato ashes. The calcium carbonate releases the goodness of the coca leaves."

"What does it taste like?" I asked.

"It tastes a little strange at first, but the flavour is neither here nor there once one becomes used to it. I enjoyed chewing coca leaves during my previous expeditions years ago but, when Amazonia became my home, I naturally chewed the leaves constantly. It's what all the men there do. There are many medicinal benefits, you know."

"Such as?"

"Coca can help in overcoming sickness and chills. It's the perfect antidote to tiredness and leaves one with a pleasant sense of alertness. The Amazonians have chewed coca for centuries."

"Then it must be a good thing," said Mrs Garnett. "Do they also partake of coca wine in the Amazon?"

"No, that appears to be a European invention. Although they do enjoy a cup of coca tea in some parts of South America."

"I should like to try that," said Mrs Garnett.

"The problem is getting hold of the leaves over here. Perhaps there's a wholesaler somewhere in London. I shall have to search for one."

"Or perhaps we could plant a coca tree in my backyard, Mr Green."

My father laughed. "If only the conditions of your backyard matched those of the Andean slopes, Mrs Garnett. That would really be something!"

As I watched the pair laugh again, their good humour enhanced by the coca wine, I recalled my Father's sombre mood on the day of my wedding once again.

"A place like that does something to you," he had said. "It's quite strange and rather difficult to describe. While I was brooding over my predicament and trying to curry favour with the tribe, I was also struck by the overwhelming beauty of the place. I have always loved the jungle, and was no stranger to Amazonia, though I had only ever experienced it as a visitor. As each day of me living among the tribe passed, I learned to live as they did. I discovered how the forest provided them with everything they needed: all their food and clothing. It was quite a pleasant way to live, with no bustling streets, fog, noise or filth, and no concern about planning my next expedition or raising the necessary funds for it. It made me realise how busy my life in England had become.

"I loved the sounds of the jungle at night and the welcoming sounds of the animals around me as I woke each morning. Yes, there are leeches and all manner of devilish insects to cope with, most of which are many times the size of the insects one might find in this country. It's damp in those hills, and it can be infuriatingly hot during the day and cold at night. But somehow I grew accustomed to it.

"I'll never forget the day that I spotted the most amazing

orchids during one of my little strolls. I had no plans to pull them up this time; I intended to leave them where they were, in their natural habitat, so I could visit them each day and watch them grow and bloom. It was a wonderful feeling to be there in that place and make it my home.

"I was eventually allowed to share meals with certain members of the tribe, which was a great honour. I tried to do whatever I could to help them with their labour and found myself working alongside the women; helping to keep things tidy and carrying out bits of general maintenance here and there. I would never have been permitted to hunt with the men, as I had no skill in that area, but I could collect firewood, fix and strengthen the huts, and carry water.

"I also remained something of a curiosity. I had a loyal band of children who followed me about and asked me to perform one or two of my tricks every day. We even began to learn a little of each other's language. I taught the tribes-people a few words and the children were remarkably quick at picking them up. It was a long time before I could converse with anyone, but it made me realise how effectively humans can communicate without words. A simple gesture or facial expression conveys so much that words are superfluous in many respects. That was certainly the case when I met Malia."

"Your common-law wife?"

"Yes, I suppose that's what she is." He shook his head. "It makes me sound like such a scoundrel. I'm so terribly sorry. I really didn't intend to hurt you or your sister... or your mother. I really didn't. I never set out to do any of this."

"But you were attracted to her."

"Yes, I was. It would be foolish not to admit that. I didn't want to admit it to myself for a long time because I kept thinking about my precious family, but I couldn't help it. It

75

was such a long time since I had left British soil, and it seemed much longer than it actually had been.

"I suppose Malia was drawn to me because I was a foreign curiosity. I can't say the tribal elders approved of our mutual attraction, and for that reason I was extremely keen to deny my feelings for her. I was worried about upsetting them, you see. It wouldn't have done at all if they'd thought I was trying to steal away one of their women! But I'm ashamed to say that from the moment I woke each morning I looked forward to seeing her. We often worked alongside each other, though it was never just the two of us, as I was never allowed to meet with an unaccompanied woman. There were others I got along well with, but there was something different about Malia. There was something in her eyes and smile that was quite intoxicating. Oh, how odd it seems to be relating such thoughts to my own daughter!"

I smiled but said nothing.

He had rested his hand on my shoulder at that point. "I'd like you to know, Penny, that I'm exceptionally proud of you. I remember how fearlessly determined you were to make your name as a writer, and I did my very best to dissuade you when you were a young girl. I regret that now, but I felt then that the life of a reporter would not be at all suitable for you. And now you have married so well and Inspector Blakely seems like such a remarkable young chap, who obviously cares a great deal for you. I don't think he cares much for me, however."

"I'm sure he will once he gets to know you, Father. He feels rather angry that you allowed us to think you were dead for all those years."

"Understandable anger in a husband who loves his wife. It was never my intention that you would all grieve for me. In fact, nothing that occurred over the past ten years was my intention; it's just how my life unravelled. I could make a hundred excuses for my behaviour, but none would ever be good enough. I was selfish and, in reality, it goes no further than that. I sincerely apologise for my actions and hope that both my daughters will eventually accept me back as the father they once lost. That's my hope, though I would fully understand if you decided to have nothing further to do with me."

As I watched my father chat with Mrs Garnett in her parlour, I realised I had already more or less forgiven him. I found no lingering anger or resentment when I searched my heart. I wondered whether I was too gullible and naive, and if I was foolish for forgiving him so readily. Eliza, James and my mother had little good to say about him. Perhaps they saw something in him that I had missed.

It was difficult for me to consider my father as a malevolent man. He was far from perfect, but the same could be said of most people. His flaws were clear to see, but so was his regret. Turning him away now would have meant losing him all over again.

"I do apologise, Penny," he said, topping up his and Mrs Garnett's glass with coca wine. "Here we are gossiping away like old women and I haven't even asked the purpose of your visit."

"I thought it might be a good time to discuss the book."

"Ah yes, the book. I'm very flattered that you've undertaken such a task. Aren't I a lucky man, Mrs Garnett, to have such a clever daughter?"

"It was certainly a pleasure to have your daughter living under this roof for so long," she replied. "She was always a good tenant, even though her typewriter was a little noisy at times and she was occasionally late in paying the rent."

My father gave me an understanding wink.

"That only happened once or twice," I added, "when I was out of work for a little while."

My father shook his head. "The precarious nature of writing."

"You must be extremely relieved that she's married now, Mr Green," said my former landlady. "We were all convinced that she would remain a spinster for the rest of her days."

"Not that it was anyone else's business," I muttered.

My father laughed. "Oh, come now, Penny. People only have your best interests at heart! At least you'll never miss paying your rent again."

"I paid everything that was due in the end."

"That's right," said Mrs Garnett. "And it wasn't as though her father was around to help."

My father's face grew sullen. "No. There were a lot of things I wasn't around for. That will always be a deep regret of mine."

"Life's too short for regrets, Mr Green," said Mrs Garnett. "What matters is that you're here now. I never imagined the great plant hunter, Mr Frederick Brinsley Green, would be renting a room from me!"

"I'm no great plant hunter any more, Mrs Garnett. I haven't done anything like that for many years, and I'm not sure I was ever really great."

"But you were famous."

"Was I? Only in botany circles and, even then, only among botanists with a particular interest in orchids. Those days are far behind me now."

"You don't think you'll ever go plant hunting again?"

"Do I look as though I could?" He lifted up his walking stick. "It's a young man's business."

Well, you made it back in one piece, Mr Green, and that's all that really matters. You're lucky those jungle people didn't boil you up in a large pot."

"They're not cannibals, Mrs Garnett."

"That's what happened to Captain Cook."

"Actually, it wasn't."

"On the Sandwich Islands. I remember hearing a joke that any foreigner who set foot there would end up in a sandwich."

"It was the island kingdom of Hawaii," replied my father, "though Cook named the islands after the Earl of Sandwich."

Mrs Garnett laughed. "So he came up with the name himself and then ended up being eaten there!"

"Not *eaten*," my father corrected her, growing slightly exasperated. "Without going into too much detail, parts of him were burned and other parts buried, all in keeping with the traditional rituals of those islands. The people who live there aren't cannibals either."

Mrs Garnett grimaced. "What a thought. Well, there are certainly cannibals in other parts of the world, so you're quite lucky you didn't stumble across any of them, Mr Green. Although it would have made for quite an interesting chapter in Mrs Blakely's book."

"Ah yes, the book. Right, let's get on with it, Penny. Where would you like to begin?"

I pulled a bundle of papers out of my carpet bag, along with some of his diaries.

"Gosh, I didn't realise there was quite so much material to work from."

"Here are the pages I've typewritten so far," I said, placing them on the table. "They're transcriptions from some of your letters and diaries. I'm hoping to put them together in chronological order so I can recreate your adventures."

He picked up one of the diaries and began to thumb through it. "These are quite something. It's funny how I can clearly recall writing some of these entries, while there are others I have no recollection of at all. I wonder why the mind chooses to store some memories over others."

"Some of your papers and sketches are on display in the natural history department at the British Museum in South Kensington," I said. "Perhaps we could pay the museum a visit and take a look."

He lowered the diary he had been leafing through. "I'd be delighted to! Yes, I should like that very much. When shall we go?"

"I'll write to the curator to arrange a time."

CHAPTER 13

The following day my thoughts returned to Mary Steinway's murder. According to the newspaper reports I had read, Mary had been estranged from her sister, Mrs Anne Pelham-Heathcote, so it was possible that Mrs Pelham-Heathcote would be reluctant to speak to me. Back then she had lived on Well Walk in Hampstead. I decided I had nothing to lose in trying to find her and journeyed toward Hampstead, emerging from Hampstead Heath station on a sunny afternoon.

The name Well Walk suggested to me that Mrs Pelham-Heathcote's home was close to Hampstead's famous wells. The clean air and mineral waters had drawn many people to these parts during the seventeenth century. The area had become extremely fashionable as a result, counting Constable and Keats among its best-known residents. As in many parts of London, the arrival of the railway had brought with it a flurry of house-building. Much of the land was criss-crossed with streets comprising large, terraced homes for well-heeled families.

My route took me uphill, with Hampstead Heath on my

right. So far, the new building projects had not encroached upon much of the heath, and I hoped it would remain that way.

Number thirty-six Well Walk was a smart, brown-brick, three-storey townhouse, but when I knocked at the door the housekeeper told me the Pelham-Heathcotes no longer lived there.

"They moved to West Heath Road," she explained. She wasn't able to recall the number but described the home as a large red-brick house with pretty turrets.

I listened carefully to the directions she gave, thanked her for her help and continued on my way. I visited the nearby Chalybeate Well before leaving the street. The plaque informed me that the well had been donated to Hampstead's poor by the third Earl of Gainsborough in 1698, along with six acres of land. I knew the spa had closed, as the popularity of Hampstead's waters had long been in decline.

I continued up the hill, walking ever closer to the heath. After walking for a further twenty minutes, I felt thankful that I had chosen to wear my most comfortable boots.

West Heath Road led me out into the countryside. The heath continued to my right, while to my left were green fields and the occasional large house. I was beginning to wonder whether the housekeeper on Well Walk had sent me all this way as some sort of practical joke when I reached a large home that was under construction. Beyond it were several other newly built houses, and I was relieved to see one made from red brick with two impressive turrets. It had a wide frontage and stood three storeys high, with large windows, a steeply pitched roof and tall chimneys. Between the turrets, an elaborate barricade ran along the second storey, providing Mrs Pelham-Heathcote with a balcony to stand and wave at passers-by from if she so wished. As I stood in front of the house, I was struck by the contrast between the locations of the two sisters' homes. I wondered why their fates had been so different.

The housekeeper who answered the bell listened to my introduction with pursed lips, making it clear that she had little enthusiasm for my visit. I couldn't tell from her expression whether she had known Mary Steinway or not, and I decided not to draw her on the matter. Despite her mild hostility, she invited me into the hallway and agreed to take my card to her mistress. There was a tiger-skin rug on the tiled floor and a vase of lilies adorned the table at the foot of the curved staircase. As I examined a portrait of an austere gentleman, I imagined my visiting card being presented to Mrs Pelham-Heathcote on a silver platter. I couldn't imagine the housekeeper encouraging her to see me. Perhaps I should have done more to win her over when I had the chance.

The housekeeper's return was fairly swift. "I'm afraid Mrs Pelham-Heathcote is otherwise detained at the present time."

"Would it be convenient for me to arrange another time to visit?"

"That won't be necessary. Thank you." She opened the front door.

"I'd like to help," I said, aware that I was being spurned. "Perhaps you could inform your mistress of that."

"She doesn't require any help, thank you."

"I meant regarding her sister's murder. I'd like to help her find the person who did it."

"It was a long time ago, Mrs Blakely." She peered out through the door, as if she were looking for my waiting carriage. "How did you get here?" she asked.

"I walked."

"From where?"

"The station."

"Goodness, what a long way! I'll ask Horace to take you back down in the dog cart."

"Oh no, there's really no need. I'm very happy to walk."

"He's about to leave on an errand and will be passing the station. You're welcome to wait here until he brings the cart around to the front."

Not only was the housekeeper keen to see the back of me, but she clearly wanted to ensure that I was escorted off the premises by Horace and his dog cart. I decided to simply thank her rather than argue.

A short while later, a two-wheeled vehicle pulled by a black horse arrived at the front of the house. The dog cart was little more than a small chassis with a seat just wide enough for two people. Wearing red and black livery, Horace helped me onto the seat, gave me a blanket to cover my knees and gently flicked the horse's haunches with his whip. He appeared to be a man of few words.

The cart made short work of the downhill journey to the station. I held on to my hat, grateful that my return home would be swift. I felt a deep sense of discontent, however, that my visit to Hampstead had been in vain.

CHAPTER 14

There were a good many things I had been hoping Mrs Pelham-Heathcote would be able to tell me about her sister; not least the name of the man Mary had married.

I felt downcast as I walked home from the train station. I wasn't quite sure what I had expected when I decided to look into the death of Mary Steinway, but I'd certainly hoped people would be more helpful. Perhaps I had expected too much.

I was grateful that Mary's landlady and her daughter had been willing to speak with me. When I considered what Mr Nicol had told me and James, however, I realised he had actually told us very little that wasn't already public knowledge. *Was he just ashamed that the case had remained unsolved all these years, or did he have something to hide?*

I reached the top of Avenue Road; the site of the Steinways' burned-out family home. I wondered whether Mary's sister had visited the ruins yet. She would no doubt have been upset when she'd heard what had happened, but there was little chance of me finding out exactly how Mrs Pelham-Heathcote felt.

I was already running out of possible avenues to explore. *Who else could tell me more about Mary Steinway's life?* My mind returned to the cook I had spoken to while the house was still aflame. It wasn't unusual for servants to gossip and I felt sure that she had more useful information up her sleeve or knew someone who could help. The question was whether she would entrust me with the information. *Would she decide to keep quiet once I revealed my true interest in the case?*

I also had to consider the fact that the cook lived locally. It was likely that she would tell other people about my enquiries, and possibly even her employers. If I were not careful, I could earn a reputation for being nosey. Previously when I had made such enquiries it would have been for an article I was writing for the *Morning Express*. With no such commission now, my only motivation was personal curiosity. Perhaps that didn't give me the right to ask painful questions of people. Perhaps it was unfair of me to dig up the past. I had told myself I was seeking justice for Mary Steinway, but I had to question whether I was really doing this for her. *Perhaps I was only really doing it for myself?* I felt a sudden heaviness in my chest. Maybe I felt so adrift now I had no official employment that I was looking for any opportunity to fill my time.

I thought of the people who had been hostile toward me and understood their sentiment. I had been carrying out my enquiries as though they were some sort of hobby. For Mr Nicol, on the other hand, investigating this murder had been an important part of his job. For Mrs Pelham-Heathcote, Mary's death was a family tragedy. Perhaps the rough man on St George Street had also known her well. I had no idea how most people felt about Mary, yet here I was travelling about

London expecting them to speak to me a full twenty years after her death had shaken their lives.

I began to feel ashamed of myself. Perhaps it was time to heed the warnings of those who had told me not to interfere. James had been supporting me, but I knew that he didn't see a great deal of sense in what I was trying to do.

I had just about resolved to give up on my investigation when St Paul's church loomed into view. I immediately thought of Mary Steinway's wedding day. Her family had lived on this street and marriage ceremonies typically took place close to the bride's home. *Was this the church she had been married in?*

Despite my misgivings, I reasoned that I had little to lose by making a few enquiries at the church. The parish registers would surely contain the details of her marriage and should at least reveal her husband's name.

The church was of a modest size and appeared reasonably modern. Within its gloomy interior I found two ladies rubbing down the pews with cleaning cloths. They wore aprons over their smart day dresses.

When they looked up and acknowledged me, I introduced myself as Mrs Penny Blakely, a local parishioner. "I wondered if I might look someone up in the parish register," I said. "Actually, it's an event I'm interested in – a marriage – but it occurred more than twenty years ago. Would the register for that time still be available for me to look at?"

"Yes, I don't see why not," replied one of the ladies. Her grey hair was pinned into neat curls and she wore half-moon spectacles. "The registers are kept in the vestry, but I'll need to fetch a key because the cupboard's locked. Do excuse me for a moment."

She exited through a small door to one side of the nave, leaving me and the other, rather stout, lady to make small talk.

"Are you new to the area?" she asked. "I don't recall seeing you at church before, though your surname sounds familiar."

"Yes, I am new. Perhaps you've come across my husband, Inspector Blakely."

"Oh, yes!" she said with a smile. "That's the chap. A very nice young man indeed. You've married well there."

"I like to think so." I returned her smile.

"Of course. I don't often see him at church, however. Perhaps you've been attending St Stephen's."

"We do our best to attend whenever we find the time," I replied, realising the last time we had attended church was on our wedding day. "The nature of his work means my husband is often occupied at the weekend."

"Well, yes, I can imagine that being the case. Criminals don't simply stop committing crimes on a Sunday, do they? More's the pity! I'm Mrs Cartwright, by the way. It's a pleasure to meet you."

The grey-haired lady reappeared with a key in her hand.

"This is Inspector Blakely's wife," said Mrs Cartwright.

"Is it indeed?" The grey-haired lady also gave me a smile. "Such a nice man. You must be the news reporter we've all heard about, in that case!"

"Well, I was until we married. How did you know?"

"Oh, word soon spreads. You've made yourself a good match with Inspector Blakely."

As she led me over to a door beside the altar, I made a mental note to ask James how he had managed to charm the ladies of St Paul's to such an extent.

The grey-haired lady introduced herself as Mrs Wilson and bade me to sit at a small table at the centre of the vestry room while she unlocked a cupboard. The other furniture in the room included a wardrobe – presumably used to store the clergy vestments – and a writing desk.

"Which year did the marriage you're enquiring about take

place?" she asked.

I had to think about this for a moment. Mary had died in 1865, by which time she had become estranged from her husband. She had only been twenty-two when she was killed, so I imagined she could have been married no earlier than 1862.

"I'm not quite sure," I replied. "Can I try 1862?"

"You don't know the exact date of the marriage?"

"No."

"In that case, the marriage banns register might be more useful to you."

A large volume was brought out and placed on the table. Mrs Wilson turned to the first record in January 1863. The names of each couple were written out alongside the three dates their banns had been published. I began to read the names, searching for those of Mary Steinway and her mysterious fiancé.

"I shall continue with my chores," said Mrs Wilson. "Do let me know when you've finished."

I thanked her for her time and continued to look through the records.

Half an hour later I had looked through every record between 1859 and 1865 several times but there was no sign of Mary Steinway's name. Mrs Wilson looked in on me once or twice, and I eventually informed her that I had been unable to find the relevant record.

"Oh dear. Are you sure they were married at this church?"

"Actually, I'm not certain of that." I was about to ask whether she had heard about Mary Steinway and knew anything of her marriage, but I checked myself, worried once again that I might gain a reputation as a gossip.

"Perhaps it took place at St Stephen's," she suggested.

"Yes, it may well have done." Having intimated to Mrs Cartwright that James and I might sometimes attend St

Stephen's, there was no way of asking for directions without embarrassing myself. "I shall check there," I said breezily. "Thank you both very much for your time."

I continued down Avenue Road, looking for someone to ask about St Stephen's church, and paused beside the ruins of the Steinway home. Half of the facade remained, but blue sky was visible through the blackened upper-storey window frames. A few charred rafters remained where the roof had been and the once-grand driveway was covered in rubble. The house had been reduced to a shell and the memories once held within its walls were gone for good. I felt thankful that no one appeared to have been caught up in the fire, although the mystery remained of how it had started.

I walked on a little further and passed a gentleman who was tapping his walking cane on the pavement as he ambled along. I asked him for directions to St Stephen's.

"Why, you're almost upon it!" He laughed, then turned and pointed toward a lane with his stick. "It's rather tucked away I'll grant you that but, if you follow that alley, you'll come to it soon enough."

I turned down the lane and was soon greeted by a much more impressive church than St Paul's. With its three tall gable ends and a towering spire, it was clearly more sizeable, and was also enclosed within a pleasant green setting, surrounded by mature trees. But what I really needed to know was whether Mary Steinway had been married here.

The elderly sexton, Mr Farthingly, assisted me, and once again I found myself seated in the vestry pouring over the marriage banns. I forced myself to blink several times when I found the name Mary Ellen Steinway, just to be sure that my eyes weren't playing tricks on me. The dates the marriage banns had been published were recorded as the second, ninth and sixteenth of February 1862. Mary's name was written next to these dates, just beneath the name Edwin Thomas Loach.

According to the register, the pair had married on the twenty-second of February.

I took my notebook out of my carpet bag and smiled to myself as I wrote this information down.

CHAPTER 15

"Edwin Loach," I said to James before dinner that evening. "Do you know the name?"

"I can't say that I do."

"If he were a curate when he married, he could be a vicar by now. Revd Loach, perhaps?"

"I don't recall any Revd Loach. I'm not sure why you think I might."

"I thought he might be the vicar of a local church."

"I don't know a great deal about local churches." He made a fuss of Tiger, who had jumped up onto his lap.

"The ladies of St Paul's speak very highly of you, by the way," I replied with a smile.

"Who on earth might they be?"

"A couple of helpful ladies who happened to be polishing the pews today. I wondered what you must have done to impress them so."

"Nothing specific, really. I just tend to impress people in general."

He gave me a wink and I shook my head in mock dismay.

I told him about my visit to Hampstead and the search through both sets of marriage banns.

"Good grief, Penny. You're busier now than when you worked at the *Morning Express*."

"Not really. I just thought I'd make a few more enquiries, although I'm not sure where they really got me."

"You managed to find out the name of Mary's husband."

"But can you imagine him agreeing to speak to me about her? He didn't even turn up to the inquest."

"You'd have to find him, first of all. He may have gone off to start a ministry in America or New Zealand for all we know."

"Why would you say something like that? It doesn't make me feel any better, you know. In fact, I started questioning why I was doing all this earlier today."

"A valid concern."

"You think I'm being foolish, don't you?"

"When did I say anything to that effect?"

"You didn't, but it's obviously what you think. It's what everyone thinks. No one understands why I should want to look into a murder that was committed twenty years ago."

"It wouldn't be *my* first choice of activity if I had a bit of time on my hands."

"There you go, you see. You think I'm foolish."

"I never said that!"

"But you think this is all a big waste of time."

"I didn't say that either."

"You just about said it, though not in so many words."

"I said it wouldn't be my first choice of activity if I had a bit of time on my hands, but that's only because you and I are different, Penny. You have far more patience and perseverance than I do."

"Now you're just using flattery to distract me from being annoyed."

He laughed. "Penny, I don't think you foolish for pursuing this. But I do think it'll involve a lot of hard work, and there's no guarantee that you'll find the answers you're seeking at the end of it."

"Do you think it wrong of me to question people who were affected by Mary Steinway's death?"

Deep in thought, he stroked Tiger's head before replying. "I think you always do so with great respect and consideration."

"But do you think what I'm doing is wrong?"

"No, it's not wrong, though I think you'll need to tread carefully. But that's what you do so well, Penny. I shouldn't worry about offending Mary Steinway's sister, if I were you. She refused to see you, and you have respected her decision. The thing you need to be most wary of is encountering someone who might resent your questions and wish to cause you harm."

I immediately felt a pang of guilt for not telling him about the broken-nosed man who had accosted me on St George Street.

"That's certainly something to be aware of," he added.

"Perhaps I shouldn't work on the case any more," I said.

"But you've already accomplished so much!"

"But there's very little chance of me finding out anything more, isn't there? I've become too caught up in the idea that I can do something about Mary Steinway's death. The fact of the matter is that I can't."

"But you might be able to. You've already found out the name of her husband."

"And where will that get me?"

"We don't know yet."

"Probably nowhere. As you say, he may be in America or New Zealand by now."

"I didn't mean to put you off when I said that. Are you

going to give up because of one thoughtless comment from me?"

"No, I was thinking about doing so anyway. It's a pointless pursuit. I wish I could do something about it, but I just need to accept that I can't. Mary Steinway's death was a tragedy, but many others have met their end in unfair and unresolved circumstances. Tragedy and suffering are part of life, and we must learn to live with them rather than fooling ourselves into thinking we can somehow alleviate them."

"Sometimes there are things that can be done," replied James. "We don't always know until we've tried."

"Well, I've tried my best," I responded, "but I don't think it'll get me anywhere. I'll concentrate on writing my book about Father instead. I'd best make the most of the time we have while he's in England."

"Has he told you when he intends to return to South America?"

"No, not yet. Though I expect his wife and children will be missing him."

"Given that he's chosen to have a family on either side of the Atlantic, someone will always be missing him, won't they?"

James had been unable to forgive my father for his conduct so far. I wasn't sure that he ever would.

"And you'll need to be discerning about any contribution he makes to the book," continued James. "He may try to ensure that he's painted in a favourable light."

"*I'm* writing the book," I said. "He's merely assisting me with it."

"Does he realise that?"

"Yes, I've explained it to him."

"That doesn't mean he won't try to influence the way he's portrayed."

"I can stand my ground. He needs to accept that he hasn't always behaved perfectly. But then again, who has?"

"No one's perfect, that's true. But not many commit the crime of bigamy, do they?"

I sighed and said nothing. Father hadn't committed bigamy, as he had never officially married his common-law wife in Colombia, but I had already explained this to James. He and I had bickered over my father's shortcomings many times, and our discussions rarely came to anything.

The evening's conversation had left me feeling restless. I got up from my seat and announced, "I'd better try to finish my article on summer hedgerows before dinner."

"Oh, don't look so downhearted, Penny. I thought you'd finished your hedgerow article."

"I had, but maybe I could rewrite it in a more interesting way."

CHAPTER 16

"A book? About me?"

I had watched tears spring into my father's eyes when I first told him I was working on the book, the same day he had moved into my old room at Mrs Garnett's house. He sat on one of his battered cases, which had not yet been unpacked.

"That's such an honour, Penny. I didn't think you would ever want to write anything about the father who let you down so badly."

"To be honest, my work on the book began when I thought you were dead."

"Ah, I see." He wiped his eyes with a crumpled hand-kerchief.

"I had collected your diaries, papers and sketches together, and couldn't help but think how interesting they were. I made slow progress, as there was always other urgent work to see to, but that was while I was a news reporter, so life was far busier back then. Now I'm a married woman I have a little more time to be working on it. And now that you're here, you can contribute!"

He laughed. "Gosh! You mean you still intend to write it?"

"Yes. It'll be easier now that you're here to help me. I can include your account of living with the Amazonian tribe. Not many Englishmen can lay claim to experiencing ten years of that."

"No, I don't suppose they can. Well, I'm terribly flattered, Penny. Thank you. I have a good deal of time available to me at the moment. I made an appointment with my former employers at Kew Gardens and have received various invitations to speak at events and dinners, but I'm not sure what to do about those yet. It feels rather odd to be living in a big city again; I'm quite unaccustomed to it. I do like your little garret room here, however. It feels like a secret hideaway."

"It's not mine any more."

"Perhaps not, but I like it all the same. Were you happy here?"

"Yes, I was. This room suited me and my cat Tiger very well."

"Good." He nodded. "Very good. I like being able to picture the life you've been leading here in London."

"Why did you come back?" I asked.

The abruptness of my question appeared to startle him and he shook his head rapidly, as if he were trying to shake his thoughts into order.

"I always intended to come back, but I suppose there was never a good time after so many years had passed. Would you rather I hadn't?"

"No, I'm glad you're here. It was an enormous surprise, but I'm still pleased you came back."

"I suppose I should have done so much sooner."

"Yes, you should have."

"I wanted to, of course. I always wanted to, and yet I never acted upon it. It was as though I didn't know how to go about it. I realise that sounds foolish coming from a seasoned traveller like me, but I was worried about the reception that awaited me on my return. Desperately worried, in fact. Would I be ostracised? Punished? Ridiculed? Fined? Had I committed a crime? I wasn't sure. The more I put it off, the more fearful I became. I kept writing letters and then destroying them. Each time I wrote one, I felt as though the words on the page were not enough. I wanted to explain what had happened to you in person, because written words could so easily be misconstrued. And you'd have had so many questions that couldn't be immediately answered."

"At least we'd have known you were alive."

"Yes. There is that, I suppose. But I certainly didn't want you risking your lives travelling across the Atlantic in an attempt to find me. I realise I've been extremely foolish and rather cruel in allowing my family to believe that I was dead. I don't think I ever imagined you would fully believe that, though it wasn't an unlikely scenario given the circumstances. A good number of plant hunters never returned to British shores. My poor guide, for one. It's a dangerous and rather silly business, really.

"I have to say, your friend Mr Edwards gave me quite the surprise. I encountered a few Europeans during my time there; more in recent years, I should add. In fact, Europeans seem to have the measure of trampling through Amazonia now. But when Mr Edwards introduced himself to me as a friend of yours... well, I was quite astonished. I hadn't told the previous Europeans I met who I really was. I came up with a false name, as I didn't want them returning to Europe and spreading the word about where I was."

"Why not?"

"Because I wanted a chance to explain myself!"

"You could have explained yourself to them."

"I couldn't, Penny. Not in the right way, anyhow. None of them were British, for a start, and I wasn't sure if I could trust them. Perhaps the tribe's wariness had rubbed off on me by that point. But when Mr Edwards arrived with your blessing, that was a different matter altogether. He was an easy fellow to talk to. I felt I could trust him to impart the true story of my experiences. And by the sound of things, he's done just that.

"After he left, I felt it would be rather unfair on the fellow to bear the sole responsibility of informing my wife and daughters of my fate, so I followed swiftly after him. I had hoped to catch him up, but as I made enquiries along the way I realised he was always one step ahead. It would have been marvellous if we'd been able to board the same ship back to Britain; however, it wasn't to be. My steamship left a week or two after his, but I got here in the end.

"I made enquiries at some of the newspaper offices on Fleet Street when I arrived. Mr Edwards hadn't mentioned which you worked for, or even if you were still employed. I didn't tell them who I was, of course."

"They might easily have guessed. How many other sun-beaten old men would have been asking after me?"

He laughed. "Less of the *old* if you please, Penny. Mind you, I suppose I am rather old. It's funny, because I don't feel it. Anyway, I spoke to a very pleasant but rather uptight lady at the *Morning Express* offices, and imagine my surprise when she told me you were about to be married! She gave me details of the service and I made her swear not to let it slip that I had arrived. I didn't want you finding out I had returned just ahead of the most important day of your life! That could have caused a few ructions."

"Your appearance on the day certainly caused a few ructions."

"It did rather, didn't it? Your mother didn't know what to say. But then again, why should she have? It was comforting to meet her new gentleman companion. I'm not surprised she has found such a friend; in fact, I'm pleased for her. What I did to her... to you all... was unforgivable." He shook his head and looked down at the floor.

"What about Malia? And your children?"

"Ah, yes. You know about them, then."

"Francis told us."

He scratched at his chin and sighed. "The children are delightful and have kept us very busy over the last few years. Rearing children in the jungle is rather different from bringing them up in Derbyshire, you understand, though I must say there are more similarities than you might think."

"Have you told them about us?"

"Yes, I have. I told Malia some years ago, and she seemed quite accepting of the fact. She must already have assumed that I had a family back home. A tribe of my own, if you could call it that. But being so far removed from the life we were leading, I don't suppose she gave it an enormous amount of thought. As far as we were both concerned, it was like a different lifetime. You were always in my thoughts, of course, but you were so very far away.

"I felt such great emotion when Edwards explained who he was, and I wanted to hear all about you and Eliza. I was so proud of you when he told me how well you had both done. And I felt so awful about the manner in which I had treated your mother. I don't suppose I shall ever be at peace with that, but there's not a great deal I can do to change things now."

"When will you return to Malia and the children?"

"I haven't decided yet. I do hope Eliza and I can be reconciled before then, but that's her decision. I suppose I shall wait about a little longer for an opportunity to meet with her and explain myself, as I have done with you."

"Perhaps she'll make contact with you once her anger has subsided. I feel fairly sure that she will."

"I hope so. Why were you so willing to speak to me, Penny, when your sister refused to do so?"

"I was interested to hear your version of events. I can't deny that it was awful not knowing what had happened to you, but I wanted to understand why you never made contact. I think I understand a little more now. It seems you were too ashamed to admit to your family what had become of you."

"Shame is the right word," he had said with a nod. "Yes, I feel a great sense of shame."

CHAPTER 17

"I wonder what excitement lies in store for you today," I said to James as I watched him button his collar onto his shirt.

"I'm going back to the jeweller's on Bond Street that was burgled on Monday night," he replied. "The thieves made off with a great many valuables, and the jeweller is rather frustrated that we haven't found the culprits yet. We're also looking into an interesting case of blackmail. I'd love to tell you more about it, but that would be against the rules!"

"That's a shame," I said, resting back against the pillows. "I'd love to hear more about it."

"What are *you* working on today?" he asked as he wrapped his tie around his neck.

"An article about soap."

"Soap?" He laughed, then quickly straightened his face when he noticed my glum expression. "I suppose there are many important things a skilled writer could say about soap."

"It's for the *Lady's Pictorial* magazine."

"Does that mean there'll be a picture of the soap, too?"

"Now you're just ribbing me."

"I'm not!" James desperately tried to suppress a giggle, but, failing terribly, he was forced to turn his back to me.

"The only consolation is that they're paying me a reasonable sum to write it," I said. "And I shall be quite the expert on soap by the time it's complete."

"Then your time is being put to good use after all." He turned to face me again, his face almost recovered. "Have you seen my cufflinks?"

"Which ones?"

"The ones I always wear... with the silver knots."

"I may or may not have done."

"Are you being deliberately unhelpful?"

"Yes. It serves you right for laughing about my soap article."

He smiled. "Oh, I'm sorry, Penny. It was difficult not to." He sat down on the bed. "It's quite a departure from the subjects you used to write about."

"I don't need reminding of that, James."

"I can't help but feel responsible. If I hadn't asked you to marry me, you wouldn't have had to leave your job, and you wouldn't have ended up writing about soap and hedgerows."

"It's not your fault. We both wanted to be married, didn't we? I'd hoped I could continue my job at the *Morning Express,* but it wasn't to be. I'm sure I'll find something more interesting to write about soon. Perhaps once a dashing young detective has managed to catch a jewel thief or trap a blackmailer."

"Which dashing young detective would that be?"

"Oh, I don't know," I replied with a smile. "But I do know that you left your cufflinks on my vanity table."

"Thank you." James leaned forward and kissed me before getting up to retrieve them. "Perhaps you need to approach publications of a more academic nature," he suggested.

"I could do, though I'm no academic myself."

"But you are intelligent. Or perhaps you could review books or plays."

"Yes, I suppose I could. But as interesting as books and plays are, they're not quite the same as real-life experiences, are they? They wouldn't encourage me to get out and about on the streets of London, visiting places I've never been before and encountering people I'd never otherwise have met."

"Perhaps it's not the writing you enjoy, but the adventure."

"It's both."

James checked his pocket watch. "Oh dear. I'm supposed to be at Bond Street police station in ten minutes. It'll take me that long just to walk to the train station." He took his jacket out of the wardrobe and kissed me goodbye. "Enjoy your day, dear wife. And good luck with your article."

I wrote for a little while after breakfast about the benefits of soap on the complexion, after which I stepped out into the garden for a breath of fresh air. Tiger sauntered out to join me as I seated myself on the little bench beside the sweet peas. She stretched herself out lazily across the warm paving slabs and closed her eyes. I watched her belly slowly rise and fall with her breath and thought of the grimy rooftops she had once traversed. Our marital home with its little garden had given her a much more pleasant space. Despite the pugilistic local cats, Tiger seemed more contented here than she had at Mrs Garnett's place.

Feeling restless, I decided to go out for a walk. Although Mrs Oliver bought most of our groceries, I felt sure there must be some butter, biscuits or jam I could go out to fetch.

The high street was just a short walk away, and once I'd purchased my groceries the distance didn't feel long or satisfying enough. I was standing at the crossroads wondering which direction to take when someone called out to me. I turned to see a broad-shouldered lady wearing a bonnet and shawl, carrying a shopping basket laden with vegetables. I recognised her as the cook I had spoken to on the day of the fire at the Steinway home.

"It's Mrs Blakely, ain't it?" she asked.

I couldn't recall telling her my name.

"I'm Mrs Jones. D'you remember us meetin' afore?"

"I do."

"Found out you're a news reporter, I did!"

"That's what I did before I was married."

"Fancy that, a news reporter! And I 'eard you're married to that Inspector chap from Scotland Yard. I reckon the pair o' you must live on 'Enstridge Place. You shoulda told me all that first time we met!"

"Should I?"

"Seemed real interested in the Steinway home, you did. I remember you askin' me a lotta questions."

"Oh dear, I am sorry. The habit has stuck with me, I'm afraid."

"Ain't no need for apologies, Mrs Blakely. I like to ask a lotta questions meself. 'Ow else can I find out what's been goin' on?" She gave me a wide grin. "I got time to tell you all about Mary Steinway now. I remember you was askin' me about her but Mrs Grosvenor was acallin' for me. She's the 'ousekeeper. Now *she's* someone who don't see the point o' chattin'. Everythin' she says is just a couple o' words."

The cook proceeded to recount what she knew of Mary Steinway's death, which was reassuringly similar to what I had already learned.

"I heard she was married," I commented once Mrs Jones had finished speaking.

"Yeah, that's right." She gave a sharp intake of breath.

"Loach were his name. The Steinways 'ad 'igh 'opes for that gal, but it all wen' wrong."

"Do you know why?"

"I've only 'eard rumours; I can't tell yer nothin' for certain. Lived over the other end o' Primrose Hill, they did, and I know the Rendells worked for them."

"Rendells?"

"Mr and Mrs Rendell. Only they wasn't married back then."

A pause followed, as if she were waiting for my next question. I recalled my new resolve to stop working on Mary Steinway's case and remained silent.

"I'd best be gettin' back." She pointed at her full basket. "Gotta get preparin' this lot. They'll be eatin' well tonight, Mrs Blakely. You know my mistress... she don't 'alf like her food!"

"I'm not sure that I do know her."

"Name's Mrs Cartwright. I 'eard you seen her in church. She said you was lookin' at the parish registers."

I pictured the stout lady who had been cleaning the pews.

"Oh yes, I remember now. Mrs Cartwright, of course."

"Well, I'd best be gettin' off now. Nice to see yer again, Mrs Blakely."

Mrs Jones took a step away and I wondered if I was losing a good opportunity to find out more. I opened my mouth to speak, then closed it again. It really wouldn't do to ask any more questions. I imagined Mrs Cartwright and her cook gossiping about my nosey behaviour. They had clearly already been discussing me.

All of a sudden, she leaned back in toward me. "Workin' at the zoo, 'e was, last I heard."

"Who was?"

"Mr Rendell. After they was married 'e took a job down the zoo."

"I see."

"I thought you might wanna speak to 'im, seeing as you was askin' about Mary Steinway and her husband." She smiled. "You *are* a news reporter, ain't you?"

"*Was*. Thank you, Mrs Jones."

CHAPTER 18

I paused under the shade of an oak tree to allow a large, lumbering elephant to pass. A grey-whiskered man in shirt sleeves, a brown waistcoat and a blue peaked cap was guiding it along. Six children sat on the animal's back in two rows of three with their little legs thrust out in front of them. A small group of people followed close behind.

"Hold on tight!" a woman with a parasol called out, no doubt concerned that her child was about to plummet from the elephant's back to the ground.

I gave the children a wave as they passed and a little boy waved back.

A week had passed since I had spoken to Mrs Jones, during which time I had attempted to persuade myself that there was no need to speak to Mr Rendell about the time he had spent working for the newly wed Mr and Mrs Loach. But the more I tried to push the thought away, the more it had pestered me. Thoughts of Mary Steinway had even infiltrated my dreams. Despite my best attempts to forget about her, something was refusing to let me, so I had reluctantly taken myself off to London Zoo.

I walked on toward the monkey house with its arched glass windows. Its occupants were throwing themselves against the bars of their large iron cages and a bitter odour hung in the air. The enormous hippopotamus was languishing beside his pool, while the giraffes arched their long necks over the wall of their enclosure to nibble at visitors' hats.

Another group of people had gathered around a zookeeper, who was holding a monkey on a chain. The little animal was dressed in a red velvet jacket and smoked a pipe. I passed the wombats and kangaroos then crossed a little bridge over the Regent's Canal to the aviary, amid a torrent of squawks and shrieks. Two keepers leading camels with children on their backs passed me before I reached the bear pit. It was feeding time for the bears and a large stick with chunks of meat speared onto its end was being passed around the visitors. The bears had clambered up a tall, dead tree trunk at the centre of the pit to fetch the meat. Their eyes were dark and shining, and the sight of their fearsome teeth and claws up close was quite thrilling.

A lady next to me clapped her hands with excitement when a bear growled in frustration as it tried to grab the meat.

"Isn't this a wonderful place?" she said. "I came here often as a child, and now my own children simply adore coming here. They're too young to have seen the quaggas, though."

"Quaggas?"

"A combination of horse and zebra. They had three here at one time, but I think the last one died about ten years ago. They're extinct now. Not a single quagga exists anywhere in the world. Isn't that sad?"

"Yes, it is."

"It's sad that they sold Jumbo to Barnum last year, too. The children used to love riding on Jumbo."

Jumbo had been a popular elephant at the zoo but had

eventually joined PT Barnum's circus in America. I wondered whether he preferred the circus to the zoo, then decided he would most likely have preferred to roam freely on an African plain instead.

I wondered whether the bears missed the forest. Perhaps they had been born at the zoo and had no notion of it. I watched a gentleman cruelly tease one of them with a stick, holding the meat close to his mouth, then moving it away before the bear could reach it. I turned away, too upset to watch any more, and walked on.

The lions and tigers were dozing in their cages and a lady sold ice creams from a cart. I passed the parrots' house and walked toward the enclosure where the elephants and rhinoceroses were kept.

Before long, the elephant returned with its keeper and the children disembarked via a tall set of wooden steps. A crowd gathered around the animal and offered it fruit, bread and ice cream. Then the grey-whiskered keeper led the animal back inside its enclosure for a well-earned rest.

When he re-emerged without the elephant, I approached him. "Mr Rendell?" I asked.

He appeared startled; no doubt surprised by a stranger addressing him by name.

"I'm Mrs Penny Blakely," I said. "A journalist. I'd like to ask you a few questions about Mary Steinway. Or Mary Loach, as she may have been called when you knew her."

He blinked rapidly, as if a memory had been reawakened.

"Mary Loach?" he eventually replied. "I haven't heard that name in a long, long time."

CHAPTER 19

Mr Rendell had agreed to meet me in nearby Regent's Park once he finished for the day. I waited beside the bandstand, observing the trees and grass as they bathed in the golden early-evening sunshine.

As the grey-whiskered man approached me, he removed the pipe from his mouth and said, "You do realise she's dead, don't you?"

"Yes."

"Then why are you asking me about her?"

"I'm trying to identify the person who killed her."

He raised an eyebrow, shook his head and pulled on his pipe. "Well, I can't tell you that," he said eventually. "Did you think I'd be able to?"

"Of course not. I'd just like to learn a little more about her for now. I spoke to Mrs Jones, a cook who works for my neighbours, the Cartwright family. Mrs Jones told me you worked for Mary while she was married to Mr Loach. He was a curate, wasn't he?"

"That's right." He gave a faint smile. "Millie Jones," he

said. "I was fond of Millie; haven't seen her for a few years. How's she doing?"

"She seems well to me."

"The Cartwrights are still there, then. Millie used to visit us in our rooms above the stables when she got a bit of time off. There wasn't much time off in them days, but we enjoyed ourselves all the same."

"You were a coachman, were you?"

"Yeah, for the Thirsk family, neighbours of the Steinways. I always loved horses. And now I love all animals, from horses to elephants." He grinned. "I grew up on a farm in Somerset, the youngest of five. Five what made it to adulthood, anyway. My brothers took over the farm and I thought I'd try me luck as a coachman in London, seeing as I already knew how to drive horses. A busy job, it was. I always had to keep the carriage immaculate and they had a pair of horses what always needed grooming. London streets are so filthy it was a job to keep the carriage and horses tidy, but that's what I done and I liked spending time with them animals."

"Were you still a coachman when you worked for Mr and Mrs Loach?"

"No, they never had no carriages. No horses, neither. I did odd jobs for them, mainly because I was keen on their maid, Katie Hicks. She's me wife now. Been me wife for eighteen years. She stayed with Miss Steinway after she became Mrs Loach."

"You mean she moved from the Steinway household with Mary Steinway?"

"Yeah. After she got married."

"So your wife worked for the Steinways prior to that."

"Yeah. Come and speak to her about 'em, if you like. There's a bit of time yet before she goes to work at the Anchor. She's a barmaid there. She won't be able to tell you who murdered Mary, but she was real fond of the girl."

"Perhaps you could ask your wife if she'd be willing to meet me sometime."

"Just come down with me now."

"Won't she mind me turning up unannounced?"

He laughed. "Course not! I wouldn't of invited you otherwise, would I? Our place is only five minutes' walk from here."

Mr Rendell told me about the elephants as we walked toward the eastern end of the park. Rows of grand houses overlooked the vast green space, but the character of the area soon changed as we approached Regent's Park Basin, where factories and warehouses lined the waterside. Enormous carts laden with hay and straw sat in Cumberland Market, and rows of cramped, grimy terraced houses lined the maze of streets. Before long I heard the rumbling and whistling of trains leaving Euston station.

Mr Rendell paused outside a little house marked number sixty-four. "This is our place," he announced proudly. "You'd better join us for supper."

"Don't you want to ask your wife first?"

"She won't mind at all. I insist on it, and she would as well. Come on in!"

I needn't have worried about how Mrs Rendell would receive me. She was as welcoming as her husband had said she would be. Perhaps she was accustomed to him bringing guests home as she didn't seem terribly surprised by my appearance. She was astonished to hear that I was a journalist, however.

"I've never met a lady journalist before," she commented as she served up bowls of mutton broth in their small, neat parlour. "I've known some clever ladies in my time, but never a journalist." She gave me a proud smile and ladled an extra serving of broth into my bowl.

She was a diminutive lady with unruly waves of grey hair, which she had unsuccessfully attempted to pin into place. She had a round face and friendly green eyes, and I liked her at once. I wondered if her demeanour would change when I asked her about Mary Steinway.

We discussed the fire at the Steinway home as we ate.

"Terrible news, that was." Mrs Rendell shook her head. "I had to go and have a look when I heard. Wish I hadn't now. Almost completely gone, isn't it? No hope of rebuilding it, neither. They'll have to pull it down. Old Steinway would of been heartbroken."

"What was he like?" I asked.

"He was a solicitor. Quite reserved. Strict but fair. I liked and respected the man, but he didn't have much humour about him. Perhaps that's to be expected from a man of the law. Mrs Steinway was the kinder of the two. I was right fond of her."

"I heard she died some years ago," I said, recalling what Mrs Jones had told me.

"Yes. That was the first Mrs Steinway, and what a lovely lady she was. Treated the servants like we was part of the family and always remembered our birthdays! I've never known a mistress like that since. She was a good-natured, generous lady, and she loved her children dearly. Took such an interest in them. She was a rare find." Mrs Rendell paused and gave a rueful shake of her head. "I absolutely adored her. We were all heartbroken when she passed away. The second Mrs Steinway died as well, but that was much more recent. Couldn't tell you when, exactly."

She offered me and her husband some bread before taking a slice herself and placing it on top of her stew. "They were happy days when I joined the Steinways. It was my first job and I'd been right nervous about leaving home. I was lucky to find such a good position."

"How old was Mary when you started working for the family?"

"About eight, and she was very sweet. I was only six years older than her. I'd just turned fourteen, which pleased my mother, 'cause it meant I'd reached an age when I could earn a bit of money for the family. It was badly needed, as my father died shortly after my youngest sister was born and we didn't have a penny to our name. Mother began taking in laundry, but it was never enough. When I started with the Steinways, I was pleased to be earning a bit of money for my family and happy to escape the house. I didn't like being a nursemaid to my little siblings! My younger sister Jenny had to take over. Whenever I had an afternoon off, I'd go back home and Jenny would stare at me, all jealous like! I knew she wanted to be working, same as me, and it weren't long before she was. The family she served wasn't as nice as mine, though. I still reckon I struck gold there.

"Mary was the youngest of the seven. The two oldest brothers, William and John, were at university. They visited now and then but spent quite a bit of time up in Cambridge. And even when they were in London, they were busy with trips to the theatre and restaurants.

"The younger Steinways had a governess. The boys went to school and the girls went for a little while too when they were young. Then when they got to ten or so they were taught at home by the governess. Mary had her lessons with her older sisters, Anne and Peggy. The two boys just above Mary – Joseph and Robert – were still in school. The governess thought herself very important compared to the likes of us common servants. But she was good with the little ones and gave the girls a good education, from what I seen. I remember listening in to their French lessons, and a bit of arithmetic and grammar.

"Mary didn't have much interest in her lessons. She liked

to be out in the garden playing with the dogs. Could never keep herself clean and tidy, that girl! Her aprons had to be changed a good few times a day and her hair got so knotted a brush couldn't get through it! The nursemaid used to cut the knots out with a pair of scissors. Mary loved to talk and sing, and she was very good on the piano. Quite the little entertainer, she was. Noisy and not that well behaved, but then she was the baby of the family, and she played up to it. The older ones would tell her off, but she weren't bothered by them. Some found her company annoying at times, but I always found her fun to be around.

"Then Anne and Peggy went off to finishing school in Switzerland. Both them girls married well. Anne lived with her husband in Hampstead and Peggy moved to Greenwich. Mary went to finishing school as well, but it all went wrong from there."

CHAPTER 20

"Why did it go wrong?" I asked.

"Mary come down with scarlet fever. She was in a bad way and Mrs Steinway was so worried she went all the way to Switzerland to bring her home again. I always thought Mary was her favourite, and I was proved right the way she went over there to bring her girl home. Mary was right poorly; we thought we might lose her. But Mrs Steinway nursed her, day and night, and eventually the poor girl recovered."

"But then Mrs Steinway come down with it," added Mr Rendell with a sigh.

"She did. She was right bad with it, too. She never recovered."

"How sad," I said. "How old was Mary when her mother died?"

"About seventeen, she would've been. I'd been working for the Steinways about nine years by then and I knew them all pretty well. Mrs Steinway was everything her husband weren't. Where he was cold, she was warm. When he was strict, she was generous. I didn't take to him much. But he absolutely adored his wife, I will say that. Completely devastated when she died, he was. Blamed Mary, of course."

"That seems terribly unfair."

"He was grieving at the time and couldn't see sense. He said they shouldn't never have brought her home. Reckoned she should have stayed in Switzerland and been nursed back to health there. That's what he'd wanted to happen, but Mrs Steinway cared so much for that girl she just wanted her home again. She insisted on doing most of the nursing herself. She would've done anything for Mary, and she ultimately paid for it with her life.

"Mary felt awful guilty about her mother's death, and there was definitely bad feeling about her in the family. It was an sad twist of fate because life changed a lot after Mrs Steinway died. Until then they'd been a happy family. The children were all clever and charming in their own individual ways. And Mr and Mrs Steinway were very much in love, which ain't always common in a marriage. Although there was a nursemaid and a governess and plenty of other servants to look after the children, Mrs Steinway'd always liked to do a lot herself. That all changed when the second Mrs Steinway came along, of course."

Mrs Rendell gathered up our empty bowls and glanced at the clock on the mantelpiece. "I'd better start getting ready to leave in fifteen minutes."

"Oh yes, of course. Your husband mentioned you were working as a barmaid. Thank you both for your time. I shall leave you to get ready, Mrs Rendell."

"But we're not finished, Mrs Blakely! You sit yourself back down. I've got fifteen minutes yet! Where'd I got to? Ah yes, the second Mrs Steinway."

"When did they marry?"

"Six months after the first one died. The new one was a Miss Griffiths; a spinster who lived in Notting Hill with her brother. A cousin of Mrs Steinway's, she was. She'd been a regular visitor ever since Mrs Steinway died. I think she had designs on Mr Steinway straight away. Her brother had a bit of money, but Mr Steinway had a lot more."

"She married him for money, then?"

"That's what we all reckoned. There might've been some affection there. She enjoyed his house and money, but not his children, and it was only Mary left at home by then. The second Mrs Steinway soon had plans for her. She wanted her out the way."

"Was Mary still seventeen at this point?"

"She'd just turned eighteen. The second Mrs Steinway wanted Mary to marry the son of a family friend, Mr Loach. We all thought it was a decent match; he was right charming and well educated. He was a curate and seemed just the right sort of chap to help Mary cope after the death of her mother. There's no doubt the marriage was fixed to take Mary off of Mr and Mrs Steinway's hands, but it still seemed like a good match."

"What did Mary make of it?"

"She weren't quite herself at the time. The bright, lively, happy girl had gone by then. The illness had changed her and the death of her mother had left her bereft. She seemed to accept it was part of all this change that was happening to her. It took her a long time to recover from her mother's death; in fact, I'm not sure she ever did. I didn't see Mary in her last few years of life, but I imagine she never would of stopped mourning her mother. We all thought the marriage'd be just what she needed. Within a year of Mary's illness her mother had died, she had a new stepmother and not only was she married herself, but she was also with child."

"She was a mother?" I replied, surprised at this news. I

wondered what had become of the child, presumably now aged twenty-three or so.

"She was. Poor Mary wasn't well during her confinement and had to spend a good while in bed. Mr Loach was most understanding about it and made sure she didn't want for nothing. And the baby was a delightful little boy..." Mrs Rendell's voice cracked and she pulled a handkerchief from her pocket.

Mr Rendell got up and placed a comforting hand on his wife's shoulder. "I think that'll have to do for now," he said quietly. I felt a horrible sense of dread that something had happened to the child.

"Of course," I said, readying myself to leave. "I'm sorry if I've caused any upset—"

"No, course not, Mrs Blakely," he replied. "Not your fault at all. It's just that the loss of a child is something my wife feels keenly."

"Oh, goodness." I felt a lump rise into my throat as I got to my feet. The young adult I had pictured in my mind quickly faded. I considered how awful it must have been for Mary and her husband. "Thank you both very much for your time and hospitality," I flustered. "I appreciate you telling me so much about Mary."

Mrs Rendell wiped her eyes. "Oh, there's no need for you to go, Mrs Blakely. I do apologise for my tears. I can tell you more if you like."

"Not this evening," her husband interjected with another gentle pat on her shoulder. "Perhaps we can invite Mrs Blakely back another time."

"There's really no need," I replied. "Not if it's too upsetting—"

"Oh, you mustn't mind silly old me," said Mrs Rendell. "I'm just a bit tired today, that is all."

I thanked and bid them both farewell. I had desperately

wanted to hear more, but I knew it wasn't the right time to probe. I left my visiting card in the hope that they might contact me another day to continue the story but, in the meantime, I would have to discover what had happened to the Loaches by some other means.

CHAPTER 21

"I wonder how the Loach marriage ended," I said to James that evening. I had told him about my encounter with the Rendells at their home in Euston while he was eating his supper.

"I'm sure you'll find out one way or another," he replied dismissively.

"Why are you taking that impatient tone with me?"

"I'm not taking any sort of tone."

"Yes, you are."

James sighed. "Well, perhaps I am a little. But only because I thought you'd decided not to look any further into Mary Steinway's death. Only, you've now learned everything that happened to her by the time she reached the age of eighteen."

"I didn't purposefully go looking for the information on this occasion. *It* found *me*."

He laughed. "You attract these stories somehow."

"I do seem to, yes. But I'd quite decided not to do anything further when Mrs Jones the cook happened to mention the name of a former servant at the Steinway house.

But then he happened to be working at the zoo, which is only a short walk from here. I felt there would be no harm in speaking to him. And as it turned out, he and his wife were very helpful."

"I presume you're back working on this again, in that case."

"I feel I have to, James. The story is unfinished."

"And it may remain so, however much you work on it."

"Perhaps you're right."

"Something clearly went wrong with the Loach marriage," said James. "The baby sadly died and the couple became estranged. Mary must have left their home and somehow ended up in the East End."

"But why there?"

"The lodgings are cheap, the population is transient and people daren't ask too many questions. It's an easy place to hide."

"Do you think Mary was hiding from someone?"

"She changed her name, didn't she?"

"But who would she have been hiding from? Her husband?"

James shrugged. "It's possible, although it could have been just about anyone."

"Perhaps she confided in Molly Gardstein."

"The mysterious Molly you were told you have no chance of finding?"

"I'd still like to try."

"And supposing you do find her... will you ask her directly whether she murdered Mary Steinway?"

"Well, no, I don't think so. I don't know yet, James. I think I'd want to hear what she had to say first. I realise the chances of finding her are slim," I noticed his sceptical expression, "but I always like to remain hopeful about these things. I intend to visit the East End again tomorrow to make further enquiries."

"Please be careful, Penny."

"Of course I'll be careful. I'm quite familiar with the place, you know. And I'm not thinking solely about Mary Steinway's murder. I've arranged a meeting at the natural history department so my father and I can look at the papers they have of his."

"That sounds as though it could be quite interesting. Is it to help with your work on the book?"

"Yes, but I also think Father would like to see his papers again."

"You've been very good to him, Penny."

"I don't know about that. I just feel as though I should make the most of this time while he's here in London."

"Has Eliza visited him yet?"

"Not yet, and I'm not sure she ever will."

"You don't have to make up for her absence, you know."

"No, I realise that, but he doesn't have a great many friends in London. Apart from Mrs Garnett, who appears to be a good buddy of his now. That's the power of coca wine, I suppose!"

CHAPTER 22

Mary's former landlady, Mrs Walcot, had told me that the large Gardstein family lived just off Cable Street. The street was north of Ratcliffe Highway and ran parallel to it, eastwards from the City of London to Limehouse. Mrs Walcot hadn't given me a street name, which was unfortunate given that Cable Street was about a mile in length. I decided to begin my enquiries along the stretch closest to St George Street, steeling myself to be met with bemusement, ignorance and hostility. I reasoned that if I was particularly fortunate, I might find someone who was willing to help.

Cable Street was similar in character to St George Street, with countless little shops offering a variety of services for sailors, along with a good number of alehouses. It was a warm morning and gentle sunlight filtered through the pall of smoke that hung above the rooftops.

I asked various shopkeepers and people I encountered in the street whether they knew of anyone by the name of Gardstein. A grocer suggested that I try Watney Street, which took me past Shadwell station and beneath the railway lines. An old man I spoke to told me the Gardstein family had once lived on Station Place, which I discovered to be a narrow lane that ran between a row of cramped terraced houses and railway arches. Grubby-faced children paused their games to watch me pass, while two young women sat sewing nearby. I asked them if they knew whether any members of the Gardstein family still lived on the street.

One of the women turned to the other and shrugged.

The other, who had a gaunt face and thin lips, pondered this for a moment. "I've 'eard the name," she said cautiously.

"Would yer ma know?" asked her companion. She had wide blue eyes and an angry-looking rash on one side of her face.

"Maybe."

The two women conversed about who else might be of help before the gaunt-faced woman got up, walked a few yards down the road and hammered on a door.

As she spoke to whoever had opened it, a little boy toddled up to me, barefoot, and grinned. A train rumbled over the arches above our heads.

The gaunt-faced woman returned with an older lady, who wiped her hands on her apron and adjusted her bonnet as she prepared herself to address me. She bore a strong resemblance to the younger woman, though her face was heavily lined.

"Gardstein?" she asked. "You askin' about Molly Gardstein's family?"

"Yes. I believe they lived on this street twenty years ago."

"All long gone now. Moved away, they did."

"Do you know where they moved to?"

"Couldn't say."

"Did you know Molly?"

"Of sorts."

"I understand she went missing after the death of her friend, Mary Steinway, who called herself Jane Stroud."

"Yeah, I remember. Why yer askin'?"

I explained who I was, and that I was interested in finding out more about Mary. She said nothing in response but raised a doubtful eyebrow.

"When did you last see Molly?" I asked.

"Same time everyone else did; when that Jane lass got poisoned. People said Molly done it."

"How well did you know her?"

"I knew 'er quite well, and if yer ask me it weren't 'er. Molly wouldn't never 'ave done nuffink like that."

"Did you know Jane at all?"

"Met 'er once or twice. Can't say I took to the girl."

"Why not?"

"Bit of a madam, I reckon. Never quite knew where you was wiv 'er. Word was, she kept looking' at the other gals' men."

"What do you mean?"

"Exactly what I says!" She laughed. "Yer know the type, don't yer? The type what's always after yer 'usband."

"Do you remember Jane doing anything like that, or was it just a rumour?"

"Oh yeah. Kemp, I think 'is name was." She paused to think for a moment. "Joshua Kemp, that's it. 'E'd been keepin' company wiv Sally Walcot 'til that Jane come along."

"Sally Walcot? The daughter of Jane's landlady?"

"Dunno, but Sally Walcot was 'er name."

Miss Walcot had omitted to mention this fact to me. *Had she forgotten about it or just considered it irrelevant? Or had she purposefully concealed it?*

"Thank you for your help," I said. "Do you know of anyone else who might know where Molly went?"

She shook her head. "Ain't no one's gonna know that."

"Who was she friendly with at the time, aside from Jane?"

The wrinkled woman placed her hands on her hips and sighed. "She took up with some fella called Burns, that much I know. But you won't get nothin' out of him, I'm sure."

"Does he still live around here?"

"Ask down the Moon an' Seven Stars."

"Is that a public house?"

"Yeah, the one just off Cable Street. They know 'im in there."

I followed the woman's directions to the Moon and Seven Stars, which was located in another narrow lane just off Cable Street. With only a small sign outside and the curtains drawn at the windows, it appeared to be the sort of establishment that would not be terribly welcoming to unfamiliar faces.

Thoughts of the man who had threatened me on St George Street returned as I paused just outside it. I knew I would be risking another such encounter by stepping inside the place, but if Mr Burns were there, and able to tell me more about Molly, it would be a risk worth taking. I took a deep breath, gripped the handle of my carpet bag tightly and pushed the door open.

As I had expected, everyone looked up at me as I stepped inside the alehouse's dingy interior. My eyes took a moment to adjust to the gloom and I felt disarmed by my obscured vision.

"Yer in the wrong place!" a gravelly voice called out from a dark corner of the pub.

A cackle of laughter followed, and I smiled in an attempt to make light of the situation.

"Yer ain't gonna get us along ter church," shouted out another voice, "and we don't want none o' yer pamphlets. We can't read 'em anyway."

Although I was growing a little tired of being mistaken for a missionary in squalid parts of London, I could see why it was the most obvious explanation as to why a well-presented, middle-class lady should wish to enter such a place.

A man in a colourful waistcoat approached me. He was about forty, with neat grey hair and whiskers. He held a cigar in a hand adorned with several gold rings. He smelled strongly of eau de cologne, and I didn't like the way his keen eyes looked me up and down.

"How can I help you, madam?"

"I'm looking for Mr Burns."

"Are you, indeed?" He sucked on his cigar, then slowly released a ring of smoke from between his thick lips. "What for?"

I hesitated for a moment, unsure whether to tell him who I was and why I was asking. For a brief moment I yearned to turn tail and dash out of the alehouse as quickly as possible. There was something about the man that made my flesh creep. But it was possible that he knew Mr Burns, and it was possible that Mr Burns could lead me to Molly.

"I'm looking for Molly Gardstein," I explained, "and I understand that Mr Burns might be able to help. Do you know him?"

"Everyone knows Burns." He grinned, displaying a row of small, yellow teeth.

"Do you know where I can find him?"

"I'm not telling you where he lives. He won't thank me for that."

"Perhaps you could pass a message on to him for me."

"A message?" he repeated slowly. "What do you think I am, the telegram office?" He seemed determined to draw out our encounter for as long as possible.

I pulled my purse out of my carpet bag and found a

shilling, which I held out to him. "I realise it wouldn't be an official service, but I'm willing to pay for it all the same."

He grinned again, wrapped his palm around my outstretched hand and gently pushed it back toward me. "What message do you want passing to him?" he asked.

I didn't like the way he kept hold of my hand. He wasn't holding it tightly, but the contact made me feel decidedly uncomfortable. It was all I could do to keep my voice steady and calm, and to keep my eyes fixed on his. I didn't want him to realise I was afraid.

"I'd be very grateful if you could simply tell him to contact me." I pulled my hand away from his, dropped the shilling into my bag and pulled out one of my old visiting cards. I handed it to him and watched as he carefully considered everything that was written on it. My old cards still bore the address of the *Morning Express* offices, and I drew some comfort from the fact that I was rarely there these days.

"Miss Green..." he said. I didn't correct him, preferring to keep my married name to myself. Then he lifted the card to his nose and sniffed it.

It was impossible to hide my disgust at this gesture. He let out a loud laugh in response to my repulsed expression.

"I'll pass this on to him, Miss Green. He's a lucky man to have a lady like yourself searching for him."

"Thank you for your help, Mr..."

"Willis. That's what they call me."

I wondered who *they* were and whether this clarification implied that Willis wasn't his real name. I thanked him for his time and left the alehouse.

Once outside, I ran along Cable Street until I felt I had put enough distance between myself and everyone at the Moon and Seven Stars.

CHAPTER 23

A few days later I met Eliza for an excursion to Greenwich. We walked around Greenwich Park, enjoying the view from the Royal Observatory and admiring the classical splendour of the Queen's House and the Royal Naval College. We made our return journey by steamboat.

"You must enjoy being a lady of leisure these days, Penelope," observed my sister as we watched the wharves and jetties of the northern riverbank slip by. We leaned against the rail and held on to our hats as the wind whipped around us. "When I think about all the dangerous situations and people you encountered, I struggle to believe you spent all those years working as a news reporter. What a hazardous profession it was for you."

"It is nice to have a little more leisure time," I responded. I decided not to tell her about my investigation into Mary Steinway's murder as I knew she would react with scorn.

"How's Francis?" I asked.

A smile played on my sister's lips. "He seems well."

"Have you seen much of him recently?"

She gave a brief laugh and a little colour appeared on her cheeks. "I don't think one would use the word 'much', as such. I have seen him, but... We're nothing more than friends, Penelope." She turned to me, her face appearing bashful. "There really is nothing more to it than that."

"But you are fond of each other."

She giggled uncharacteristically. "I'm fond of him, yes. I couldn't possibly say whether he's fond of me or not."

"Of course he is."

"Oh, Penelope, don't say such things! Now you're just teasing."

"I think your friendship is a wonderful thing, and perhaps when your divorce is over and done with—"

"Exactly! I can't consider anything of the kind until that day arrives."

"I'm sure he'll wait patiently for that day."

"That's enough now. Francis happened to mention that he'd seen you at the library. Have you found it impossible to stay away?"

"I haven't completely stopped writing, Ellie. I'm still putting together articles for ladies' periodicals and that sort of thing."

"He told me you were looking up newspapers from twenty years ago."

"Yes, I was doing a little research." I made a mental note to be careful about what I told Francis. It seemed any information of this kind would quickly find its way to Eliza.

"You should help me with the work I'm doing for Miss Barrington now that you have some more time on your hands. She's just bought a row of houses in Lambeth to be let out to the poor and needy. There's an awful lot to do, and we need new members at the West London Women's Society, too."

"I see."

"You don't seem terribly enthusiastic about the idea, Penelope."

"It's just that I have a fair amount of work to do, and I'm also rather busy working on Father's book at the moment."

"You still consider him the sort of man who deserves to have a book written about him, do you?"

"Yes. He's led a very interesting life."

She gave a hollow laugh. "You could call it that."

"And besides, I'd begun working on it before he even returned."

"Yes, I suppose you have been committed to the project for a while now."

"He'd really like to see you, Ellie."

"Has he told you that?"

"Of course. He's not expecting you to, but—"

"Good. Then he won't be disappointed."

"But I know he's hoping you'll change your mind."

"I'm sure he'd like us all to forgive him as well. The truth is, I'm rather busy at the moment, Penelope, what with my work for Miss Barrington and all the meetings I've been having with my lawyer. The divorce case is due to start soon."

"You have no time to see Father, then?"

"I shall have to decide if I even want to first."

My sister's stubbornness was beginning to irritate me. I stepped back from the rail for a moment and glanced around at the other passengers. A tall man of a shabby-genteel appearance wearing a top hat caught my eye. He seemed to be looking directly at me but, as he appeared unfamiliar, I had no desire to invite an approach of any sort.

I turned back to face Eliza and addressed her calmly. "How would you feel if Father returned to South America tomorrow, Ellie?"

She considered this for a moment. "But he can't be," she

said eventually. "You told me you intend to meet him at the museum in South Kensington to look at his work."

"He may suddenly decide to leave tomorrow or the day after that. How would you feel about that?"

"Now you're just trying to make me feel guilty about not seeing him."

"Not at all. I'm just trying to help you understand how important your relationship with him is."

"He's my father! We'll only ever have one father, Penelope."

"My thoughts exactly. So why let pride get in the way?"

"Pride? I'm not proud! Anyway, that's quite enough about Father. We're approaching Temple Pier."

The boat slowed as we passed a group of watermen congregated on Temple Steps. The boat let out a great rush of steam and juddered slowly to a halt.

"Please don't be angry, Ellie," I said as my sister readied herself to disembark.

"I'm not angry."

"You seem it."

"Are you getting off here?"

"No. I'm going on to Charing Cross so I can meet James at Scotland Yard."

"Do pass on my regards to him, Penelope."

I waved to Eliza once she reached the jetty, at which point the boat moved off again. As it did so, I became aware of someone standing just to my left. I turned to see the man in the top hat who had been watching me earlier.

"Mrs Blakely," he said with a smile. "Just the lady I want to speak to."

I felt a pang of alarm. "How do you know my name? Who are you?"

CHAPTER 24

He was a tall man of about forty-five. His features had probably once been handsome, but his skin was coarse and his greying whiskers covered heavy jowls. The jacket and waistcoat he wore were well tailored, but tight-fitting and worn with age. He gave the impression of an affluent man about town who had fallen on hard times.

"Terribly rude of me to strike up a conversation without introducing myself, wasn't it? Masefield's the name. Mr Robert Masefield. I hear you're interested in hearing about Mary Steinway."

I was quite startled. "How do you know that?"

"Word spreads."

"Who did you hear it from?"

He gave a shrug and lit his pipe. "That would be telling."

"Did you know Mary?" I asked.

"I might have done."

"Is that a yes or a no?"

"That'll depend on whether you can make it worth my while." He looked out over the railings and puffed on his pipe.

"Is it money you're after?" I asked.

He gave an uneasy laugh. "Makes me sound like a mercenary, doesn't it?"

"But you'd like some money, all the same."

"Who wouldn't?"

I turned away from him. It was entirely possible that he would be of no help to me at all. I decided that if it was money he was after, I was probably more useful to him than he was to me. "If you don't mind, I should like to enjoy the rest of the trip in peace," I said.

"But you don't have long, Mrs Blakely. We'll be at Charing Cross pier shortly."

I surmised that he must have overheard my conversation with Eliza. "Have you been following me?" I asked.

"Yes, but only because I think it'll help if you hear what I have to say."

"How do I know that you have anything useful to tell me?"

"Maybe I haven't. Have you found out why she changed her name yet?"

"I assume she didn't want people to know she was estranged from her husband."

"In which case she'd most likely have used her previous name, Steinway. But Jane Stroud is a different name entirely, isn't it?"

"Why did she change her name, then?"

"Ah, well that would be telling, wouldn't it? I'll let you in on the fact that someone else was involved. Someone quite well-known, I might add."

"Who?"

"A member of parliament."

"But you're not prepared to tell me who until I give you some money. Is that right?"

"A fair deal, wouldn't you say?"

"A shilling. That's all I have."

"Well, that's a start."

He gave an insincere smile and I wondered whether I could trust him or not. I considered it fairly unlikely, but reasoned that I would be foolish to turn down his offer if a shilling were enough to buy me a crucial piece of information. I had almost given the lecherous Mr Willis the same amount, after all. I reached into my carpet bag for my coin purse.

Mr Masefield clearly had no qualms about accepting money from a lady. He pocketed the shilling, then rested his forearms on the railings. "Sir Octavius Harvey," he said. "Member of Parliament for Southwark. Do you know him?"

"Not personally, but I've heard of him. A Liberal, isn't he?"

"Yes. He was Under-Secretary of State for Foreign Affairs until quite recently. He's also a member of the Privy Council."

"And he knew Mary?"

"Oh, yes. Extremely well, in fact."

The most I knew about Mary's adult life was that she had been married and given birth to a son, who had subsequently died. *How had she become acquainted with a politician?* I wondered.

"Gus was always set to be successful. He had that air about him."

"Gus?"

"That's what we called him. Octavius is quite a mouthful, wouldn't you say? We knocked about together twenty years or so ago."

"Doing what?"

"It was all a bit of a party, really. Staying up until dawn, sleeping until mid-afternoon. That sort of thing. There was always a party somewhere; here in London or out in the countryside when the season ended. We went to all sorts of fine houses. Sometimes I wasn't even sure who owned them! Invitations would simply turn up, and off we all went. There was a group of us chaps from school. Quite a loose-knit group, I'd say. We didn't live in each other's pockets, but we had a lot of fun when we got together. There were a few girls, too. Mary was one of them."

"How did you get to know her?"

"It's hard to recall, really. She just sort of appeared with one or two other girls. I think they all worked at a hotel or club of some sort. One of the chaps must have invited them along for an evening, and that was that. They were all good company, and Gus was very fond of Mary. She was a fine girl."

"Did you learn much about her?"

"Not a great deal. Her father was a lawyer, I believe."

"Were Sir Octavius and Mary courting?"

"Yes, but not officially. By which I mean that Gus hadn't told his folks about her. She was a girl with a past, as I understand it."

"She had been married."

"I only discovered that a while later. When I knew her, she had gone back to using the name Steinway rather than her married name. She enjoyed a drink as much as the rest of us. Some of us drank to be merry... I was one of those. Others drank to forget, and that's certainly the impression I got from Mary."

"What did she want to forget?"

He spread his palms out wide. "Who knows? The girl was a bit of a mystery on that front. I don't think many of us were bothered either way, to be honest. Those were rather indulgent days. We were only thinking about ourselves and the next party, or the next pretty girl to sit on our knee. Terrible when I say it aloud, isn't it? I can't say I'm proud of those carefree days of youth, but I had a thoroughly enjoyable time back then."

"Did Sir Octavius enjoy it in equal measure?"

"Oh yes! Gus loved every minute of it. He was supposed

to be attending Cambridge at the time, but he'd dropped out. His behaviour was a little unruly for a while, but he eventually managed to get back on the straight and narrow. He was the son of a baronet, you see. It was rather easier for him to regain a bit of respectability than it was for me." He gazed out across the water, as if reflecting on a life of regrets and missed opportunities. "We spent the late summers of '63 and '64 at Blinker's place. He had an enormous estate in Somerset."

"Blinker?"

He turned to face me as he clarified this statement. "John Cecil-Palmer. We called him Blinker because he was always doing this." He blinked his eyes in quick succession.

"I see."

"The place had a fantastic lake, and there was some pretty good shooting, too. Picnics, boating and parties... lots of people there. Half of London, I'd wager!"

"Half of London's *wealthiest*, perhaps."

"Ah, yes. That goes without saying. Anyway, the place emptied out rather swiftly after old Blinker died."

"He died?"

"Haven't you heard the story?"

"I can't say that I have."

"He drowned in the boating lake. He was pushed in late one evening."

"Was the culprit ever caught?"

"Oh, yes. A chap named Derricks swung for it. He was a worker on the estate."

"Goodness! He was hanged for Blinker's murder?"

"Yes. Derricks admitted to it, hoping his life would be spared, only it wasn't. It was a silly, spur-of-the-moment sort of thing. There had been a great deal of drinking, of course. Then there was an argument and he just pushed Blinker in. I don't suppose he ever thought the poor chap would drown.

The house was sold after that, and once Derricks was hanged the rest of us didn't want much to do with each other."

"Was Mary staying at the house when Blinker died?"

"Yes, we all were; all the usual crowd. His death put an end to the parties, that's for sure. Everyone went off in pursuit of marriage and sensible professions after that. Everyone except me, that is."

"Why didn't you do the same?"

"The old drink had a hold over me by then, to be quite honest with you. I was in a bit of a state, in fact. I discovered a temper I never knew I had." He shook his head. "Those were dark days."

The steamboat was drawing close to Charing Cross Pier.

"Did you see much of Sir Octavius and Mary after Blinker's death?"

"I saw them once or twice. There was the funeral, of course. We all attended that. And then we met up in London, but it wasn't the same. It can't be, can it? Gus was terribly affected by what had happened. He didn't laugh much; there was no lightness about him at all. Perfectly understandable, really. Seeing each other again only served to remind us how awful the whole business had been. Gus decided to make a serious go of it in politics and I had no interest in such things, so I wished him well and that was the last I saw of him. About eighteen months later I read in the newspaper that he was married. Not to Mary, though, so I can only imagine they went their separate ways shortly after that last rendezvous. He ended up marrying the daughter of a wealthy industrialist."

"And Mary?"

"She was saddened by Blinker's death, like the rest of us, but I have no idea where she went. I heard she had died some weeks after it happened."

"Why did she change her name?"

"Most of the girls did after all that business down at Blinker's place. No one wanted to admit they'd been there, and rumours abounded that Derricks had been forced into making a confession. Gus's father ensured that there were no reports of his son being present at the time. We all had to distance ourselves from it. I took myself off to Greece for a year."

"Do you think Mary's murder might have had something to do with Blinker's death?"

He shrugged. "How should I know? That's a question only the police could answer... or perhaps a keen reporter like yourself. I think it's time for you to disembark, Mrs Blakely."

The gangplank was laid down and a number of passengers began to walk down it onto dry land.

"Thank you for your help, Mr Masefield," I said, unsure what to make of all that he had told me.

He doffed his hat. "Pleasure."

CHAPTER 25

"It worries me enormously to hear that this Masefield chap has been following you," said James as we sat in his draughty office at Scotland Yard. "How did he find out that you were looking into Mary Steinway's death?"

"He wouldn't tell me," I replied. "I've asked a few people about her now, so I suppose he heard that way."

James tapped his pencil impatiently against the desk. "Well, I don't like it. I don't like it at all."

"I didn't get the impression there was anything malevolent about him," I said.

"But how would you know?"

"He just didn't seem terribly nasty. There was something rather sorrowful about him, actually. He seemed to be one of those people who gets left behind while the rest of the world moves on."

"What sort of people, exactly?"

I shrugged. "People who haven't made the most of the opportunities available to them. He told me the drink had taken hold of him for a while."

James gave a knowing nod. "I'd say he's the sort of chap who would best be avoided from now on."

"I'd have no idea where to find him again even if I wanted to."

"Good. Let's hope he doesn't find you again either."

"But what he told me was rather useful."

"If it's even true."

"Why wouldn't it be?"

"He wanted a shilling out of you for it."

"That isn't an enormous sum of money, James. And some of what he said could be easily verified. I'll visit the reading room tomorrow to do some research. Do you recall hearing about the murder of John Cecil-Palmer in Somerset?"

"No. But then I suppose it happened more than twenty years ago now, and some distance from here."

"I shall look it up in the old newspapers tomorrow."

From what Robert Masefield had told me, I deduced that John Cecil-Palmer's death had taken place during the late summer of 1864. Once again, Francis helped me gather together a number of heavy volumes in the newspaper room, and it wasn't long before I found the relevant reports from the August of that year.

I read about the sorry incident as well as the inquest, which recorded that William Derricks had confessed to pushing Cecil-Palmer into the lake at Mordaunt House, near Bridgwater in Somerset. The report stated that John Cecil-Palmer and William Derricks had been lakeside that evening with two unnamed acquaintances. I scoured the reports for further details of who these people might have been, but I found nothing to that effect.

Everything else was just as Mr Masefield had told me.

Contrary to James's opinion, he had proven himself a reliable informant. *But what had been his motive for telling me so much? Had he only been interested in the money?* I struggled to believe a shilling would have been reason enough for him to speak to me. I felt sure there had to be another motive, but I couldn't think what.

I browsed various current south London newspapers to find out whether Sir Octavius Harvey had any public appointments planned. I was pleased to read in the *Southwark Gazette* that he was due to attend a public meeting at Bermondsey Town Hall the following week. I made a note of the date and time.

Once I had finished in the newspaper room, I found an empty desk in the reading room and wrote a letter to Mrs Anne Pelham-Heathcote in Hampstead. I explained that I was looking into the death of her sister Mary and would welcome an opportunity to meet. Then it suddenly occurred to me that there was another line of research I could pursue.

"Is there a directory for clergymen?" I asked Francis.

"Anglican clergy?"

"I assume so. I'm looking for a Mr Loach, who was married in an Anglican church."

"You need *Crockford's Clerical Directory*. I'll go and fetch it for you."

He soon returned with a heavy-looking book. "Twenty-year-old newspapers and a directory of vicars, eh, Penny?" he whispered. "What are you writing about?"

"Oh, it's just an article I've been commissioned to write."

I should have liked to discuss Mary Steinway's case with Francis, but felt sure that Eliza would soon hear of my work and scold me for putting myself in danger once again.

"About vicars?" he asked.

"Yes."

"I see." He didn't seem entirely convinced, but he pushed

his spectacles up his nose nevertheless and smiled. "I shall leave you to it."

"Thank you, Francis."

Crockford's Clerical Directory proved straightforward enough to consult, and I soon found Revd Loach's name. He was listed as 'Loach, Edwin Thomas', and his address was recorded at St Saviour's Vicarage in Chalk Farm. I smiled. He was nowhere near America or New Zealand. Indeed, he was just a few miles from our St John's Wood home.

CHAPTER 26

Sir Octavius Harvey was a smooth-featured man with neat whiskers. He looked about forty-five years of age and his sleek, side-parted hair was sandy brown. He and four other men were seated at a polished table on a small stage in Bermondsey Town Hall, listening intently to a discussion on improvements to public baths and washhouses. When he spoke, his voice was eloquent and mellifluous. He projected authority and gravitas and I imagined his constituents placing a great deal of trust in their member of parliament.

Could this be the same man who had attended disreputable parties with Robert Masefield? Despite his professional manner, I decided he could well be. Experience had taught me that appearances can be deceiving.

I had purposefully arrived late so I didn't have to sit through any lengthy debates that applied only to Bermondsey residents. I was keen to speak to Sir Octavius after the meeting, however. As I listened to the ongoing discussion, I wondered how graciously he would receive my questions.

It took a while to find this out. Judging by the number of

constituents wishing to speak to him once the meeting had concluded, Sir Octavius was a popular man. Among those requesting an audience was a large man who spoke of setting up a new society for dock labourers and a well-dressed lady who objected to the closure of a ragged school.

Sir Octavius placed his top hat on his head before responding briefly yet politely to each person in turn before an officious, grey-suited assistant asked them to arrange a meeting via the MP's secretary if they wished to take the discussion further.

Once the crowd had dispersed, I stepped forward and introduced myself as Mrs Penny Blakely, explaining that I was a journalist. "I wondered if I might speak to you about Mary Steinway?" I asked.

If the name provoked a reaction within him, he showed no sign of it at all. His calm green eyes rested unblinkingly on mine. "Now that's a name I haven't heard in a long time. May I ask what has sparked your interest in Miss Steinway?"

I provided the same explanation I had given the other people I had spoken to.

Sir Octavius responded with a nod and pushed his lower lip out as he pondered my words.

"Do you live in this constituency, Mrs Blakely?" asked the uptight assistant.

"No. I live in Marylebone."

"In which case, you'll need to raise the matter with your own member of—"

Sir Octavius held up a hand to stop him. "It's quite all right, Cooper. I'll deal with this." He pulled a gold watch from his pocket and glanced at it. "The hour is growing late and my carriage is waiting outside to take me to Mayfair. Perhaps you'd like to join us, Mrs Blakely? We can talk on the way. You have a fair way to travel this evening. My carriage can take you home once the driver has dropped me at my club."

"That would be extremely kind," I replied. "But only if it's not too much trouble."

"It's no trouble at all! Do join me. I'm intrigued to find out more."

The grumpy assistant joined us in the landau, which was pulled by a pair of well-groomed horses. The two men sat opposite me, and Sir Octavius lit a cigar.

"You don't mind if I smoke, do you, Mrs Blakely? I find I'm always in rather dire need of a little tobacco after a public meeting. Though I suppose there are worse things to be in dire need of." He smiled. "Now, what was it you wished to ask me?"

"I was recently approached by your old friend, Robert Masefield."

"Masefield approached you? How very odd. I'm sorry to hear that, Mrs Blakely. He always was that sort of chap, I'm afraid." His voice had lost its clipped edge and he sounded a little more relaxed now that he was smoking a cigar in his private carriage. It was rather easier to imagine him partying with Mr Masefield now.

"He somehow heard that I was investigating Miss Steinway's death," I said, "and he told me you had both known her."

"He gave you my name, did he?"

"Yes."

"How interesting." He puffed on his cigar.

The grumpy assistant glowered at me, as if he resented my presence.

I glanced out of the window at the busy street. The shopfronts glowed orange in the setting sun and the alleyways were already dark. I recalled walking these very streets in search of the Bermondsey poisoner.

"I knew Mary all right," Sir Octavius eventually said. "It was a long time ago now. I heard about the murder and was terribly saddened by the news, though I hadn't seen her for a good while before then. I always presumed they would catch the person responsible, but to learn that no one has been brought to justice all these years later..." He pulled on his cigar again and shook his head. "It's terrible," he uttered through a cloud of smoke. "Did Masefield ask for money in return for his information?"

"Yes."

He cackled. "He hasn't changed a bit! I take it my name was included in the information you paid for."

I nodded.

"Well, you've been sold short there. I'm not sure I can tell you anything you don't already know."

"When did you last see Miss Steinway?"

He spluttered on his cigar. "Goodness! That's the sort of question a police officer would ask. I hope you're not implying anything, Mrs Blakely."

"No, not at all. I'm simply trying to find out what her life was like in the months leading up to her death."

"I couldn't tell you much about that because I hadn't seen her in a long while, as I've already explained. It would have been..." He closed his eyes as he tried to recall. "The end of '64." His eyes opened again. "Not quite the end, actually. I'd say it was about October time. Who on earth would harm a girl like that? She was delightful company."

"Have you ever heard the name Molly Gardstein?"

"No. Who might she be?"

"A friend of Miss Steinway's. She went missing around the time Mary was murdered. Many people believe Miss Gardstein was the killer."

"Never heard of her. Any idea why she might have done such a thing?"

"There were rumours of a disagreement."

"I see."

"Miss Steinway wasn't exactly earning a reputable living before she died. She was arrested a number of times for thieving."

"Oh dear. That is sad news."

"And the drink had apparently taken hold of her."

"I'm afraid to say there were signs of that back when I knew her. She always enjoyed a drink, though I must highlight the word *enjoy*. She wasn't a miserable, solitary drinker; she merely drank with her friends on social occasions."

"With you?"

"Yes, we were friends. Very good friends, I should add. That's not common knowledge, by the way." He added emphasis to his words by pointing his cigar at me. "And I would take a dim view if that were to be mentioned in a newspaper. I wasn't married back then, or even betrothed to be married, so there was no wrongdoing on my part. But the association wouldn't do me any favours."

"I understand."

"Good. I'm extremely devoted to my dear wife, Julia, and to our children. Julia and I have been married for fifteen years now. I'm a very different chap from the one who knew Miss Steinway way back when."

"I see."

"I had to pull myself together in the autumn of '64. I'd gone off the rails a little, so to speak. What young man doesn't at some time or another? But with my father being who he was, and a certain weight of expectation resting upon my shoulders, I had to do the right thing, and that meant ending a number of relationships."

"Including your relationship with Miss Steinway."

"Yes. She was a delightful girl, you understand, but not the sort I could marry."

"Was she upset when you ended it?"

"Yes, I would say that she was a little upset. But we both knew it had to happen. It had become rather inevitable, you see, after a particularly unpleasant incident that had taken place earlier that summer."

"The death of John Cecil-Palmer, you mean?" I ventured.

He gave a wry smile. "Masefield told you about him as well, did he? Yes, that was the catalyst." He turned to look out of the window as we crossed London Bridge, the lights from the boats and wharves reflected in the river. "You'd be wise to watch what Masefield tells you," he added, still looking out. "He's the sort of chap who bears a grudge."

"Are you inferring that he had some sort of ulterior motive in speaking to me?"

He laughed. "Masefield always had a motive, all right!" He turned his face toward me again. "He was perpetually driven by self-interest, and I can't imagine he's changed a bit."

"Might some of the things he says be untrue, in that case?"

"I won't call the chap a liar, but he just has a tendency to frame events in a way that paints him in a favourable light."

"I found him to be quite self-deprecating."

"It's all an act, Mrs Blakely. All an act. I don't suppose he mentioned that Mary rejected his advances, did he?"

"No, he didn't tell me that."

"Just one example of his framing, you see. He was quite offended when she turned him down. There was no expectation on my part that she should, you understand. I enjoyed the company of various ladies in those days, and I didn't expect any loyalty from them, if you catch my drift. I do hope you're not offended by all this, Mrs Blakely. Our morals were rather loose in those days." He glanced across at his assistant and gave a conspiratorial chuckle. "As a journalist, I imagine you've seen a good deal of what humanity has to offer, and

I'm sure you have a fair idea of what young men can be like, too." He looked me up and down, then gave a wolfish grin. "I wish you the very best of luck in finding Mary's murderer, Mrs Blakely. It won't be an easy task, especially considering the length of time that has passed since then. You'll let me know if there's anything I can do to help, won't you? I can't help feeling partly responsible for what happened to her."

"Why?"

"I didn't exactly help the girl's reputation; I probably made it worse, in fact. I'm ashamed to say that we practically lived as man and wife for about a year. I should have behaved more considerately and given the poor girl a chance. The trouble was, I liked her too much, and I'm ashamed to say that I behaved rather selfishly. Mind you, I had no idea she'd been married before. It was a surprise when I found that out."

"Were you invited to speak at the inquest?"

"There was never any question of me doing so. My father had a word with the coroner to ensure that my name was entirely left out of it. I was just beginning my career in politics and it wouldn't have looked good. Besides, there was nothing useful I could have said, was there? She was living a completely different life at the time of her death. Ratcliffe Highway, of all places! The poor girl. Her path really did take an unfortunate turn.

"I suppose the only way to make amends now would be to find out who was behind her tragic death. It sounds as though this friend of hers needs to be found. What did you say her name was?"

"Molly Gardstein."

"There are certainly some questions for her to answer, the first being why she ran off like that. But I don't suppose we can assume that Miss Gardstein was responsible for Mary's death. There must be other suspects to consider. If I'm to help you, Mrs Blakely, I require your explicit assurance that the contents of this conversation will remain private. Is that clear?"

"Absolutely."

"I shall do whatever is in my power to help you find out what happened to Mary, but I must do so quietly, and from the sidelines. I'm sure you'll agree that my behaviour hasn't been too terrible in the grand scheme of things, and there are many chaps who would happily admit to the same. But the public expects a good deal of its public servants these days and would be likely to take a dim view of my antics, youthful and foolish as they were."

"People might be more forgiving than you expect."

"I have no wish to find out one way or the other! Now, there's to be no mention of our conversation this evening, please, but I shall see what I can do. Which police division does Ratcliffe fall under?"

"H Division."

"I see. In that case I'll begin with the commissioner at Scotland Yard. We're members of the same club."

"I'll be interested to hear what he has to say. My husband is an inspector at the Yard. He hasn't been able to find out much about the original investigation yet, as the Yard wasn't involved."

"Was it not? That doesn't seem right. Your husband's an inspector, you say?" He sat back and looked me up and down again, as if viewing me from a fresh perspective. "Interesting. Given your and your husband's professional abilities, I'd have thought you might have been able to crack this one, but I take it the case isn't as simple as it first seemed."

"No, it isn't. Especially when it comes to investigating it twenty years later."

"Which begs the question: why do it at all? Don't doubt me for one moment; I'm sure your actions are honourable.

But so many years have passed since this terrible event! I imagine you would have been rather young back then."

"*Fairly* young."

"There's no need to tell me how old," he said with a grin. "I'd never ask a lady to reveal her age. Leave it with me, Mrs Blakely, and I'll see what I can do."

CHAPTER 27

"We've had an interesting character in here asking for you, Mrs Blakely," said Mr Sherman, my former editor. We sat in his office after he had summoned me that morning by telegram. "I think he was under the impression that you still worked here."

"Did he mention the name Burns?"

"He did, as a matter of fact. He said that Mr Burns is willing to meet with you." He passed me an envelope. "And he left you a message."

"Thank you."

"I can't say that I like the idea of this messenger chap, whoever he was, and Burns, whoever he might be, thinking that the work you're undertaking is associated with the *Morning Express*."

"You did agree to publish an article about Mary Steinway if I managed to find out any useful information, sir. And I'm pleased to say that I have found out a great deal since we last spoke."

"I'm sure you have, Mrs Blakely. Knowing you, you've been shaking the tree quite vigorously. But I don't want people thinking your work has been commissioned by this paper."

"I can't see how I might have given anyone that impression. I've explained to everyone I've spoken to that I'm undertaking this work for myself." I realised as I said this, however, that perhaps I hadn't made this clear enough.

"Then why did that unsavoury messenger turn up here?"

"Most likely because I gave one of my old visiting cards to a gentleman – not that I feel entirely comfortable describing him as that – a *man* at an alehouse on Cable Street. I didn't want to give him one with my new address on."

"Because he seemed like an untrustworthy type?"

"Yes. I didn't like the look of him."

"So you thought it would be appropriate to give him the address of the *Morning Express* offices instead, creating the impression that the investigations you were undertaking in an insalubrious part of town had been sanctioned by me?"

"I'm sorry, sir. It was never my intention to implicate this newspaper in my work. I didn't think it through properly when I gave him the card. To be quite honest, I didn't give it much thought at all. I needed information, but I had found myself conversing with an unpleasant man in unpleasant surroundings, and I wanted to get out of there as quickly as possible."

He sat back in his chair. "Still out there taking risks, then, Mrs Blakely."

"It has to be done on occasion. I'm only sorry that I appear to have misled such a shady character."

"There's no need to be sorry for misleading characters like that, Mrs Blakely. You should be sorrier that you've put the reputation of this newspaper at risk."

"I conducted myself quite properly, sir."

"I'm sure you did. But when word gets around, and it surely will, that the *Morning Express* newspaper is investigating the death of Miss Steinway, it'll give people a false impression about the paper, wouldn't you say? I could suddenly find myself answerable to all sorts of people, not least the Metropolitan Police. Do you think they'll take kindly to an established newspaper investigating a case they failed to solve?"

"No, but then they should have done the job properly in the first place."

"I hope you haven't been casting aspersions like that in the name of this newspaper."

"Of course not. I have only ever voiced that opinion to you just now, sir."

"I'm sure H Division wish that a better job had been done back then, but we're talking about a case from two decades ago, Mrs Blakely. We can't go around correcting all the mistakes that have ever been made by the police, pleasing as that might sound."

"I apologise for implicating the newspaper in my investigation, sir. That certainly wasn't my intention. I won't go distributing any more of my *Morning Express* visiting cards."

"May I also suggest that if you meet a man so deeply unpleasant that you prefer not to give him one of your own cards, you might be better off avoiding him altogether? Or perhaps you should ask your husband to deal with him. Does Inspector Blakely know you've been meeting with such unsavoury characters?"

"He has a reasonable idea."

He gave a mild snort. "I suspect you haven't told him the full story. I know you wouldn't want to worry him, but you must be careful, Mrs Blakely."

"I realise that, but nothing untoward has happened so far."

"How very reassuring."

"Mr Burns may be able to tell me where Molly Gardstein is. She was the main suspect in Miss Steinway's murder."

"I see."

"I'm confident that I'll be able to gather a good deal of useful information, sir. Enough for a full article, perhaps."

He leaned forward across his desk. "I must stress to you, Mrs Blakely, that I cannot guarantee the *Morning Express* will be able to publish any such article."

"I was under the impression that you were interested in doing so, sir."

"It's certainly an interesting case, but I can't be certain that it'll be publishable. No doubt the information you've been uncovering is most useful, Mrs Blakely, but it's also based on the word of others. And these people may well have an interest in influencing what gets reported. You can't trust everything they tell you, you know."

"I realise that, sir. But I've been speaking to a lot of people, and between them I believe I'll be able to build up a viable picture of what happened to poor Mary."

He sat back in his chair again. "Very good, Mrs Blakely. I wish you all the best with it."

"Is there a possibility that you would be willing to publish it?"

"I really can't say at this point. Even if you managed to find Miss Gardstein, what then?"

"She may be arrested!"

"On what evidence? She's had twenty years to hide anything that might incriminate her."

For some reason, Mr Sherman no longer seemed supportive of my work, but I couldn't understand why. I picked up my bag and rose to my feet. "I'm sorry if I misinterpreted what I considered to be enthusiasm on your part when I first discussed this case with you, sir. I shall ensure that the name of the *Morning Express* is never mentioned again in the course of my investigations. In fact, I shall leave my old cards with you now." I began rummaging about for them in my carpet bag. "You can make sure they're properly disposed of. You could even throw them on your fire," I glanced at the small hearth. "That way you can be certain they've been completely destroyed. Here you are." I began to deposit the cards on his desk with a slap of my hand. "I think that's all of them."

I looked down at my bag again, and from the corner of my eye I noticed Mr Sherman shifting uncomfortably in his chair.

"I'm sure there's no need to burn them, Mrs Blakely. I can entrust you with the remaining cards—"

"No, it's quite all right, sir. After all, I don't work for this newspaper any more, do I? It was foolish of me to mention it to anyone. Old habits die hard, I suppose." Tears pricked the backs of my eyes as I snapped my bag shut and walked toward the door.

"Before you leave, Mrs Blakely, there was something else I wanted to mention to you."

I paused with my hand on the door handle.

"I had a conversation with Mrs Curridge from *The Lady's Review*, and she seemed extremely interested in hiring you as a regular writer. She wanted to invite you to meet her at their offices on Friday morning."

"I can't," I replied curtly. "I'm meeting my father then."

"I see. And how is your father?"

"He's very well, thank you."

And with that, I left.

I opened the envelope the messenger had brought to the *Morning Express* offices during my train ride home to St John's Wood. Written in a scrawling hand, the misspelled message suggested an unusual meeting place, along with instructions on how to locate it.

CHAPTER 28

"I can't understand why Mr Sherman has suddenly lost all enthusiasm for the article," I said to James over dinner that evening. "He seemed keen to publish something a few weeks ago. Perhaps I misunderstood him."

"I shouldn't think so. It sounds as though something has made him change his mind."

"It must have been that messenger turning up at the office after I handed out one of my old visiting cards. I realise it was rather presumptuous of me, but I didn't think he'd take such offence at it."

"It seems most unlike Mr Sherman," said James. "I don't know him terribly well, but I can't imagine him being so offended that he would no longer be interested in your article."

"Perhaps something else has changed his mind."

"Or maybe he just has his doubts about it."

"He made a comment that suggested he was worried about upsetting the police."

"Quite understandable."

"Once again, I find myself wondering whether it's worth

my while continuing with this work, especially if nothing will ever be published about it. That doesn't really make me a journalist, does it? It makes me a... I'm not sure. Little more than a nosey parker, I suppose."

"Nonsense! You've been doing the job for eleven years."

"But I'm not officially a journalist any more."

"Who decides whether you're official or not?"

"Well, I'm not receiving a regular salary from any of the publications."

"Does that mean you're no longer a journalist?"

"No, I suppose not. I must keep telling myself that I'm still a journalist."

"Of course you are. You need to keep believing in your work, Penny."

"It was just easier when I could name the newspaper I worked for, wasn't it? It gave me better access to people and places."

"From what I can see, you haven't had any difficulty accessing people or places over the past few weeks. I think you're creating difficulties in your mind that don't exist. You are a journalist, Penny, and a good writer. You have an inquiring mind, a strong sense of justice and an unrivalled determination to seek out the truth. Just think about every-thing you've achieved in the time we've known each other."

"But what do I do about Mary Steinway? Is it worth my while continuing with this?"

"Are you the sort of person who stops halfway through an investigation?"

"No."

"Then there's your answer."

"It's just that it seems to be becoming increasingly diffi-cult. Let me show you the message I received." I got up from the table and went to fetch Mr Burns's message.

There was a deep furrow in James's brow once he had read

it. "A door will be left open for you in the Crescent?" he queried. "At four o'clock on Wednesday? The message says it will only be unlocked for a short period of time, and if you're late it'll be locked again."

"That's right."

"And there's a staircase for you to walk down. I don't like the sound of this, Penny. What is this place? Who is this person?"

"Mr Burns."

"And who might he be?"

"He was Molly Gardstein's companion."

"I don't like the idea of you meeting him alone."

"I'm not sure you could really come with me. He probably wouldn't take kindly to a police officer accompanying me."

"Of course not. But where is this place, exactly? Tower Hill?"

"Yes, that's what the message says."

"I need to be there."

"But he won't want you to be present."

"No, of course not, but I can hide somewhere nearby. First of all, we need to find out where it is. I have a map of the City somewhere."

James went off to find the map while I read the message again. It sounded as though the meeting place was underground. *Why the need for such secrecy?*

Mrs Oliver came into the dining room and glanced at James's empty chair and our uneaten food. "Something wrong with the beef?" she asked, hands on hips.

"Not at all, Mrs Oliver; it's delightful," I said. "We were just busy discussing something."

"I hope the food will hold its heat in that case." She bent down to make a fuss of Tiger whose nose was twitching at the smell of roast beef.

James returned with a map, moved his plate to one side

and opened it out on the table. "Let's see if we can find the location he mentions."

The five-sided citadel of the Tower of London was easy to find on the map. Just north-west of it was the oval of the green in the middle of Trinity Square, and to the north-east was a jumble of buildings.

"There's the Crescent," said James, pointing to a row of buildings in a half-moon shape. The half-moon was interrupted by an oblong running west toward Trinity Square. The structure appeared to be subterranean, as it ran beneath a street called Trinity Place. "That's the Tower of London train station," said James. "Its main entrance is on Trinity Place."

"The station that was closed?"

"Yes. Just last year, wasn't it?"

"It was fairly recent."

"Well, that's where he wants to meet you. The staircase must lead down from the Crescent to the station platform."

"And the station has no roof to it," I said, "so you'll be able to find yourself a vantage point to observe our meeting."

"Yes. I'll try not to make myself too conspicuous, but I suspect I'll be able to position myself somewhere on Trinity Place so I can keep an eye on you both."

"Your meat and potatoes will be stone cold by now, sir," said Mrs Oliver.

"I'm sorry, Mrs Oliver. We won't be a moment."

The housekeeper shook her head in bemusement and left the room.

Once we had finished discussing where the unusual meeting was to take place, we returned to our food.

"You appear to have had quite an impact on Sir Octavius," said James. "The commissioner told me the MP has requested that the circumstances of Mary Steinway's death be revisited."

"And has the commissioner agreed to do so?"

"Yes. I'm not quite sure what H Division will make of it, but it's good news in terms of the work you're doing."

"Good news indeed." I rested my knife and fork on the plate as I considered this. "I'm very grateful to Sir Octavius for taking such swift action. He told me he would, but I wasn't quite sure whether to believe him or not."

"He's a member of parliament, Penny. Surely you should believe everything a politician tells you?" James gave a wry smile.

CHAPTER 29

I received a reply from Mary Steinway's sister, Mrs Pelham-Heathcote, turning down my request for a meeting. Her response was brief and she gave no reason for declining it.

I scrunched the letter into a ball and threw it onto my writing room floor. Tiger leaped off her chair and began to pat the ball of paper around in circles with her paw. Resolving to make the day profitable, I decided to pay a visit to Revd Loach.

As I walked across Primrose Hill toward Chalk Farm, I considered the welcome news that the commissioner of Scotland Yard intended to ask H Division to look into Mary Steinway's murder once again. Perhaps this meant my own investigation was over, though I couldn't imagine H Division being pleased about the extra work involved. They no doubt had enough to do as it was. *Would they take a proper look at the case?*

I decided to continue with my own investigations for the time being, at least. I felt pleased with what I had discovered so far and knew there was a lot more that could be done. I resolved to carry on until my input was no longer needed.

St Saviour's Church was set on a triangle of land bordered by three pleasant streets. Each street was lined with trees and a number of large, detached residences. The vicarage was the largest house I could see. As I knocked at the door, I surmised that Revd Loach must have done rather well for himself.

A humourless housekeeper answered and took my visiting card. She soon returned to say that Revd Loach would be pleased to see me. I wondered how pleased he would be once he heard Mary Steinway's name mentioned.

I was shown into a drawing room with large windows that looked out onto a well-tended garden with an emerald-green lawn.

Mrs Loach entered the room first. She was a slight lady with neat, mid-brown hair, and she wore a plain cotton dress.

"My husband won't be a moment," she said once I had introduced myself. Her voice was high and feeble-sounding, and she lacked the formidable presence of some vicars' wives. "He's a busy man."

"I can imagine. How long has he been vicar of this parish?"

"Oh, it must be about twelve years now. Quite some time." She smiled broadly at me, as if unsure what else to say.

"It's a lovely parish."

"This bit is, most certainly, but it's not without its problems. Venture over to the other side of the train station from here and you'll find households with a great many difficulties. We do what we can."

"Of course."

The door opened and Revd Loach entered the room. He was a tall, slender man with a sharp nose and a small chin. His thinning brown hair was brushed forward, as if to create the impression that there was more of it than there actually was. He looked to be about fifty years of age.

"Mrs Blakely, how nice to meet you. How can we help?"

Tea was brought in as I explained that I was trying to track down Mary Steinway's murderer. Revd Loach remained impassive throughout.

"We don't talk about her as a rule," said Mrs Loach once I had finished, "but it's a very sad story." Her eyes remained on mine for a moment before she gave another of her smiles.

"I read about her death in the newspaper," said the Revd. "Terribly sad. There was an awful inevitability about it, I'm afraid to say."

"Why do you say that?"

"Well, there was only one way it was all heading."

"I'm not sure I understand."

"Lunacy," he said quietly. "The poor girl was gradually losing her mind. It was a great shame when her mother died. She was such a lovely lady."

"Did you know the Steinway family well?"

"Our families were close friends. My father was the vicar of St Stephen's for a time and the Steinways were regular churchgoers. They were a very respectable family. Sadly, Mary never recovered from her mother's death. I think much of it was to do with the guilt she felt about passing that dreadful sickness to her. It quite damaged her mind."

"Did you realise that before you were married?"

"No, I had no idea at all. I'd known her since she was about twelve years of age, though I was eight years her senior. We married when she was eighteen, and she seemed rather happy about the situation. In fact, it was the first happy event she'd experienced since her mother's death. Mr Steinway had remarried by then, and his new wife was extremely supportive of our union. I found Mary to be an attentive wife, and the first few months we spent together were very happy. She was musical and loved playing the piano, and I enjoyed her conversation. She was well educated, as you would expect from a member of the Steinway family.

"I was a curate at All Saint's Church in St John's Wood at that time. A junior clergyman, if you will. It was my intention to have a parish of my own, so Mary needed to take on the duties of a vicar's wife. We had discussed it at length before we married, and I think she was looking forward to it. She joined a few committees and carried out a number of good works before her confinement.

"She suffered a little with her health around that time and had to take a fair bit of rest. She became rather bored and read a great many books, but they weren't books I considered suitable for a vicar's wife. I told her that if she had the time to read, I had a list of perfectly proper books. A number of them, though not all, were ecclesiastical, but still quite accessible for a lady. I gave her the ones that I felt would provide all the necessary education and instruction for becoming a vicar's wife. Though I still caught her reading her own choices sometimes!"

I nodded attentively and felt secretly relieved that my husband had never tried to influence my reading choices.

A brief smile flickered across the Revd's face. "She was interested in the rights of women and women's suffrage," he continued, "and I encouraged such an interest because I believed the role of a vicar's wife fitted well with such ideals."

"It sounds as though everything went well for a while."

"For a while, yes. I realise now that I was wasting my time, knowing what I now know about her lunacy." He shook his head. "I never realised how fragile her poor little mind was. She said something about her jewellery going missing; jewellery that had belonged to her mother. She blamed the servants, but they claimed she had given it to them. There was even a trial about it."

"Really?" I queried.

"It was a terrible business. Her mind was very confused."

"And then a son was born," I interjected.

"Yes. John." He nodded his head sadly. "A strong, healthy boy. No weakness in him at all. No one realised at the time that Mary's mind wasn't sound enough to care for him properly."

"Did she neglect him?"

"She kept leaving the house with him at all hours and in all weathers. We'd employed a young nursemaid to look after the boy, so there was no need for her to take him out. I couldn't understand it."

"Why did she keep leaving the house?"

"It was due to this odd madness that had taken over her, which grew worse after John's birth. Morning, noon and night she would suddenly decide to take a walk. I pleaded with her, as did the servants, but she simply wouldn't listen."

"Do you know where she went when she left the house?"

"Primrose Hill. Totally exposed to the elements in the middle of winter! She just walked about aimlessly up there. I would go out to join them, but she told me she wished to be left alone. That poor child. He shouldn't have been out in weather like that."

"Was she trying to avoid your company?"

"She was trying to avoid everyone's company! It was a terrible shame. I should have called a doctor, of course, but I didn't realise she had an illness of the mind."

"When did you first notice this supposed illness of her mind?"

"*Supposed?* A physician certified that she was suffering from lunacy. I suppose the signs were there when we first married. I hadn't realised how badly her mother's death had affected her; the poor thing was quite distraught. Her nerves suffered more and more over time."

"Did you discuss her state of mind with her family?" I asked. "Had they noticed these signs of madness?"

"I never discussed it with them, no. I felt it was rather a delicate, private matter between a man and his wife. And although it sounds rather foolish now, I suppose I was worried they might somehow hold me responsible for it. Quite ridiculous, I know. Besides, I always viewed it as a problem that would eventually be resolved. I felt that with a careful steer in the right direction, and with God's love and guidance, she would soon return to the right path. But these things are sent to try us, and my faith was sorely tested during those dark days. I could see how troubled her mind was; as if she were dwelling within some sort of inner purgatory. I suppose the long walks calmed her and made her feel better. I longed to accompany her, but she just wouldn't have it. And when poor little John came down with a fever it was the beginning of the end for him, and for our marriage.

"I was desperately sad when he died. He was just eight weeks old. The poor baby caught a chill and perished. I didn't rebuke her, mind you; her mental state was too fragile for that. I merely explained that John's death had been caused by his being taken outside in winter for long periods of time. I don't suppose she knew how to look after a baby. Why she chose to ignore the nursemaid, I shall never know. Then she felt responsible for two deaths: that of her mother and of her son. The people she loved the most had died as a result of her own actions. No wonder she completely lost her mind after that. It was a sorrowful day when she was admitted to the institution, and I felt I had somehow failed her as a husband. I hadn't been able to help her recover, as I had always hoped she would. I put so much time into it."

"How long was she kept in the institution?"

"Three months."

"And she returned home once she was discharged?"

"Yes, but only briefly. She wasn't with me for long before she suddenly left one night. I awoke in the morning and she'd packed a case and taken all her things."

He retrieved a handkerchief from his pocket and wiped his face with it.

Mrs Loach's expression was suitably solemn.

"I suppose Mary's return to our home reminded her of the little boy she had lost," continued the Revd. "I told her there would be more children, but my words were of no comfort to her, so she left. That's what lunacy does, I suppose. And I must admit that there had been increasing signs of intemperance in her."

"Was she drinking a lot?"

"Drowning her sorrows, I suppose. I tried to stop her, but she paid me no heed."

I wondered if Mary's disappearance had come as a relief to the Revd. It sounded as though she would never have coped well as a vicar's wife. "You said that Mary was responsible for two deaths," I said. "But she didn't cause them deliberately, did she?"

"Not deliberately, no."

"In fact, it really wasn't her fault at all that her mother caught scarlet fever from her."

"No, but it was impossible to explain that to her. She was convinced it was her fault, just as she was with John's death. That one was her fault, of course. We told her not to take him out into the cold, but she wouldn't listen."

"Did you ever see her again after she left?"

"No. I had to tell people she'd been readmitted to the hospital. Can you imagine what the parishioners would have thought if they knew she'd just upped and left? It was difficult enough telling them Mary was in an institution. I know that it led to a good deal of gossip."

Lying to parishioners was not a trait I expected from a

man of the clergy. "And you had no idea where she went after she left you?" I thought of Sir Octavius and wondered whether the Revd had the slightest inkling that she had befriended a man who was now an MP.

"No idea at all. The next time I heard anything of Mary was three years later, when I received a summons to attend the inquest into her death. I refused to go, naturally. There was nothing I could tell them about her, given that I hadn't seen her for three years. And I was a vicar by then. My attendance at the inquest would surely have set tongues wagging."

"Had you tried to seek a divorce prior to her death?"

"The thought had occurred to me, swiftly followed by further concerns over what my parishioners would think. I knew Mary would be presumed dead after an absence of seven years, and then I would be free to marry again. Not that I wished any of that time away, of course. I always lived in the hope of her returning someday. I can't tell you how upset I was when I heard about her death."

"Have you any idea who might have harmed her?"

"Absolutely none at all. I knew nothing of her life during those last three years. From what I've since heard, the intemperance continued and she clearly fell in with bad company. As I said at the beginning of our conversation, there was an inevitability about it all. I don't mean that I could have predicted what happened, but when I realised she was a lunatic... I suppose it could never have ended well."

Mrs Loach showed me out once my questions had come to an end.

"I apologise for the difficult conversation," I said to her. "And I appreciate the time you and your husband have offered me today."

"You're very welcome, Mrs Blakely. It's the least we could do."

I paused just before stepping out of the door. "How long have you and Revd Loach been married?"

"Nineteen years."

"Did you meet him at St Saviour's?"

"No, we actually met in east London."

"East London?"

"Yes, at the Salvation Army shelter in Whitechapel. I used to volunteer there and he paid us a visit one day."

"Thank you, Mrs Loach. Farewell."

CHAPTER 30

The Crescent was hidden away between Trinity Square and a railway goods depot. James and I walked beneath a bridge that carried the railway toward Fenchurch Street Station.

"Perhaps there isn't any need for me to meet Mr Burns after all," I said.

"But we're almost there! Are you feeling nervous?"

"A little. I'd prefer not to go anywhere subterranean again." My stomach gave an uncomfortable turn as I recalled the tunnels beneath the River Fleet, which I had been forced to walk along a few months previously by members of the Twelve Brides gang.

"I can't say I blame you, Penny, but at least the disused station is open to the elements, as it has no roof. And I'll be able to keep watch over you from Trinity Place."

The Crescent was quite grand, or at least it had once been. The elegant four-storey, eighteenth-century houses were bordered on the north side by railway lines, and the smooth curve of the crescent was interrupted where some of the buildings had been demolished to make space for the Tower of London railway station.

We stopped to survey the scene. At one end of the wall was a small, black door.

"I suppose that's the door he's left unlocked," I said.

"Yes, it must be. I'll wait here," said James, peering around and stepped back into a doorway. "Once you're through the door, I'll rush over to Trinity Place and keep a lookout."

"Thank you." I stepped into the doorway to give him a kiss.

He squeezed my arm. "Good luck, Penny."

I tentatively crossed the cobbles leading up to the small door. There was no handle on it, only a lock. I pushed against the door and it swung open.

It was dingy on the other side, with just enough light to reveal an iron staircase spiralling down beneath me. The lower steps were barely visible in the grey daylight. I closed the door behind me, my heart pounding in my throat as I gradually navigated my way down the staircase. I gripped tightly to the handrail and walked slowly, careful not to miss a step. As I reached the bottom of the staircase, I found myself standing on the sloping edge of a platform. I saw faint footprints in the layer of soot and bird droppings that covered the ground.

The rails on the track began to hum as they vibrated, a gust of air whipping out of the tunnel to my right. Then came the unmistakeable sound of an engine. I stepped back against the wall as the train thundered past, smoke and steam billowing. The pound of pistons and rush of air filled my ears and, for a brief moment, my senses were overwhelmed.

I released the breath I had been holding as I watched the guard's van retreat into the tunnel at the far end of the platform. I thought it rather sad that the trains no longer stopped here since the new Mark Lane station had opened close by.

I took a few steps along the platform, feeling a gritty sensation beneath my boots. The opposite platform looked lonely, with nothing but fading advertisements pasted onto its gloomy walls. There was no sign of Mr Burns, however. I glanced behind me, worried he might suddenly appear. *Was he watching me from the shadows?*

Above my head, a bridge ran across the centre of the station. Recalling the map, I realised this was where Trinity Place crossed the railway. James would hopefully be in position up there by now. I glanced upwards and, as the steam from the train cleared, I saw the head and shoulders of a man silhouetted against the grey sky.

It had to be James, but I daren't make any attempt to acknowledge him. It was important not to draw Mr Burns's attention to his presence.

But where was Mr Burns?

I walked on a little further. Above the tunnel at the far end of the platform I saw the outline of a little ticket office. Stairwells had once led down to the platforms on either side of it, but the steps had since been removed.

Everything seemed to fall silent for a moment. All I could hear was the flutter of pigeons somewhere above me.

Then a door slammed, followed by echoing footsteps. A broad figure strode into view at the far end of the platform opposite me. It was a man wearing a long, dark overcoat and a wide-brimmed hat. He had a clay pipe tucked between his lips.

He climbed down from the platform, nonchalantly stepped over the railway tracks, then effortlessly hauled himself up some way down the platform I was standing on. As he approached, I saw how tall and powerfully built he was. He slowed his step as he drew closer.

"Mr Burns?" I queried.

He stopped and removed the pipe from his mouth. He had a long, square-jawed face with rough, textured skin, which was heavily lined. His left eye was partially closed, suggesting it had been injured in the past.

"Mrs Blakely, ain't it?"

"Yes." The question unnerved me, as the visiting card I had given Mr Willis at the alehouse on Cable Street had recorded my name as Miss Penny Green.

Mr Burns took a few steps closer and surveyed me carefully. "And you're lookin' ter find Molly Gardstein."

"Yes."

"So'm I," he replied.

The railway lines began to hum again, and I knew there would be no use in trying to continue our conversation until the train had passed us by. This time it came from a westerly direction and the whistle sounded. I caught a glimpse of the driver watching us from the footplate as it rushed past.

"Why did you choose to meet me here?" I asked as the turbulence from the train subsided.

He gave a shrug. "Nice an' quiet. An' out the way o' prying eyes." He lifted the pipe to his mouth again, as he did so I caught a glimpse of his tattooed fingers. "You're an interesting sort, ain't you, Mrs Blakely?" he said, the smoke escaping from his mouth. "I've 'ad you looked into."

"Really? Why?"

"I does it whenever anyone goes 'round askin' questions. I ain't answerin' no questions till I knows who I'm talkin' to." He stared down at me. "You look 'armless enough, but you ain't. Married to a copper, ain't you? An' not just any old copper; 'e's CID down the Yard."

"That's right," I replied, pretending not to feel unnerved by his research. "I can tell you a little more about myself if you like."

"Dunno if I can trust what ya say, though, do I?" He glanced around, as if looking for someone. "I spect 'e's close by," he commented. "There ain't no man in 'is right mind who'd let 'is wife meet a man like me alone. Copper or no copper."

I decided to come clean. "You're right; he is close by. But this conversation is entirely between the two of us, and neither I nor my husband have any interest in your business. It's only Molly I want to find out about."

"I ain't seen sight nor sound of her fer twenny years."

"Did you ever see her after the death of Mary Steinway, or Jane Stroud, as she called herself?"

"No."

I began to wonder if I was wasting my time, and whether he also had companions watching from close by. "But you knew Mary, did you not?"

"I knowed 'er as Jane. Can't say as I took to 'er, meself. She were a good friend ter Molly, though. Molly liked 'er. They 'ad their fallings out, though, an' Jane liked a good row when the drink got 'old of 'er."

"Why didn't you take to Jane?"

"It were the way she looked at me now and then. Thought 'erself a bit above ev'ryone else, she did. We all knowed she comed from money. She never told us, but we knowed it any'ow. She'd been ter school and everythin', but then she'd fallen on 'ard times. I ain't sure she understood that, mind. Still thought 'erself a cut above, if yer know what I mean. She didn't treat Molly all that nice neither. Lady Muck, I called 'er."

"Do you know why Molly ran away?" I asked.

"She didn't want ter get 'erself nicked."

"Do you think she murdered Miss Steinway?"

He stared at me for a moment, and I began to wonder whether or not there was an eye beneath the semi-closed lid.

I felt a nauseous shudder but managed to hold his gaze all the same.

"Nah, I don't reckon she done it," he eventually replied. "It jus' weren't the sorta thing she'd of done."

"Then why did she run away?"

"'Cause they'd 'ave made her swing for it anyways. You know what them coppers are like, don't yer? Mind, I'm probably askin' the wrong person, seein' as you're married to one."

"I heard Miss Gardstein and Miss Steinway had a disagreement around that time."

"Them two was always arguin'!"

'But they remained friends all the same?"

"Yeah, they was always fightin' over nuffink, an' they always made it up after. There ain't no way Molly done it."

"And you'd also like to find her?"

"I've always wanted to find 'er. I was real fond of 'er. We lived as man and wife, an' she was always my favourite."

I took this to mean that he had been associated with a number of other female companions.

"Good comp'ny, she was," he continued. "We was good comp'ny for each other. Broke me 'eart when she left."

He paused to suck on his pipe and I wondered if this show of affection was genuine. It seemed odd coming from such a tough-looking man.

"Where do you think she went?" I asked.

He shrugged. "I was out lookin' for 'er and the coppers was out lookin' for 'er, but none of us found 'er. She didn't go to 'er folks... they was lookin' for 'er, too. Myst'ry, it was. I even tried lookin' down Kent way. She used to go 'oppin' there ev'ry year. Same place each time. I went lookin', but they 'adn't seen no sign of 'er."

"She picked hops?"

"Yeah. Ev'ry September. 'Er family'd always done it."

We paused our conversation once more while another train passed through the station.

"I was 'opin' you might be able to tell me summink about 'er, Mrs Blakely."

"I discovered that Miss Gardstein's family lived in Station Place, close to Shadwell train station."

"I coulda told yer that."

"Whereabouts in Kent did she go hop-picking?"

"Sarsden Farm, it were."

"And where is that, exactly?"

"You thinkin' o' goin'?"

"I might."

"In that case, you'd 'ave ter take a train down Faversham way an' then ask directions from there. Wiley's the farmer's name, far as I remember. That was twenny years ago now, though. Might be one of 'is sons these days, if the family's still there." He looked around again. "So where's this fella o' yours, then? I'd like ter say good day to 'im."

I glanced around and felt relieved to see that there was no sign of James. "I honestly don't know. I didn't think you'd want to speak to the police."

"I don't norm'ly like speakin' to coppers' wives, neither, but you ain't too bad, far's they go. Yer'll tell me if yer find Molly, won't yer?"

"Where will I find you?"

He turned to walk away. "Yer found me before, an' yer'll find me again."

CHAPTER 31

"An interesting incident seems to have occurred in the Ratcliffe area," announced James as he read the *Morning Express* over breakfast the following morning. "Someone by the name of Sally Walcot has appeared at Thames Police Court. Didn't you meet with her?"

I paused with my cup of tea lifted halfway to my mouth. "Yes. Sally is the daughter of Mary Steinway's old landlady."

"Miss Walcot was summoned before magistrates for assaulting a woman named Harriet Goodstone during a quarrel at the White Swan," said James. "She was ordered to pay a fine and court costs, and has been bound over to keep the peace for six months."

"I can't imagine her assaulting anyone. I wonder what caused the disagreement."

"It's rather difficult to guess without having met either Miss Walcot or Miss Goodstone. The fact she's been bound over to keep the peace suggests she's done this sort of thing before. It's not commonly imposed for a first offence."

"Perhaps H Division would have the relevant arrest records," I said.

"I think I could probably get away with enquiring about them in this instance." He folded the newspaper back on itself and passed it to me so I could read the article for myself. "It'll be interesting to find out a little more about her."

"But even if we discover that she regularly gets into fights with people, it won't necessarily mean she's capable of murder," I reasoned.

"Yes, that's a good point."

"And poisoning someone is rather different from striking them."

"True. It's a certain sort of person who poisons, isn't it? It's a measured, calculated form of murder. Rather different from an impulsive punch or kick."

I lowered my cup onto my saucer as I read the article. I recalled the sharp-faced woman in Shadwell telling me that Mary Steinway had kept company with a man named Kemp, whom Sally Walcot had been fond of. *Was it possible that Miss Walcot had exacted her revenge on Mary for this reason?*

❧

I stood waiting for my father outside the British Museum's Natural History department in South Kensington later that morning. As I watched people passing by, I concluded that Mr Burns wasn't as intimidating as he had first appeared. His unusual choice of meeting place was probably intended to daunt me, but I had found him reasonably respectful and forthcoming, and he appeared to have genuinely cared for Molly Gardstein. Perhaps his sole reason for agreeing to meet with me stemmed from a hope that I might be able to find her.

I asked a passing gentleman for the time. It was ten minutes after ten, which meant that my father was late for our meeting. I occupied myself by surveying the impressive museum building before me, which had only recently been completed. Two Romanesque towers rose up on either side of the grand entrance, and countless plants and animals had been carved into the museum's granite-and-cream stonework.

I recalled the proud moment when Eliza and I had first visited this place to view Father's papers and sketches on display. We had dearly hoped he was still alive but could have never imagined that he would ever be found. So much had changed since then, and my father was now residing in the same city as my sister. Despite the tears she had shed for him back then, she resolutely refused to meet with him now. While it seemed unlikely that she would ever forgive him, passing up the opportunity to listen to his account of events seemed foolish to me. I could only conceive that a combination of pride and resentment was preventing her from seeing him. I simply couldn't understand why she would allow her emotions to control her actions in such a way.

I rested back against the museum wall, took my notebook out of my carpet bag and flicked through the notes I had made. Mr Burns had been quite specific about the Kent location where Molly Gardstein had gone hopping. I wondered whether it would be worth my while travelling down there to ask the Wiley family about her. It could be a trip for me and James to take together at the weekend if his work didn't detain him in London.

I asked for the time once again and discovered that it was half-past ten. I scoured the faces of the passers-by, but there was no sign of Father. *Had he forgotten our meeting? Or had something else detained him?*

I decided to wait another five minutes, though I was beginning to think my time would have been better spent with Mrs Curridge from *The Lady's Review* after all. I was beginning to regret being so surly with Mr Sherman when he had mentioned the appointment to me. Perhaps I had foolishly turned down a fruitful opportunity, and perhaps my trust in Father had been misplaced. The only other person who seemed to share my fondness for him was my former landlady, Mrs Garnett. I had chosen not to listen to James and Eliza when they criticised him, but perhaps this was a mistake. Perhaps I had been so desperate to see the good in him that I had willingly overlooked his faults.

Having waited for thirty-five minutes, I started walking toward South Kensington train station to return home.

CHAPTER 32

I hadn't been home long before Mrs Oliver came to find me in my room.

"A visitor for you, Mrs Blakely," she announced. "An ordinary woman, with no visiting card. Says her name's Rendell."

I felt a skip of excitement. With a bit of luck, Mrs Rendell would be able to give me further insight into the Loach marriage. I felt sure Revd Loach had given me an edited version of events that had been curated to fit his own requirements.

I thanked Mrs Oliver and asked her to show my visitor into the front room. Then I splashed some water onto my face, re-pinned my hair, smoothed out my dress and went downstairs to meet her.

"You've a nice house here, Mrs Blakely," said Mrs Rendell, standing stiffly at the centre of the room. She wore a neat skirt and blouse with a paisley shawl.

I thanked her and gestured for her to sit.

"I've come to say sorry for cutting short your last visit," she said.

"There's no need to apologise, Mrs Rendell," I responded. "I hope you haven't been worrying about it."

"No. Well... only a little bit."

I noticed the glisten of a tear in her eye. "Please don't give it another thought," I said, keen to reassure her. "The information you gave me was extremely helpful. I'm so grateful that you were able to tell me so much about Mary Steinway, and for sharing your wonderful stew."

"It was a pleasure." She gave a bashful smile and wiped her eyes. "Thank you, Mrs Blakely. You're a kind lady."

Mrs Oliver brought in a tea tray.

"Oh, you shouldn't have gone to no trouble for me!" exclaimed Mrs Rendell. "I wasn't expecting refreshments!"

"It's no trouble at all," I said. "please do stay and have tea with me. You may be interested to hear that I visited Revd Loach a few days ago."

Her eyes grew wide. "You spoke to him about Mary?"

"I did. I was sure he would refuse to speak to me; after all, he had refused the summons to attend her inquest. However, he told me quite a lot about their life together. Perhaps the passage of time has mellowed his attitude toward her a little."

Mrs Rendell tutted. "I'd be surprised if it had."

"Why do you say that?"

"He probably didn't tell you the full story, did he?"

"I imagine he omitted anything that might have been detrimental to his reputation. He appeared to be greatly worried about his parishioners' opinions."

"Yes, that sounds just like him!"

I poured out the tea. "What do you think he might have omitted?" I asked.

"He was cruel to her," she replied, her jaw firm and her eyes defiant. "I didn't get round to telling you that, did I? But he was cruel to her, and she kept trying to leave him. There was nowhere for her to go, though. Her sisters let her stay with them a few times, but when they noticed she was turning to the drink they didn't want nothing else to do with her."

"In what manner was he cruel?"

"He had no patience with her. She was still very upset about her mother's death, but he taunted her all the same. Told her she had to get over it and stop being so miserable. Said she would never be a proper vicar's wife, and that he regretted their marriage."

"And what of Mary's lunacy?"

"Oh, that was something he made up. Mary showed no signs of lunacy before her mother's death, and after that she was consumed by grief, not lunacy. There were times when her behaviour was a little hysterical, and that's when the doctor would be called."

"The one who certified her as a lunatic?"

"That's what Revd Loach said. If you ask me, he did his best to make sure she was locked up in that asylum to keep her out the way for a while."

"Did he ever strike her?"

"I never saw it, but I heard it. She wanted to get away with the little baby, John. She stayed out the house as long as she could and always took the baby with her. She didn't trust him with John. But then the baby caught a chill and died."

She gulped back a sob, and I waited in silence while she wiped her face with her handkerchief and tried to compose herself.

"Did Mary go to the asylum before or after John died?"

"After. Her mother died, her husband was cruel to her and then her son died. If she really was a lunatic, she was driven to it! I think she could've been cured of it with the right treatment, but he was the wrong man for her. That's what I wanted to finish telling you, Mrs Blakely. Men like him should never be vicars or priests. How can they be men of the cloth?

How can they represent God on earth? It don't make no sense to me."

A telegram arrived for me shortly before dinner that evening. It was from my father:

My apologies for this morning. I was waylaid. Next Tuesday?

I put it to one side while I gave this some thought.

CHAPTER 33

"Who or what could possibly have 'waylaid' him?" I asked James as we travelled to Kent by train the following day.

The sky lightened as we left the smoky chimneys of London behind, and green fields greeted us after Bromley. The railway line followed a similar route to the Great Dover Road; an ancient route that connected London with the port of Dover.

"Anything's possible with your father," said James, "but failing to give a proper explanation is rude."

"I suppose it's rather difficult to provide a proper explanation via a telegram."

"That may be so, but it was certainly rude of him to leave you standing there for more than half an hour."

"I suppose I shall have to wait to find out what happened."

"What's the point? He obviously felt he had something more important to do."

I felt hurt by this thought. "More important than seeing his own daughter?"

EMILY ORGAN

James shrugged. "He's the sort of man who allowed you to think he was dead for ten years."

I turned my face toward the window, blinking back a tear. I felt sure my father had a good reason for not turning up for our meeting, but perhaps I was simply trying to see the best in him once again. Maybe James's dismissal of him was justified.

James rested his hand on my arm and I turned back to face him.

"I'm sorry," he said. "Your father just makes me angry."

I nodded and swallowed the lump in my throat. "Revd Loach," I announced with a slight crack in my voice. "He could have murdered Mary Steinway, couldn't he?"

"Ah, I see we're back to solving this murder again. Don't you want to discuss your father any more?"

"Not particularly."

"Mary Steinway's case will provide a welcome distraction, in that case. From what you've told me about Mrs Rendell's account, Revd Loach is rather an unpleasant man. He appears to have been cruel to his wife and to have felt deeply ashamed by her descent into lunacy."

"If you believe she actually was a lunatic, that is."

"You think that was something he invented to explain the failure of their marriage?"

"Either that or he eventually drove her to it. Or both. Poor Mary must have been so desperately unhappy. It doesn't seem as though anyone had her best interests at heart."

"If the Revd is a murderer, what would his motive be?"

"He wanted to be rid of her. Mary could never have been the vicar's wife he had hoped for, and then she disgraced him by leaving."

"But did he feel disgraced?" replied James. "He appears to have framed it quite cleverly with his claims of her madness.

And he probably garnered a good deal of sympathy from his parishioners as a result."

"Yes, he managed the situation carefully so that he didn't have to bear any responsibility for it. But even so, her actions may have angered him. Perhaps he sought revenge."

James nodded. "It's possible."

"And let's not forget that he had most likely already met his current wife," I said. "Mrs Loach told me they'd been married for nineteen years, so they must have wed a short while after Mary's death. Perhaps they were acquainted before Mary died and wished to marry but couldn't because he was still married to Mary."

"He could have applied for a divorce."

"But that would have been widely reported in the newspapers, and he wouldn't have liked that at all. His claims about her madness might have been examined in more detail, and perhaps he was worried that they didn't amount to enough. He certainly wouldn't have been happy about the scrutiny. Besides, Mary would presumably have been given the chance to present her side of the story. There was a risk that his might have been discredited."

"I agree. It must have seemed better for him to be abandoned by a mad wife than to seek a divorce within the public eye."

"And he wanted to be rid of her so he was free to marry again."

"So he thought it better to become a murderer than a bigamist?" James laughed. "I'd say the former was rather more serious than the latter."

"In the eyes of the law, yes. But if he could commit a murder no one would think to attribute to him, he'd get away with it, wouldn't he? There would have been no need for him to become a bigamist and his first wife would no longer have been a problem. He told me himself that Mary would have been declared dead after an absence of seven years. Perhaps he simply didn't wish to wait that long."

"Supposing he did do it," said James. "How could a clergyman have poured poison into a drink, unnoticed, inside a busy alehouse?"

"I have no idea. And while it's not unheard of to see a man of the cloth out trying to save souls in a debauched alehouse, I feel sure that the other drinkers there would have noticed him."

"Maybe he disguised himself as a dockyard worker to avoid drawing attention to himself."

"It's quite possible, I suppose. If he'd dressed in scruffy clothing and a cap, no one would even have glanced in his direction. It would have been easy enough to buy some old clothing from the rag shops in that area."

"It would be interesting to hear whether he provided an alibi for the evening Mary was murdered," James mused.

"It would be rather difficult to find that out after so many years."

"Something significant must have happened that evening. Perhaps he was at a meeting or a dinner party."

"We could ask him, but I'm fairly sure he'd take great offence at the suggestion and refuse to answer any more questions."

"Yes, I imagine he would. He has a reputation to uphold, after all. We could ask if we found we had nowhere left to turn, but I would only do so as a last resort. As you say, the merest suggestion that he might have had something to do with Mary's death would put an end to any co-operation from him. I think he must simply remain a person of interest for the time being."

CHAPTER 34

We passed through the historic town of Rochester and the dockyard town of Chatham. An hour and a half after leaving Victoria station we reached the small market town of Faversham.

Once the train had pulled away, I took a deep breath of fresh air. We were only a few miles from the north Kent coast and, perhaps it was just fancy, I felt sure I could smell the sea.

A pony and trap took us through the rolling green hills to Sarsden Farm. Fortunately, the driver had heard of it, as the place was popular with Londoners visiting to pick hops in late summer. We passed the hops as the trap travelled along the bumpy track leading down to the farm. They were planted in long, neat rows, and were growing up poles of about fifteen or twenty feet high. I could just about see the pale green flowers among their rich foliage.

On arrival at the farm, three circular buildings appeared in our view; each topped with a peaked conical roof. These were the oast kilns, where the hops were dried after picking.

"You wouldn't know this place come September," commented the driver. "Thousands of 'em'll be down from

London. They lay on extra trains for 'em. There'll be a bit o' trouble in the evenings sometimes. All our fresh air and beer goes straight to their 'eads!"

We were greeted by several barking dogs, which were soon placated by the tall, wide-shouldered farmer with a sun-tanned face. Once we had explained who we were, he introduced himself as Thomas Wiley and showed us into a low, timber-ceilinged front room.

"My father probably knew the Gardsteins," he said, hands on hips at the centre of the hearthrug. "But he's no longer with us. I'll fetch Mother."

Mrs Wiley looked to be over seventy, but although she walked with a stoop, there didn't appear to be any great frailty about her. She had a sharp glint in her eye, and I could imagine her being in full command of the hop pickers at harvest time.

While the younger Mrs Wiley brought in tea, the elder Mrs Wiley sat in an easy chair and attempted to recall summers past.

"The Gardsteins came down 'ere for years," she said. "I've not seen none of 'em for a long time, but we 'ad several generations o' the Gardsteins. It was proberly the forties when they first started coming 'ere. I married my William in '35."

"William was my father," clarified Thomas Wiley.

"And I don't suppose it was long after we was married that the Gardsteins started comin'," she added.

"Did you know the family well?" I asked.

"As well as any other. You want to know about a partic'lar one, though, don't you? Which one is it?"

"Molly Gardstein," I replied. "I imagine she first came here as a child."

Mrs Wiley gave a nod. "They all 'elp down 'ere. Soon as they can walk, they're picking hops."

"I heard Molly was still picking hops here about twenty

years ago," I continued. "I'm not sure how exactly old she was, but she would have been a young woman. Possibly about twenty-two or twenty-three."

"She may well 'ave been, dear," replied Mrs Wiley. "I don't remember her specifically, though. There was a lot of them Gardsteins."

"Do they still come here to pick hops?"

"No," she said scornfully, as though this was a foolish question. "No, dear. They must've stopped coming about twenty year ago now."

"Do you know why?"

"'Aven't a clue." Her response to my question was swift, and it almost felt dismissive.

"Why're you so int'rested in *Molly* Gardstein?" asked Mr Wiley.

"She vanished twenty years ago," I replied, "just after the death of her friend, Mary Steinway. Mary was murdered and the police assumed Molly was the culprit, presumably because she was nowhere to be found."

"'Ow did Miss Steinway die?" he asked.

"She was poisoned. It's believed the poison was mixed in with her drink at the alehouse. Molly was present at the time, but so were a good many other people. While most are still convinced that Molly poisoned her friend, I've come across several who don't believe it was her at all."

"Why're you tryin' to find out twenty years later?" asked Mr Wiley. "Surely it don't matter no more."

"Because I believe someone got away with murder, and I don't think that's right. I've found myself visiting all manner of people and places, but I never imagined my search would bring me to a hop farm in Kent. And my husband here has been forced into accompanying me."

"I can't say that I mind being forced to visit a hop farm," said James. "It's a very pleasant place indeed."

"You're a police inspector, ain't you?" Mr Wiley said to James. "You plannin' on arrestin' Molly if you find her?"

"No, not at all," he replied. "This isn't an active case, and it's not even *my* case. I work for Scotland Yard and Mary Steinway's murder was the concern of H Division of the Metropolitan Police. There would need to be an agreement between the two forces for me to start investigating and arresting people. And there's no evidence at all that Molly poisoned her friend. The fact that she ran away when Mary died does look suspicious, but there may have been another explanation. I may be a police inspector, but I'm here today in support of my wife."

"We came to Kent in the hope of finding some answers," I added.

"It's right noble of you, Mrs Blakely," said Mrs Wiley. "I ain't too sure you're gonna get anywhere with it, but it's right noble of yer all the same."

After our brief conversation with Mrs Wiley, Thomas showed us around the farm before taking us back to Faversham. I gave him my calling card in the hope that there might be something else he could tell me in the future, but I left Kent with more knowledge of hops than of Molly Gardstein.

CHAPTER 35

The following Monday, Mr Sherman invited me to join him for lunch at the Burton Dining Rooms in Gough Square, close to Fleet Street. I hoped this meant he had experienced a change of heart and was interested in publishing my work on Mary Steinway once again.

My former editor was already seated at the table when I arrived. He stood to greet me, but his smile was guarded. We made small talk while bread and wine was brought to the table.

Once we had ordered our food, Mr Sherman leaned in toward me and spoke in a lowered voice. "I fear that your investigation is having far-reaching consequences, Mrs Blakely."

"What do you mean?"

"Many more people are involved than you might have anticipated."

"I realise that. I've already spoken to a good number of them."

"Not everyone is happy about the circumstances of Miss Steinway's death being revisited."

"True. And some, namely her sister, have refused to meet with me at all. You'd think she would welcome an opportunity to find out what happened to Mary."

"Doesn't that tell you something?"

"Yes. It tells me that a number of people may have something to hide."

"But you're not a police detective, Mrs Blakely."

"I realise that."

"In which case, you're treading on rather dangerous ground."

I sat back in my chair and studied him for a moment. His face bore an expression of concern I hadn't often seen before. "When I last met with you, sir, you said there was no guarantee that you would publish my investigation into Miss Steinway's death. Was that decision made at someone else's request?"

"I'm not at liberty to disclose any conversations I've had on the topic, Mrs Blakely."

I smiled. "I'll assume your answer is a yes."

"That would merely be an assumption."

I noticed how carefully he was choosing his words.

"I assume that if someone has made this request, they must have a reputation to protect," I said. "I can think of two people that might apply to: Miss Steinway's estranged husband, Revd Edwin Loach, and the MP, Sir Octavius Harvey."

"Is that so?" he replied, as though he were hearing these names for the first time.

"I find it odd that either should contact the *Morning Express*, given that I'm no longer employed by the paper."

"It wasn't quite as official as that."

Then a realisation dawned on me. "Isn't the commissioner of Scotland Yard a cousin of yours, Mr Sherman? I know that Sir Octavius met with him recently."

"The commissioner informed me of that meeting."

"And apparently he intends to ask H Division to take another look at the case, which is excellent news."

"Yes. Excellent news indeed."

"And presumably you were asked to inform me that my work in relation to this case is no longer welcome."

"As I've already mentioned, Mrs Blakely, I'm not at liberty to disclose what was discussed."

"But that's what you're asking me to do, isn't it? This goes a step further than before. Not only are you refusing to publish my work on the case, but you're asking me to stop my work on it altogether."

"I can't very well do that, Mrs Blakely, but—"

"Only, you *are* asking me to stop. For some reason Sir Octavius doesn't want the case to be reopened."

"But it's already been referred to H Division!"

"Yes, but we both know how unlikely it is that they'll have time to properly revisit the case. And Sir Octavius probably guessed that, too. He's pretending he wants to help, but he's actually doing the exact opposite."

"It's a police matter now, Mrs Blakely," said Mr Sherman. "And in all fairness, it always has been."

"But you're a journalist, sir. I'm sure you must agree with me that the police didn't carry out a thorough investigation twenty years ago. And you're usually so supportive of any journalistic work that questions the actions of the authorities. Part of our job is to help the public hold them to account."

He shifted in his seat, and I could see that this was a difficult conversation for him.

"I suppose your family connection creates something of a conflict," I added.

"No more so than yours," he shot back. "You happen to be married to an inspector of the Yard!" He lowered his voice further. "This is a little more than a mere conflict of loyalty, Mrs Blakely. It's becoming rather dangerous."

"Why do you say that?"

"Please just take my word for it."

"Because Sir Octavius has spoken to your cousin, you mean?"

"No, it's more than that. There are lawyers involved now, and they've been speaking to the *Morning Express'* proprietor, Mr Conway."

"That all seems rather unnecessary."

"To you, perhaps, but it's happening nonetheless. And if pressure can't be brought to bear the official way, unofficial means may be used."

"Have you been threatened, sir?"

"Not directly, no."

"From what I understand, then, Sir Octavius objected to being asked about Miss Steinway. He has subsequently instructed his lawyers to threaten the *Morning Express* newspaper and asked the commissioner of the Yard to have a word with his editor cousin."

We paused the conversation while our food was brought to the table.

Mr Sherman picked up his glass of wine and sat back in his chair. "This must be rather an uneasy time to be an MP," he said.

"It's not like you to have sympathy for politicians, sir."

"Oh, I don't. I'm just trying to explain the matter from an MP's point of view."

"Sir Octavius's, you mean?"

He shrugged before continuing. "There'll be a general election this autumn, and the Redistribution Bill means many constituencies are being reorganised. If you were to take Sir Octavius as an example, his Southwark constituency is to be divided up into West Southwark, Rotherhithe and Bermondsey. The parties are busy selecting their candidates, and those who have traditionally held seats are facing a lot more competition. Re-election isn't as much of a certainty as it has been in previous elections. And when you also consider the Third Reform Act, which has extended suffrage to a great many more men, it means this year's election will be very different from the one we had five years ago. Different constituencies and more voters... it's a worrying time for some people."

"Much-needed reform," I said.

"Yes, I agree with you. These changes were badly needed."

"And many more. Extending the franchise to women would also be a great help."

"Although I agree with you on that, Mrs Blakely, now is not the time to discuss women's suffrage. I'm trying to explain the uncertainty facing many MPs at present."

"If Sir Octavius is worried that his name will be publicly connected with Miss Steinway's, I've already reassured him on that front," I said. "I don't see why he should have any reason not to believe me."

"It's a little more complicated than that."

"How so?"

Mr Sherman lowered his voice again. "The word is, Sir Octavius is about to be named in a divorce case."

I couldn't help but emit a quiet laugh.

"It could be ruinous for him," added Mr Sherman. "His lawyers are extremely worried."

"Perhaps he should have thought about that sooner!" I said scornfully. "Who has he had the affair with?"

Mr Sherman glanced around, as if he feared that someone might overhear us. "I couldn't possibly disclose that information," he said in an even more hushed tone.

"I imagine we'll all find out soon enough."

"That's what he's so worried about. He was already facing various challenges in his re-election campaign as it was. And with an affair about to become public knowledge, the last thing he needs is for any connection to be made between himself and the murder of Mary Steinway."

"But why should he be worried about that?" I asked. "Unless he's guilty, that is."

"We can't be sure what he's thinking, but he's at risk of losing everything at the moment. I can't help but picture him as a cornered animal; the danger being that he might lash out at any minute, and he may not go through his lawyers to do so. I know a little about the man and I fear that he may use very different tactics altogether. Tactics that would never be traced back to him."

I left the restaurant with my teeth clenched in anger. *Had Mr Sherman been threatened, despite his denial of it? Was Sir Octavius really capable of something far worse than idle threats?*

I became aware of footsteps behind me as I left Gough Square and turned into Hind Court. Thinking at first that Mr Sherman must be following close behind me, I turned but saw no one there. The lane was narrow and dingy, so I quickened my step and continued on toward Fleet Street. *Might Sir Octavius have employed someone to follow me? If Mr Sherman had already been threatened, might I be next?* My heart beat a little faster as I broke out into a jog.

I felt a sense of relief as I reached the bustle of Fleet Street, but it was short-lived, as a tall man in a top hat immediately lumbered over to me.

"Mrs Blakely!"

It was Robert Masefield.

"Did I startle you?" he asked. "You look as though you've seen a ghost."

"No, I..." I turned to look back to where Hind Court

joined the street. "Were you following me just now, Mr Masefield?"

"No. I'd decided to pay your offices a visit to see if I could find you there."

"But I don't work there any more, and I'm sure someone was just following me. It can't have been you, I suppose, because you were already standing on this street."

"You look rather flustered, Mrs Blakely."

"I am."

"Would you like a drink?"

"No, thank you."

"I'm sure it would help. Ye Olde Cheshire Cheese is close by."

"I'm quite all right, thank you. What is it you want, Mr Masefield? I apologise for being so curt, but I'm rather busy."

"I was just wondering what Sir Octavius had to say for himself."

"How did you know that I had met with Sir Octavius?"

"I was sure you wouldn't be able to resist going to see him as soon as I'd told you about his connection to Mary Steinway."

"Well, you were right," I replied rather begrudgingly. "I did go and see him."

"Did he try to deny that he knew her?"

"No, not at all. I found him to be surprisingly candid, in fact."

"He's always pretty happy to speak to an attractive lady." He winked. "I don't suppose he wanted his association with Mary Steinway to become public knowledge, however."

"No, he didn't."

Masefield chuckled. "How unfortunate that would be."

"Do you bear him any ill will, Mr Masefield?" I asked.

"No. Why should I?"

"I sense a note of sarcasm whenever you speak about him,

as if you'd like his acquaintance with Mary Steinway to be more widely known."

"No, I'd never wish a chap any ill will; it's not the done thing. However, I do feel that life isn't always fairly balanced."

I glanced at his worn clothes and couldn't help but assume that he was envious of his former friend.

"Gus got where he wanted to be because of who his father is," he continued.

"Isn't that often the way?"

"I suppose so. But when you look at what we got up to together, I've paid the price for my scrapes, while he's got away with his."

"So far."

"Yes." He grinned. "*So far*. I like that sentiment, Mrs Blakely. If you've another shilling to spare I could tell you more about Derricks."

"The man who was hanged for drowning your friend?"

"Cecil-Palmer. Yes, Derricks was hanged for the murder after he confessed."

"What more is there to tell?"

"A shilling will see you straight, Mrs Blakely."

"But how will that information help me with my investigation into Mary Steinway's death?"

"It'll help you understand the sort of characters you're dealing with."

"Sir Octavius, you mean?"

"Possibly."

He glanced away and I decided another shilling wasn't too great an outlay if he had more to tell. I passed it to him.

"Thank you, Mrs Blakely. Much obliged." He pocketed the coin. "It's about Derricks," he continued.

"I gathered that."

"He confessed to Blinker's murder, but the rumours were that he was forced to confess."

"By whom?"

"He was encouraged to do so by the police. It's believed they were instructed to ensure that a confession was made."

"By whom?" I asked again.

"Who do you think?"

"Sir Octavius?" I suggested.

"Your words, not mine."

"But he's the person you're implying, is he not?"

"He comes from a powerful family."

"Are you implying that Sir Octavius was responsible for Mr Cecil-Palmer's death, not Mr Derricks?"

"There have been rumours to that effect over the years. Worth looking into, don't you think? And guess who was with Sir Octavius when the incident took place."

"Mary Steinway?"

He nodded.

"So you're saying that the people present when Mr Cecil-Palmer was pushed into the lake were William Derricks, Sir Octavius and Mary Steinway."

He nodded again.

"Anyone else?" I asked.

"No one else."

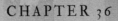

CHAPTER 36

"That's a very serious accusation," said James when I told him about Mr Masefield's latest revelations before dinner that evening. "He's suggesting the police forced a confession from William Derricks."

"Yes. And that Sir Octavius's father played a role in it."

"Did Masefield have any evidence?"

"He didn't mention that he had. I think he may be trying to cause problems for Sir Octavius because he's resentful of his old friend's success. That doesn't mean it isn't the truth, however. He told me Mary Steinway and Sir Octavius were present when Mr Cecil-Palmer was pushed into the lake. The inquest reports stated that two unnamed acquaintances were present at the time. I found it odd that they weren't named, but now I know why. Sir Octavius's father obviously wished to keep his son's name out of the reports. Everything Mr Masefield has told me so far appears to be true."

"That doesn't mean you can trust him, Penny."

"Of course not. I don't trust anyone any more; not since I was pushed beneath the wheels of that cart near St Paul's Cathedral."

James winced. "I don't like to be reminded of that. And I'm not keen on Mr Sherman's description of Sir Octavius as a cornered animal. It sounds as though he's concerned about what the MP might do."

"The man's clearly a bully," I responded, "and he's done a good job of intimidating everyone at the *Morning Express*. Going by Mr Sherman's detailed political explanation, you'd think he was making excuses for the MP."

"He's wary," said James, "and rightly so. Powerful men like Sir Octavius can pull strings."

"But they shouldn't be allowed to get away with it!"

"I doubt he will, from the sound of things. If he's about to be named in a divorce case, that'll be the end of him."

"I told him I wouldn't publicly mention his association with Mary Steinway."

"That was rather a foolish thing to promise if he turns out to be her murderer!"

"Yes, it was short-sighted of me. I was trying to encourage him to talk."

"Perhaps the reason he's become so antagonistic is that he had something to do with her death after all."

"If Sir Octavius pushed Mr Cecil-Palmer into the water, Mary Steinway must have witnessed it," I said. "She presumably lied to protect Sir Octavius, and perhaps that's why she changed her name to Jane Stroud. Then she ran away and did her utmost not to be found."

"By him?"

"Possibly. He might have been concerned that she would eventually tell the truth about what had happened. Perhaps he murdered her to keep her silent."

"That's an interesting thought."

"I wonder if your colleagues in Somerset could be of any help with this."

"In what respect?"

"With regard to Mr Derricks being forced to make a confession."

"I can't imagine many police officers admitting to that, even if it happened twenty years ago!"

"Don't you think it's at least worth asking?"

"I can't ask whether they made a man falsely confess. That wouldn't go down at all well! But I don't suppose it would do any harm to find out more about the circumstances of Derricks's arrest and conviction. I could make some informal enquiries."

"Thank you, James. I suppose there's a possibility that Sir Octavius wasn't the one behind Mary Steinway's murder at all. We also have Revd Loach and Sally Walcot to consider. I'll pay another visit to the Walcots tomorrow and try to find out more about Sally's recent conviction."

"Do you think that's wise?"

"I'll be tactful about it."

We were interrupted by a knock at the door, immediately followed by Mrs Oliver walking into the front room. "Your father is here, madam. What shall I tell him?"

"I can think of a few things," muttered James.

I gave him a sharp glance before replying. "Please show him in, Mrs Oliver."

My father bustled into the room a moment later with a paper-wrapped bundle in his hand. "I'm so terribly sorry I missed our meeting, Penny. Did you receive my telegram?"

"Yes, I did. Thank you, Father."

"Good evening James." My father followed this greeting with a wary nod. "I do hope I'm not interrupting anything. You both look terribly serious."

"We were just discussing my work," I replied.

"Always so busy!" He gave a polite laugh. "Well, I brought a little peace offering with me." He passed me the bundle. "Your very own bottle of Vin Mariana!"

"Coca wine?" enquired James.

"The very same."

"Thank you, Father."

"Perhaps we could all have a glass now?" he ventured with a rub of his hands.

I glanced at James, whose expression was frosty.

"You look as though you could do with a little cheer, Inspector," my father added.

I felt my teeth clench at the awkwardness of the situation. *Couldn't James just pretend to be nice to him? Was it fair of me to expect him to be?*

"Why not?" responded James briskly, as if reading my thoughts. He fetched some glasses from the drinks cabinet.

"There's a good man," said my father as he settled onto the settee. "Never met a police officer who doesn't enjoy a tipple!" He glanced around the room. "I see that he looks after you well, Penny. Oh, good evening, cat!"

Tiger eyed him cautiously from the far end of the room.

"What exactly were you waylaid by when you missed your meeting with Penny the other day, Mr Green?" asked James as he poured out the coca wine.

"Oh, just some silly nonsense."

"Important enough nonsense to miss a meeting with your daughter?"

"If you must know, I was detained by a chap who labours under the misapprehension that I owe him money."

"How could I possibly owe him money?" I asked. "You've only been in London for a little over a month."

"Oh, this goes way back." He brushed aside an imaginary object with his arm. "Way back before I went to Amazonia. It refers to an expedition I undertook in '73, in fact. Apparently, I didn't fulfil some of the terms of our agreement. That was news to me! I don't owe him a penny, but some people will try anything."

"Do you have any money?" James asked, handing him a glass of wine.

"Oh, yes. I've had a small sum sitting in a bank on Lombard Street for the past ten years. A nice little amount of interest it's earned, too!"

"Then you have the means to pay this man, if needs be."

"I'm not paying him a farthing!" He took a large gulp of his drink.

I'd only taken a sip of mine, which was very sweet and had a medicinal flavour to it. Even that small amount produced a soothing effect, however.

"Why have you come to see us, Father?" I asked. "Is there a particular reason?"

"No particular reason, no. I just wanted to explain myself, as you hadn't replied to my telegram about rearranging our meeting."

"Ah, yes. I've been rather busy."

"Tell me all about it!" He sat back, drink in hand. "Tell me about this important work you've been doing."

James gave me an exasperated glance, which suggested that we were likely to be in for a long evening.

CHAPTER 37

The yard behind the White Swan alehouse looked more dismal than it had during my previous visit, or perhaps it only appeared so because my head was aching a little from the coca wine.

I found Mrs Walcot at home but there was no sign of Sally.

"Ain't yer given up yet?" Mrs Walcot asked as we took a seat at her kitchen table.

"I've been close to giving up a couple of times, but on each occasion I discovered something new and found myself continuing with it."

"Any sign o' Molly?"

I shook my head. "I even travelled down to the farm in Kent where she used to go hopping."

"Why'd she be there?"

"It would have been a good hiding place."

"Mebbe for a time, but she'd of got bored soon enough. 'Ow can I 'elp yer today?"

"I was hoping to speak to Sally."

"She's out on an errand, but she'll be back afore long. Why don't yer try me for now?"

"Do you remember a man by the name of Kemp?"

"Joshua Kemp?"

"Yes."

"Course I do. What do yer want *'im* for?"

"I heard there was a disagreement between Sally and Mary Steinway – or Jane Stroud, I should say –about him."

She gave a scornful grunt. "Years ago, that were!"

"I realise that. It was shortly before Jane died, I gather."

"Who've yer been talkin' to?"

"Lots of people."

"And which of 'em's been talkin' about my Sal?"

"A family in Shadwell."

"What do folk up that way know abaht anythin'?"

As the indignance in her voice rose, I tried my best to retain an air of calm.

"I'm not sure. Local gossip, I suppose. I realise there was probably nothing in it."

"Proberly? It's more than proberly. There ain't nuffink in it, and I dunno why you're comin' dahn 'ere askin' about gossip from twenny years ago. Is that what yer wanna speak to Sal about?"

"I was planning to ask her about it, yes."

"Well, it won't get yer nowhere, and she won't take kindly to yer askin'. I hope you ain't suggestin' Kemp was the reason Jane got poisoned! That weren't nuffink to do wiv it. What's 'appened's 'appened, an' the girls sorted it out between 'emselves afore Jane died."

"Thank you for clearing that up, Mrs Walcot. I suppose I was just surprised that your daughter didn't mention the disagreement when we last spoke."

"Why should she of? It weren't nuffink ter do wi' what 'appened to Jane. She's 'ad fallin's out with a lotta folks; yer can't go over every single one of 'em. And most of 'em's been long forgotten, any'ow. Sal proberly jus' forgot all abaht it! That's what we all need to ter do now... forget abaht it. What's done's done, and there ain't nuffink what's gonna bring 'er back."

"But someone has got away with murder."

"It 'appens, Mrs Blakely. Maybe it don't 'appen much where you comes from, but it 'appens round 'ere. Go and speak ter Mrs Letts, if yer like. 'Er son got killed in a fight outside Paddy's Goose eight year ago. Just a punch, that's all it was, an' no one's ever been arrested for killin' 'im. Some people reckoned 'e 'ad it comin', anyways. Keep gettin' yerself in fights and sooner or later yer gonna come a cropper, they say. Try tellin' that ter Mrs Letts, though. She don't wanna 'ear it! Far as she's concerned, she's lost 'er son, and the bloke what did it's still walkin' these streets. Yer gonna go find 'im too, Mrs Blakely?"

Her eyes bored into mine and I lowered my gaze. I didn't wish to antagonise Mrs Walcot any further and, in truth, I found myself partly agreeing with her. *There were plenty of murderers who hadn't been caught, so why was I so intent on pursuing Mary Steinway's case? And why did I think I had any hope of getting anywhere with it?*

I felt a heat in my face, as if I'd just been scolded by a schoolteacher. I had planned to ask about Sally's recent arrest, but I didn't dare mention it after this ticking off.

Perhaps Mrs Walcot had expected me to argue with her, as my silence seemed to deflate her a little. She soon picked up a cloth and began wiping down the stove.

"If yer must know, Sal's wi' Kemp now," she said. "You can ask the pair of 'em when they get back 'ere. They won't be long now."

"It's quite all right," I replied. "I won't impose on you any further."

"Suit yourself," she said, occupying herself with a stubborn mark on the stove.

I felt a pang of sadness that the rapport between us had disappeared. I recalled how helpful Mrs Walcot had been the first time I spoke to her, but I had asked one too many questions, and now her defences were up. *Was her response typical of a proud woman who wouldn't hear a word spoken against her family? Or was I getting too close to the truth?*

I bid her farewell and left the house. If I wanted to know anything more about Sally Walcot I would have to find another source of information. I still found it interesting that Mrs Walcot and her daughter had initially been suspects in the investigation. *Did the police know more about them than Mr Nicol had shared with me and James?*

I stepped out into the dingy courtyard, where a light drizzle was falling. Refreshed by rain, the stench of filth assaulted my nose. As I strode toward the alleyway that led to St George Street, I saw the silhouette of a couple in the gloom. There wasn't enough room for us to pass comfortably in the passageway, so I waited in the courtyard for them.

As they stepped into the courtyard, I immediately recognised Sally Walcot, so I presumed the man was Joshua Kemp. I was about to greet them both when I realised that I also recognised this narrow-eyed chap with rough whiskers and a broken nose. It was the man who had threatened me after my last visit.

Sally opened her mouth to speak, but her companion simply glared at her and she quickly closed it again. I briefly acknowledged her with a nod and dashed past them into the passageway. On reaching St George Street, I ran for about fifty yards, keen to put some distance between myself and Joshua Kemp. *Had he and Sally murdered Mary Steinway? Is that why he had threatened me?* Whatever the reason, I knew he hadn't been happy to see me on St George Street again.

I slowed my pace as I heard the strains of a marching band. Within a few moments, the traffic on the road had become stationary as the musicians marched toward me. People stopped and clapped their hands in time to the music. The tune was familiar, and the thump of drums and parp of brass felt strangely comforting.

As the band drew nearer, I recognised the black uniforms of the Salvation Army. I joined in with the clapping as I watched them pass, grateful for a moment that had helped lift my spirits. As I clapped, I recalled something Mrs Loach had told me. She and her husband had met at the Salvation Army shelter in Whitechapel. Although I couldn't be sure where the shelter was, I knew that Whitechapel was close by. My clapping slowed as I considered this. *Had Revd Loach been just a short distance from his estranged wife's home at the time of her death?*

CHAPTER 38

"Revd Loach may have been in the East End around the time Mary Steinway was murdered," I said to James when he returned home that evening. "His wife told me they met at the Salvation Army shelter in Whitechapel. Why would he go there?"

"To volunteer his services, I suppose."

"Possibly. But the Salvation Army was founded by a Methodist minister, and Revd Loach is Anglican."

"Perhaps they managed to bury their differences when it came to helping east London's poor?"

"I hope you're not trying to make a joke of this. I think it's something we should look into."

"I shall treat it more seriously, in that case. You think Revd Loach may have used his visits to the Salvation Army in Whitechapel as an excuse to look for his estranged wife who was hiding close by, do you?"

"Yes."

"But how would he have known she was there?"

"I don't know. Only he could tell us that, I suspect."

"It may just be a coincidence."

"But it might not be! He was remarried nineteen years ago, and he must have met his wife in Whitechapel a year or two before that."

"Perhaps they had a very short engagement."

"I realise that's a possibility, but I still think there could be something in this. He may have positioned himself in east London to look for Mary."

"It still doesn't mean he murdered her. He may simply have wished to find her."

"Yes, that's also possible. I wish I could ask Mrs Walcot if Mary Steinway was ever visited by a vicar."

"If he did visit her, I don't think he'd have let on that he was a vicar, would he? From the sound of things, he'd done his best to disassociate himself from his wife. He would have worn plain clothes, so no one would have known whether he was a vicar or not."

"I suppose I shall have to visit the Salvation Army shelter to find out whether anyone there remembers him visiting. If I discover that he was there at around the time of Mary's death, he has to be a strong suspect, don't you think?"

"Possibly. Do you still think his motive was that he wanted to be free of his wife?"

"Yes. A divorce wouldn't have been an appropriate course of action for a clergyman, so he perhaps decided to end her life instead. He'd have had to wait several more years for Mary to be presumed dead, and I assume he wished to marry again. He must have met his current wife shortly before Mary's death, so he had even more reason to rid himself of his first wife."

"It's possible."

"I think it's extremely likely. Aren't you convinced?"

"I don't know what to think, Penny. Not when I consider what happened earlier today."

"What happened?"

"I've been over at Thames Police Station in Wapping. A man's body was pulled from the river this morning."

"They don't call you every time a body is pulled out of the river, do they?"

"No, they don't; only if the circumstances are suspicious. This poor chap's hands and feet were bound."

"How awful. Had he drowned?"

"It's assumed so, as there were no visible signs of fatal injuries. The post-mortem should be able to confirm that."

"How barbaric." I shuddered. "He must have been thrust under the water, unable to save himself."

A memory of being pushed beneath the cold, filthy water of the Thames by two members of the Twelve Brides gang entered my mind, but I quickly pushed it away. "Do you have any idea who might have done it?"

"Not yet, but thanks to some papers he had on him, we know who he was."

"Who?"

"Robert Masefield. Isn't he the man who spoke to you about Mary Steinway?"

I felt my heart begin to thud. "Are you sure it was him?" I entreated, struggling to believe this piece of news. "He would have been about ten years older than me. Clothing of good quality, though rather shabby. Greying whiskers, fairly tall. I'd say he was almost six foot."

"It sounds like him all right."

"Oh dear." I clasped my hands together to stop them trembling. "I can't say he was enormously likeable, but to die in that way. How horrible! How long do they think he was in the river?"

"Two days at the very most."

I thought back to the last conversation I'd had with him. "I saw him just a few days ago. He suggested that Sir Octavius may have had something to do with his friend's death; that chap, Mr Cecil-Palmer, who was pushed into the lake at a party. Could Sir Octavius also have been behind this? Might he have wished to silence Mr Masefield? He knew Mr Masefield had been talking about him."

James shrugged. "It's possible, I suppose, but we simply don't know."

"I hope it wasn't my fault!"

"Why on earth should it be your fault?"

"Because I started looking into Mary Steinway's death. I disturbed well-hidden secrets."

"You were always going to disturb secrets when you took on this case. But you're certainly not responsible for Masefield's death. The only person responsible is the one who bound him and threw him into the river. Nothing you've done could have caused that to happen. And besides, didn't Masefield seek you out rather than you seeking him?"

"Yes."

"He heard what you were up to and wanted to get a few shillings out of you. None of this is your fault, Penny!"

CHAPTER 39

My eyes rested on an advert for Price's Candles as I travelled along Whitechapel Road by horse tram the following day. I'd slept very little the previous night as I couldn't help turning the death of Robert Masefield over in my mind. I had believed his account beforehand, but now I was certain that he had been telling the truth. *He must have been murdered for telling the truth, but by whom?* I felt sure it had to be Sir Octavius. Mr Sherman had been right to warn me.

James had returned to Wapping early that morning to continue his investigation into Mr Masefield's murder. Meanwhile, I had decided to find out what I could about Revd Loach's work in Whitechapel.

I disembarked shortly after we reached St Mary's Church and easily found the shelter. The sign on the side of the three-storey building read 'Salvation Army', below which was another sign proclaiming 'Food and Shelter', presumably for the likes of the shabbily dressed group of men I found loitering outside it. I ignored their winks and coarse remarks as I made my way through the group and into the shelter.

After making enquiries with a man in the small office, I was introduced to a sombre lady wearing a black dress, whose name was Miss Havers. We moved into a corridor with a well-scrubbed floor to talk, the echo of banging pots and pans coming from a kitchen nearby.

"I was wondering if you happened to recall a gentleman named Revd Loach," I said.

"Why do you wish to know that?"

"It's for an article I'm writing about Christian missions in the East End," I lied. A full explanation would have taken too much time and discussion, and I wasn't sure how helpful she would be once I'd explained the true reason for my enquiry. "Do you know him?" I probed.

"He hasn't been here for many years, but he used to visit us at one time."

"I heard he met his wife here."

"Yes, he did. I can't recall her name now, but I do remember her becoming a vicar's wife."

"I was introduced to her as Margaret Loach."

"Margaret, that's right." She fixed her eye on a distant point beyond me as she tried to recall more information. "Margaret Collins, she was back then. I remember now. A good volunteer; she worked extremely hard for us. I'm sure she'll have done a great deal of good as a vicar's wife. It was just a shame she didn't marry a Methodist," she paused to give me a fleeting smile. "I've no doubt that she and her husband have made a great career out of doing excellent works, however."

"I'm sure they have." I thought of Mrs Rendell's account of the way Revd Loach had treated Mary Steinway and gave Miss Havers a false smile to cover my disdain.

"It must have been a number of years ago that Miss Collins, as she was called then, first volunteered here," I said.

"Oh, yes. I would say that it was twenty-five years ago."

"And around the same time for Revd Loach?"

"He was a little later. About twenty years, I would say. He turned up here one day looking for a friend."

"Did he mention the friend's name?"

"No, and I couldn't tell you whether he found him in the end or not. But when he saw the good work we were doing, he decided to volunteer his services every Saturday."

"You mentioned that he first volunteered here twenty years ago. Can you remember when? The exact month, perhaps?"

"No, I'm afraid not."

"Might it be written down somewhere?"

She gave a slight frown. "Possibly. Why would you need to know that?"

"I don't," I replied disappointedly. "I just wondered if it might be possible to find out. For a historical record."

"I see." She bit her lip as she gave this some thought. "There may be a mention of him in the journals or ledgers we keep here. I would need to have a look."

"I'm happy to look through them myself if it would save you time," I suggested. "If you don't mind, that is."

"I shall have a look myself. Are you in any great hurry for the information?"

"I must confess that I am. The editor of the journal I'm writing for has asked me to finish the article as soon as possible."

"I see. Well, I can't promise you I'll be able to find out that piece of information, but I'll see what I can do."

I wondered how James was faring in Wapping as I walked along Whitechapel High Street. The day was particularly hot, so I sought out the shade from the shop awnings where possible. Such was the heat that an unpleasant odour lingered in the gutter, and carriage drivers poured pails of water over their horses at regular intervals to keep them cool.

As I walked, I felt the uncomfortable sensation of being watched. Perhaps the tragic death of Mr Masefield had made me more cautious than before. I occasionally glanced behind me as I walked, but I couldn't see anyone who appeared to be following in my footsteps.

I continued on my way, but couldn't shake the sensation that someone was tailing me. I passed St Mary's Church and a row of shops, then decided to make a sudden turn to my left, which took me into a narrow lane called Spectacle Alley. It sat deep in shadow, and I didn't relish the thought of walking through it. But I continued on, stepping around a pile of discarded packing cases and broken glass.

About halfway along the passage, I stopped and turned to look behind me. I saw movement at the far end of the alley, as though someone had decided to follow, then changed his or her mind. I felt my breath quicken. *Should I return that way and find out who it was?*

I decided to do just that. Walking as briskly as I could, I returned to the opening of the passageway, then back out onto the sun-bathed street. A number of people bustled past me, but none looked in my direction.

If someone had been following me, it was impossible to tell who it might have been.

CHAPTER 40

"Masefield was last seen at a restaurant in Covent Garden two evenings ago," James told me as I breakfasted the following morning.

I had been asleep when he returned late the previous evening, and he was now readying himself to leave for Somerset.

"He was dining with a group of friends, all of whom have since been interviewed by E Division," continued James. "The last anyone saw of him was when he left the restaurant, having informed them he was going home to his lodgings in nearby Exeter Street. E Division have spoken to his landlady and the other tenants, but no one saw him return home that evening, and there was no sign of him the following morning either.

"The landlady didn't consider his absence particularly unusual, as he regularly stayed with friends overnight, apparently. She was rather unperturbed by his absence until she learned that he had been pulled out of the river."

"He just left the restaurant and disappeared into the night?"

"It seems that way."

"Where had he dined?"

"Le Réfectoire on Hart Street."

"What time had he left?"

"Just after half-past-ten. And then somehow he found his way into the river."

"Someone *threw* him into the river, you mean."

"Yes. The river is about a half-mile walk from Le Réfectoire, so he could have covered that distance in ten minutes or so."

"If he walked there, that is. Someone may have ambushed him close to the restaurant."

"They may indeed. E Division are busy talking to witnesses. There have been reports of a scuffle in the area, but they haven't been able to confirm that Masefield was involved."

"In which case, they have yet to find a witness who saw him after he left the restaurant."

"On the contrary; numerous people claim to have seen him. E Division are trying to determine which of those claims are genuine sightings. Another pertinent piece of information is that two men called at the home of Masefield's parents in Kensington last week."

"What sort of men?"

"Two unpleasant-looking types, according to the servants. Fortunately for the Masefields, they weren't at home."

"Sir Octavius has to be behind this, don't you think?"

"He should certainly be considered a suspect, but we don't know a great deal about Masefield's life yet. Although he shared with you the possibility that Mr Derricks may have been innocent, we have found nothing to suggest that Sir Octavius murdered Cecil-Palmer. We only have Masefield's word for it. It'll be interesting to speak to the police force in Bridgwater today, as it's possible that the events of twenty years ago at Cecil-Palmer's home are somehow connected with Masefield's death." He checked his inside jacket pocket. "Oh, I've left my warrant card upstairs."

As he headed off to fetch it, I read a newspaper article on the *Thornton v. Thornton and Harvey* divorce case being heard in the High Court of Justice.

Major Owen Thornton had petitioned for a dissolution of his marriage on the grounds of the adultery of his wife, Mrs Katherine Thornton, with the co-respondent named as Sir Octavius Harvey. As I spread marmalade on my toast, I read how there had been an alleged 'flirtation' between Mrs Thornton and Sir Octavius. She had reportedly 'passed nights at his house' and was 'well known to his servants'. I wondered how this could have happened when he was married with a family of his own.

"You're reading something scandalous," commented James when he returned. "I know that look on your face."

I smiled. I recalled Sir Octavius telling me how devoted he was to his wife Julia, yet here I was reading about his antics with another man's wife.

"I feel desperately sorry for Sir Octavius's family," I said.

"You don't look desperately sorry."

"I am." I attempted to straighten my face. "I'm just amused to see that Sir Octavius is finally being revealed for what he truly is. It's just a shame his family will be so hurt by this. And the Thornton family, too."

James nodded. "Men like him never consider the feelings of others. Though I need to be careful with my words here, considering that I once abandoned a lady on her wedding day."

"Oh let's not talk about *her*," I responded. "That was quite different altogether."

"Anyway, I must get to Paddington Station. I don't want to miss my train."

"Wouldn't it be wonderful if you managed to find evidence that Sir Octavius was Mr Masefield's murderer? It really would be the end of him."

"We can't be too hopeful, Penny. E Division will have to pursue other lines of enquiry as well. We mustn't assume that Sir Octavius is the only suspect."

He gave me a quick kiss before hurrying out the door.

"You seem rather distracted, Penelope," said my sister as we ate our lunch at the Holborn Restaurant. "Is everything all right? I expect you're finding married life rather different from the life you led before. It must have been quite an adjustment for you to make."

"I'm enjoying married life very much," I said, smiling to demonstrate just how much I was enjoying it.

"I get the impression you've been keeping yourself occupied."

"I have indeed."

"What could possibly have been keeping you so busy? I'd been expecting you to help me with my work for Miss Barrington. She always needs an extra pair of hands. And we need as many women as we can get at the West London Women's Society. We've lost a few of our members recently."

"That sounds rather careless of you, Ellie."

"It's not a joking matter, Penelope!" My sister frowned as she sipped her wine.

"I'm sorry. It's just that my mind is rather occupied with other matters at the moment."

"Such as? You're no longer a reporter for a busy newspaper. What could possibly be occupying your thoughts to such a degree?"

"James is paying an important visit to Somerset today.

There have been a number of developments in a case we've...
he's been working on."

"You said *we* before correcting yourself. Have you also
been working on the case?"

I relented and told Eliza all about Mary Steinway and my
search for her killer. She listened intently throughout.

"I'm impatient to hear from James when he returns this
evening to find out whether William Derricks was forced into
making a false confession or not," I added.

"I can see now why you've so little time for Miss
Barrington and the West London Women's Society. Why
didn't you tell me all this sooner?"

"Because I knew you'd scold me."

"I don't scold you, Penelope!"

"Yes, you do. You always tell me I'm putting myself in
danger and that it's not appropriate for a lady to go around
visiting dangerous parts of London."

"Well, it isn't, and I'm surprised James allows it. Actually,
I'm not terribly surprised James allows it. He knows what
you're like, and that there's little use in arguing with you.
That wouldn't make for a happy marriage, would it?"

"No, it wouldn't. He's always known that I would continue
with my work in some shape or form."

"He's quite unlike most other husbands, isn't he?"

"Of course he is. That's why I married him."

We exchanged a smile.

"Now, what are your thoughts on Father?" I asked, keen to
move the conversation along. "Have you changed your mind
about meeting him yet? I'm pretty sure he could win you over
with a bottle of coca wine. That appears to be his main plan
of attack."

"Coca wine? I don't think so."

"James has become slightly more amenable to him of

late," I said. "He overstayed his welcome with us one evening, but I think James quite enjoyed it. Once one realises that Father is irreverent, feckless and imperfect in almost every way, one begins to develop a little more affection for him."

"Oh dear. Really?"

"It's impossible to hold him to the highest standards, Ellie. I realise it's natural to consider one's parents that way, but it's not always realistic. What does Francis make of him?"

"Francis? I don't see what he has to do with this." She occupied herself with buttering a bread roll.

"He has everything to do with it! He found Father for us. And, as a close friend of yours—"

"A *friend*, Penelope, not a *close friend*."

"A *good* friend."

"Yes, a *good* friend. I'll allow that."

"What does he think of Father's actions?"

"He thinks Father has behaved most foolishly, but he doesn't dislike him. In fact, he has a sort of liking for him. There's no denying that Father has some charm about him, and I think Francis has perhaps been taken in by that a little."

"Does he think you should go and see him?"

"He has suggested it, yes. We had quite a discussion about it yesterday, in fact."

"You saw Francis as recently as yesterday?" I grinned and raised an interested eyebrow.

"Oh, stop looking at me like that!"

"Like what?"

"You know what."

"So, you discussed Father yesterday. What was the outcome?"

"Francis thinks I should meet with him, but I'm not sure about it yet."

I took a sip of wine and decided to stir up a little

mischief. "Father mentioned to me that he intends to return to Colombia next week," I said.

My sister's eyes widened. "Next week? When next week?"

"Friday. His ticket is already booked."

"He's going back so soon?"

"I'm afraid so."

CHAPTER 41

I hadn't expected James to return with a companion late that evening, and especially not a female one. When I saw her step into our front room, I assumed he had befriended her on the train and felt a pang of irritation that she happened to be such a young, attractive lady. She had brown hair and a freckled complexion and was wearing a blue flannel dress. On closer inspection, I was struck by something familiar about her.

"Mrs Worthers?" I ventured, realising she was the private detective I had encountered while reporting on the Twelve Brides gang for the *Morning Express*.

"Good evening, Mrs Blakely."

"Have you travelled all the way from Somerset?"

"Good gracious, no!" She laughed. "I've been trying to speak to your husband all day and, out of desperation, I decided to call at your home. I've just encountered him in the street outside."

"Mrs Worthers has some news for us about Sir Octavius," added James. "I invited her in so we could both hear it."

"Perfect!" I replied.

I invited Mrs Worthers to sit down and James poured us some sherry.

"Before I tell you what I know, Mrs Blakely, will you please promise me that it won't find its way into any sort of publication?" she asked. "Not just yet, at least. I intend to fully co-operate with the police," she acknowledged James with a nod, "and to be as helpful as I can, but it wouldn't help if certain matters were to be made public at this stage."

"You have my assurance," I replied. "Besides, I'm not even sure whether any publications would be interested in my work at the present time."

"Oh, I see." She smoothed down her skirts and continued. "I've been employed by Sir Octavius for a few months now. He was receiving anonymous letters and asked me to find out who had been sending them."

"What was the tone of the letters?"

"Someone was blackmailing him."

"And how did he respond?"

"He complied with the first two. They referred to some extremely personal information, and had been sent by someone who clearly knew something of his past."

"Did they relate to his alleged adultery with Mrs Thornton?"

"No. That's another unfortunate matter that has since come to light. No, the blackmail letters related to something else altogether. They threatened to reveal him as a murderer."

I gave a knowing nod.

"Were you aware of this?" she asked, her eyebrows raised.

"It's the first I've heard of the letters, but I heard a rumour that Sir Octavius might have been responsible for John Cecil-Palmer's death twenty years ago. A man named William Derricks was hanged for the crime."

"So you *do* know about that! Do you mind me asking how?"

"I'd hazard a guess that it came from the same source as the letters: Robert Masefield."

"Yes," she replied. "That's who I discovered was behind them."

"How did you find out it was him?"

"Some of the information they contained could only have been known by a handful of people, according to Sir Octavius. He gave me a list of those people, and I eventually managed to deduce that it was Mr Masefield."

"And how did you manage that?"

"I had to take him into my confidence. I befriended him by taking a job as a waitress at one of the restaurants he frequented."

"You disguised yourself?"

"Yes, it's something I have to do fairly often. His animosity toward Sir Octavius was quite evident once I got to know him a little."

"Yes, I noticed that, too."

"You also met him?"

"He approached me after he heard that I had been making enquiries about Mary Steinway's murder."

"You were investigating her murder? I didn't realise that. I've heard a little about her since I first undertook this work for Sir Octavius, and I understand she was present when Cecil-Palmer drowned. Though Mr Masefield alleged that Sir Octavius was responsible for his death."

"Did Mr Masefield receive any money from Sir Octavius in response to the letters?"

"Yes. Quite a significant sum to begin with. Sir Octavius hoped that would be the end of it. Unfortunately, Mr Masefield became greedy and asked for more. That's when Sir Octavius asked me to start investigating. The trouble was…" Her voice trailed off and she examined her fingernails, then looked out of the window. I could see that her eyes were moist.

"The trouble is what, Mrs Worthers?" asked James gently.

She turned her face back toward us. "The trouble is, I think my actions led Mr Masefield to his death. When Sir Octavius asked me to find his blackmailer, I had no idea he would go to such great lengths to have him silenced! I often investigate blackmail cases, but once I've gathered all the necessary evidence the police are usually informed and the blackmailer is dealt with appropriately. He or she receives a fair punishment and the matter is resolved. However, this time... having Mr Masefield murdered..." She shook her head. "I had no idea Sir Octavius would do such a thing! And to think I was the one who told him the name of his blackmailer..." She stretched out her palms and stared down at them. "I can almost see the blood on my hands!"

"Nonsense!" retorted James. "You did what you were asked to do. As you said yourself, you've carried out this sort of work numerous times before with no unfortunate outcome. Do you have any evidence that Sir Octavius murdered Masefield?"

"Not actual evidence, no."

"Did he tell you that he intended to harm him?"

"No."

"Then it's possible Masefield's death had nothing do with Sir Octavius."

"I suppose that's a possibility. I'd like to think he had nothing to do with it, but unfortunately I'm sure that he did."

"But you bear no responsibility for his actions," I said. "He appears to be the sort of man who takes matters into his own hands whenever there's a problem to be dealt with. But it'll all catch up with him eventually. Inspector Blakely and E Division are working hard on the case, and Sir Octavius's time will soon be up. Isn't that right, James?"

"I certainly hope so. We'll do all we can to make sure of it."

"I hope something can be done. That was all I had to impart to you for now." Mrs Worthers rose to her feet. "I've interrupted your evening enough. I'll leave you in peace."

"Please stay for a moment longer, Mrs Worthers," replied James. "If you don't mind, that is. You'll probably want to hear what I have to say. I've had an interesting day making enquiries in Somerset."

She nodded and sat down again.

"I met with a retired detective, Mr Grant, who investigated the death of John Cecil-Palmer," he continued. "I asked him about all the suspects at the time, but he said Mr Derricks was so swift to confess that he didn't consider any other suspects."

"Did he explain what happened that night?" I asked.

"There was a party at the house. From the sounds of it, there had been a party at the house most evenings that August. It was something Cecil-Palmer was known for during the summer months. His parents were overseas, so he had the run of the place. It was common for him to invite his London friends down to Somerset once the season had come to an end.

"Mr Grant was called to the house late that evening, after Cecil-Palmer had fallen into the lake. Many of the guests were under the influence of alcohol, so he initially struggled to make much sense of what had happened. But he rounded everyone up the following day and managed to establish that Sir Octavius, Miss Steinway, Mr Derricks and Mr Cecil-Palmer had been present when Cecil-Palmer went into the water. The story the three survivors told was that there had been a disagreement between Derricks and Cecil-Palmer, and that Derricks had pushed his employer into the water. Their accounts suggested that Derricks had confronted his employer about his wages, but Cecil-Palmer had been defensive and belittled him. Cecil-Palmer was then pushed into the water as a punishment, and Derricks had refused to let anyone help him.

"According to their accounts, Sir Octavius and Miss Steinway were both greatly distressed by what they saw that night. Derricks was apparently angry and aggressive, and threatened to do the same to them if they tried to help the poor man."

"You mean they had to just watch Mr Cecil-Palmer drown?" I asked, horrified.

"That's what they said. And once Mr Grant had established what had purportedly happened, Derricks's confession swiftly followed."

"But Mr Masefield claimed to have witnessed Sir Octavius pushing Mr Cecil-Palmer into the water," said Mrs Worthers.

"Is that what he told you?" asked James.

"Yes, and he was quite sure of it. He was standing on the lawn near the house at the time, and he claimed it was Sir Octavius who pushed Mr Cecil-Palmer, not Mr Derricks."

"Did Sir Octavius know that Masefield had witnessed the incident?" I asked.

"No. None of them knew he had. I think he was afraid of Sir Octavius, and that's why he never confronted him about it."

"But he and Miss Steinway were perfectly happy to see Mr Derricks convicted," I said.

"He wasn't happy about it, but I think they were all afraid. Sir Octavius was – and still is – an intimidating man. And he's not without influence, either."

"It must have been fear that made Derricks confess," said James. "And unfortunately, Grant believed the man. He considered his actions to be out of character, though. Derricks's friends and family were adamant that he would never do such a thing, especially to his own employer, but Grant blamed his irrational behaviour on the effects of the drink. After the execution, Grant learned that Derricks had told his wife and children to seek refuge with a relative of hers near Bristol, which suggests he was worried for their safety. Perhaps he'd been told that if he didn't confess their lives would be in danger. I believe the threat came directly from the culprit."

"Sir Octavius," mused Mrs Worthers ruefully. "How I wish I'd never met the man!"

"I'm sure a number of people feel the same way," replied James. "Masefield was certainly playing with fire when he put his blackmail plan into action. Let's not forget that two unpleasant men called on Masefield's parents last week. Perhaps someone was threatening them the same way that Derricks's family was threatened."

I felt a bitter taste in my mouth as my anger toward Sir Octavius intensified.

"When are you going to arrest him, James?" I snapped.

"I need to get down to Bow Street now to discuss all this with them."

"I'd better be on my way, too," said Mrs Worthers. "Just one more thing before I leave, though. Mr Masefield confessed to me that he had committed an act of arson. He didn't tell me when or where, exactly, but when I heard about the former Steinway home being burned down, I wondered if—"

"If it was Masefield!" I exclaimed. "Why on earth would he do such a thing?"

"He didn't explain himself fully. All he said was that he'd lit a fire under some long-forgotten secrets. He went on to explain that the building had been lying empty for a long time and that he had watched it burn."

"Well, it certainly caught Penny's attention," said James,

"and led us to where we are now. It seems like a very odd thing for him to do, but then again, he appears to have been a troubled man. Would you mind reporting to Bow Street tomorrow morning, Mrs Worthers, to tell Inspector Fenton about your dealings with Sir Octavius and Masefield?"

"Of course." She got to her feet, opened her handbag and took out a card. "I'll leave this with you if that's all right, Mrs Blakely."

"Thank you." I rose to my feet and took the card from her.

"I'll take my leave of you now. Apologies again for intruding on your evening."

"There's no need for you to apologise at all, Mrs Worthers," I replied. "It appears we've been working on the same case, albeit from slightly different angles."

"Indeed we have." She smiled. "Perhaps our paths will cross again someday."

CHAPTER 42

A letter arrived for me the following morning. I didn't recognise the scrawling handwriting on the envelope, but I saw that it bore a Kent postmark. The address at the top of the letter was Sarsden Farm.

I apologise for my silence when you visited. I was sworn to secrecy twenty years ago, but since your visit I've decided that sometimes an answer is deserved. Please don't acknowledge this letter, but instead direct your enquiries to Goldsworth Farm, near Welbrook.

The letter was signed by Mrs Ruth Wiley. I recalled how tight-lipped the elderly lady at the farm had been about Molly Gardstein. *Was it possible that she might lead me to her after all?*

I felt my heart skip with excitement. I longed to tell James what had happened, but he was still busy at Bow Street police station. With little else planned for the day, I decided to take the train to Faversham.

As I left the house, I reflected on the fact that Molly Gardstein had almost escaped my thoughts since my previous visit to Kent. There was no denying, however, that she might still be a suspect in Mary Steinway's death. And now there was a chance that I might finally meet her. *But would she welcome me?*

It was clear that Mrs Wiley had known something of Molly's whereabouts for a long time but had been forced to keep the secret. *How would Molly behave when her location was discovered? Would the police rush straight down to arrest her when they found out? If Molly Gardstein was innocent, who might she believe to be responsible for Mary's death?* I felt nervous about our meeting, yet hopeful that she might be able to tell me something useful.

I took a detour to the Royal Courts of Justice on Fleet Street on my way to Victoria Station. It was a building I was familiar with, as it was close to the *Morning Express* offices. The courts were striking in design, with an array of towers, turrets and soaring spires on display. The vast doorway and countless arched windows wouldn't have looked out of place on a cathedral. I waited beside the railings and watched as the gowned barristers arrived from their chambers in Middle Temple and Inner Temple across the road.

I hoped I was early enough to witness the arrival of Sir Octavius. I felt that a mere glimpse of his face would help me decide whether or not he was a murderer.

"Mrs Blakely!" I turned to see my former colleague, Edgar Fish, loping toward me with a wry smile.

"Oh, hello, Edgar."

"Are you reporting on the divorce case as well?"

"Why would I be?"

"I don't know. I thought you might have been offered a reporting job for another newspaper."

"No."

"Too busy with married life, eh? You must call on Mrs Fish sometime. She'd be delighted to see you again. You know our address, don't you?"

"Yes, I have it somewhere."

"Good. I'm sure she'd be happy to introduce you to a good number of interesting ladies. They could put the world to rights between them, I'd say. In fact, they've quite changed my mind on women's suffrage. We should go one step further and put Mrs Fish and her gentlewomen friends in government!" He laughed. "That would separate the men from the boys, wouldn't it?"

"And the ladies from the girls, perhaps."

He laughed again. "How's your schoolboy inspector faring?"

"Quite busy, as usual. He's investigating the murder of Robert Masefield."

"The chap they pulled out of the river? What an unpleasant business."

"Did you know he was once a friend of Sir Octavius's?"

"No!" His eyes widened and I wondered whether I had spoken too freely.

"It was many years ago now," I muttered quietly. "I don't think Sir Octavius wished it to become public knowledge."

"Indeed not. It turns out there several things Sir Octavius didn't wish to become public knowledge... but here we are." He gave a conspiratorial smile. "Actually, Sherman asked me to be extra careful about the way I report on this case. Apparently, Sir Octavius is feeling rather nervous at the moment, and it wouldn't do to offend. Are you coming into the public gallery? You'll need to head inside now if you are; they couldn't fit everyone in yesterday."

"No, I have somewhere else to be. I stopped by out of curiosity really, just to catch sight of him again."

"Again?"

"I'm hoping to write all about it soon, but we'll have to see what happens."

"You've got me on tenterhooks now, Mrs Blakely. I look forward to reading all about it; whatever *it* is."

"Enjoy the court case."

"I certainly will! There's no danger of me falling asleep through this one, that's for sure! It'll be more entertaining than the theatre."

We bid each other farewell, but I remained where I was for a little while longer. A number of shiny carriages pulled up outside the law courts and various well-dressed gentlemen stepped out of them before making their way up the steps. The Royal Courts of Justice only heard civic cases, so those attending did so to settle matters of family and business. There were no criminals in attendance, though some might have described Sir Octavius as such.

Two black horses trotted up, pulling a landau I had recently travelled in. Before it came to a standstill, a smooth-featured man with neat whiskers hopped out. The member of parliament for Southwark was clearly keen to get inside the court building as quickly as possible. His assistant and two sombre-looking men carrying briefcases followed him in.

Onlookers stared at the MP and muttered to one another. His brow was lowered and his jaw tense, and I noticed him swallowing uncomfortably. His gaze rose above the onlookers as he headed for the gap between the railings. His eyes briefly met mine and gave a jolt of recognition. Then his hardened stare returned and I felt my skin prickle. He turned his eyes toward the steps ahead of him and marched up them.

Was he capable of extreme cruelty? Did he have no regard for the lives of others?

I had already seen three different versions of the same man: the one who addressed public meetings; the one who recalled his wayward youth, cigar in hand; and the one who was now attempting to defend his reputation. *How many versions were there? Might I one day find myself looking at the version that had committed three murders?* I suddenly realised the figure might even be four. If he had forced Derricks to confess, he was also responsible for the poor man's hanging.

Three lives had been lost in order to absolve himself of responsibility for a murder he had committed on a lake one drunken summer evening.

I felt anger stir in my stomach and fervently hoped James would be able to persuade E Division to arrest Sir Octavius. I prayed some definitive evidence would be found against him; not just for Robert Masefield's murder, but also for Mary Steinway's and John Cecil-Palmer's. And then William Derricks could be pardoned posthumously.

I glanced up the steps Sir Octavius had just ascended and wished I could enter the courtroom he was standing in and announce to everyone what he had done. Although I knew that James and E Division were working on the case, I was worried he would somehow get away with all the despicable things he had done.

On reaching Victoria Station, I walked alongside the Dover train looking for the second-class carriages. As I stepped around a porter's trolley and various people saying their good-byes, I felt, once again, as though I were being watched. I stopped suddenly and turned, but only in time to see a carriage door being pulled closed. *Had someone jumped onto the train as soon I slowed my pace to look around?*

I walked back toward the closed door and peered inside

the carriage. A man with a large moustache glared back at me through the glass. The other forms within the compartment were too indistinct to make out. I told myself I was imagining things and walked on to find a compartment with vacant seats.

CHAPTER 43

It was raining as I approached Goldsworth Farm. The trap had dropped me at the end of a long track that had been deeply furrowed by cart wheels, with thick grass growing in the middle. I could either choose to walk through the long, wet grass or twist my ankle in the furrows. I smiled to myself as I realised how accustomed I had become to paving stones. Despite being raised in rural Derbyshire, I was far more suited to the city these days.

A small farmhouse eventually revealed itself beyond the brow of the hill. I desperately hoped that I would find Molly there, was I naive for being so hopeful? I knew that I had to prepare myself for another dead end, but I didn't want to. I wanted to meet Molly and discover what she was like. I wanted to speak with her and find some answers to my many questions.

I flinched as I saw three dogs running across a field toward me, issuing short, sharp warning barks. I looked down and tramped on, hoping they would see that I wasn't a threat. A short while later they blocked my way, their wide eyes fixed on me and their barking relentless. I stopped walking and tried to avoid their gaze as best I could. Attempting to slow my pounding heart, I took several deep breaths.

The cacophony continued, but the dogs didn't advance any further. I hoped the noise would alert someone at the house, who would come out and call them over. But no one came and I remained where I was, hoping the dogs would soon leave me alone.

Were they Molly's dogs? Had she trained them to protect her? I felt sure they would be enough to dissuade many people from visiting the farm. I presumed that if I turned back the dogs would leave me alone. They were protecting their territory and their master... or mistress.

Only I couldn't turn back. I had made a series of enquiries and travelled some distance to find Molly, putting myself at considerable risk. This encounter with the dogs was just another obstacle I would have to overcome. I stood still, feeling encouraged by the fact that the barking was becoming less intense.

One of the dogs stepped forward and tentatively sniffed at my skirts. I said hello and immediately wished I hadn't, as the sound of my voice set off a new round of barking. I would have to stay quiet and remain where I was until the dogs gave up or someone came to rescue me.

But there was little hope of rescue in this rain-drenched landscape. I had expected someone working in a nearby field to come to my aid, but I saw no one at all.

A firm breeze whipped the rain into my face as the dogs began to quieten again. One of them turned its back on me and began to sniff at the grass, and the other two took this as their cue to do the same. I exhaled with relief. The dogs were losing interest in me.

As all three animals examined the same patch of grass, I slowly began to walk on. This movement didn't escape their attention, their tails moving stiffly from side to side. I looked ahead and continued on my way, and the dogs accompanied me as I did so. They might have decided not to attack me, but they certainly weren't about to let me out of their sight.

Would I have an equally unfriendly experience with the residents of the farmhouse? Would they be hostile enough to set the dogs on me? Was it possible that I would be mauled to death in this peaceful place?

I attempted to laugh off my anxious thoughts, but struggled to find any comforting ones to replace them with. I wondered whether my attempts to investigate Mary Steinway's death had been an enormous mistake; a strange reaction to the recent change in my employment status. *Was the life of a married woman really so unfulfilling that I had willingly placed myself in danger in the wet, lonely Kent countryside?*

I began to admonish myself for being so foolhardy, reasoning that my place was at home with James now. Given that I was fast approaching the age of thirty-six, perhaps it was time to accept that my days of adventure were over. After all, this was not how married ladies were supposed to behave! I pondered why I was finding it so difficult to accept my new role.

As I moved closer to the farmhouse, I convinced myself that whatever answer I received there would be wholly unsatisfactory. Perhaps that was all I deserved for pointedly ignoring society's rules. I pictured the newspaper report describing how a recently married lady had been killed by dogs on a remote farm. It would include comments on my recklessness and lack of self-control, questioning the state of my mind. *What was Mrs Blakely even doing there? She had brought it upon herself.*

My maudlin thoughts tailed off when I reached the farmhouse gate. The dogs watched curiously, as if daring me to unlatch it. *Would it provoke them?*

I cautiously lifted the latch and pushed the gate open. It

brushed against the long grass growing beneath it. To my relief, the dogs trotted on ahead toward a door that had been painted pale blue. I knocked nervously.

The dogs skipped inside as soon as the door opened, as if tired by their little jaunt and in need of rest. A small woman with untidy grey hair stared back at me, a puzzled expression on her face.

"Molly?" I asked. "Molly Gardstein?"

Her eyes widened and she took a step back. "Who are you?"

"My name is Mrs Penny Blakely. I'm a journalist and I've been trying to find you. I heard you ran away from London after Mary Steinway was murdered, but a good number of people believe you were innocent."

She sighed and her gaze sank to the floor. "I knew someone'd come one day." She looked up at me again. "And I suppose it could've been someone worse. There's no one else with you, is there?" She peered out through the doorway.

"No, it's just me."

"I suppose you'd better come in, seeing as you're wet through from the rain." She stepped to one side. "But I should tell you now that I'm not Molly."

The dogs dozed beside the fire while the farm owner, whose name was Mrs Garner, told me about Molly. Once inside, I could see that she was a good deal older than Molly would have been. We sat in a dingy but cosy front room, the odour of damp dog lingering all around us.

"Ruth Wiley from Sarsden Farm called on me back then. She had Molly working for her at the time. Molly was scared 'cause the police were after her. It must've been Ruth who told you Molly'd come here."

"Yes, it was."

Mrs Garner nodded. "We arranged it all in secret, me and Ruth. We changed Molly's name right away. We called her Emma and she cut all her hair off." She smiled. "That was a sight, that was. But we knew the police would go to Sarsden Farm looking for her before long. Ruth saw them off; she made sure of that. She's always been very convincing, has Ruth.

"Emma told me she wanted to change her ways. She'd been given some money to leave London, and she'd always loved Kent. I didn't find out for some time that her turning up here had something to do with a murder."

"She told you about that?"

"She told me she'd been a suspect. Said that was the way it was supposed to be. She'd got herself into all sorts of trouble up there and wanted to leave it all behind, so she'd taken the money and run. She was very upset about her friend but leaving seemed like the best course of action. She said the police would only have suspected her if she'd stayed, anyway. She was sure they would have arrested her, even though she'd done nothing wrong. They'd arrested her so many times before, she told me.

"I didn't ask for details; it weren't none of my business. But I could see she wanted to do good by herself. She wanted to change. And that's exactly what I helped her do. She worked with us here on the farm. My husband and son were here back then, and we all kept quiet about who she really was. Police only visited once, and that was up at Ruth's place. We was all left well alone after that."

"Did she tell you who had given her the money to leave?"

"No. She never breathed a word of it."

"One can only presume that the person who offered it to her was connected to the murder of her friend."

"I wouldn't know about that. As far as I was concerned, we both forgot all about her life in London."

"But she could have told the police who had offered her the money, couldn't she?"

"I suppose she could've done, but she reckoned they wouldn't believe her. Apparently, she weren't on the best of terms with her friend before the girl died, and Emma thought everyone would suspect her. She was a good girl really."

"*Was?*"

"She's not with us no more. Died three years ago of rheumatic fever. We did our best to get her as healthy as us country folk, but I don't think she ever got over all them years of smoke and damp up there in London. It weren't often we saw her with any colour in her cheeks, but she was happy. I heard she was no angel up in London, but she changed her ways and found happiness here for seventeen years. Buster there loved her." She pointed at one of the sleeping dogs. "Never left her side. He pined for her after she went. We all did."

I sat silent for a moment, staring at sleeping Buster and considering Mrs Garner's words.

So Molly was dead.

My hopes of meeting her were gone.

Perhaps it had been better that I hadn't met her? From what Mrs Garner had told me, she'd been keen to forget about her life in London. She wouldn't have wished to discuss any of it with me.

Possibly I was mistaken, but I felt certain now that Molly was innocent of Mary's murder. I hoped that she had found some happiness here in the Kent countryside with Mrs Garner and her dogs.

The conversation turned to my work and what I had learned about Mary Steinway's death so far.

Mrs Garner responded with a combination of interest and surprise. "I don't know how you've found the energy to do all that. And to make such a long journey down here, too! I'm only sorry I haven't got no good news to give you."

"Please don't apologise, Mrs Garner. There's really no need. You gave Molly – or Emma, I should say – a second chance at life."

She nodded slowly. "I don't like to think of her poisoning Mary, but I suppose she could've, couldn't she? I always believed what she told me, you see, 'cause she seemed quite honest about her shortcomings. I wouldn't like to think of her as a murderer, though." She sighed. "I suppose we all believe what we want to believe, and if something don't sound very pleasant... well, we brush it under the carpet, don't we? We don't like to think about it."

"That's very true, Mrs Garner."

A young man entered the room. He quickly pulled off his cap when he saw me.

"Have you finished with that shed door, Harry?" she asked.

"Almost." He smoothed his hair flat and gave me a wary glance.

"Help yourself to bread and butter. I'll come and have a look at the shed once I've taken Mrs Blakely back to the station."

"Oh, there's really no need!" I replied. "I don't want to keep you from your work."

"Nonsense, it won't take long. You don't want to be walking all that way."

The rain had stopped by the time we departed, but Mrs Garner lent me one of her shawls and draped a good number across her own shoulders. A large bay horse called Mayoress pulled the cart.

I focused on the rolling green fields and pretty hedgerows as we travelled, reflecting on the solace Molly Gardstein must have found in this place. It was a far cry from the narrow lane beside the railway lines back in Shadwell.

CHAPTER 44

"You have a visitor, Mrs Blakely," said Mrs Oliver when I returned home that evening. "I explained she'd have to wait and asked if she'd like to return another day, but she seemed quite insistent about seeing you."

I thanked her, wishing I could change out of the damp travelling clothes I had been wearing all day. I quickly removed my hat and re-pinned my hair in the hallway looking glass. Then I walked into the front room to see a slight lady with neat brown hair and a plain cotton dress rising to her feet.

"Mrs Loach! How nice to see you again," I said, forcing some cheer into my voice. "What brings you here?"

She wasn't smiling the way she had when we first met. As we sat down, I saw that Mrs Oliver had already brought in a tea tray for her, and that the cup was empty. I wondered how long she had resolved to wait for me.

"I spoke to an old friend of mine today," she began. "Actually, she called on me. She told me she'd received a visit from a lady who described herself as a journalist." Her shoulders lifted a little, as though she were fighting back some anger.

"She works at the Salvation Army shelter in Whitechapel," she continued.

"Miss Havers?" I asked.

"Yes, Miss Havers. I presume you visited the shelter because I'd told you I met my husband there."

"I recall you telling me that, yes. And as I explained to Miss Havers, I'm writing an article about Christian missions in the East End." I smiled, doubting that my explanation would be enough to convince her.

"Yes, Miss Havers said as much. However, she also told me that you seemed particularly interested in my husband."

"Only because I happened to have met him, and it was interesting to discover that he had volunteered with the Salvation Army, which has a Methodist foundation."

"It's not unusual for Methodists and Anglicans to join forces, Mrs Blakely. Especially when they're working toward the common good."

"Of course. Has your husband ever volunteered with any other missions in the East End?"

"Very much so. Even the Jewish mission." She enunciated these last two words, as if to stress her husband's all-encompassing goodwill.

"How very noble of him."

I hoped Mrs Oliver would bring more tea in. I felt weary from the day's events and Mrs Loach was beginning to irritate me. "May I ask exactly what it was that you wished to discuss? You must forgive me for the directness of the question, but I've had rather a tiring day, and I'm sure you have no wish to be detained here any longer than you already have been."

"I'll get to the point, then."

Her lips thinned and I prepared myself for a verbal onslaught.

"I don't appreciate you making enquiries about my

husband, Mrs Blakely. To be quite frank with you, I don't believe you were writing an article about Christian missions when you spoke to Miss Havers. You specifically went there to ask her about my husband. You were gathering information about him. The fact that you turned up at our home in the first place was an imposition. And I considered it incredibly rude of you to ask a respected clergyman about his lunatic wife, though my husband demonstrated remarkable patience with you. He didn't have to answer your questions, and indeed we didn't have to invite you into our home at all!"

"I'm extremely grateful that you did, Mrs Loach."

My passive reply appeared to deflate her a little, but then her shoulders lifted again. "It was impertinent of you! And you asked me direct questions about how long we'd been married and where I'd met my husband. Then you used the information I gave you to make further enquiries about him!"

"I'm afraid that's what journalists do."

"Well, I don't appreciate it!"

"Can I ask why this has upset you so? As I explained to you at the time, I've been looking into the circumstances of Mary Steinway's death."

"But there's no need!"

"Why not?"

"Because it was so long ago, and it's quite obvious to everyone else that she was a victim of her own downfall."

"You don't think anyone else was responsible for her death?"

"Well, someone must have poisoned her, but she probably drove them to it."

"Are you saying that she deserved to die?"

"The Lord decides such matters."

I sighed. "Someone murdered her, Mrs Loach, and somehow got away with it. Your husband was in Whitechapel around the time of her death. He volunteered at the shelter on Saturdays, and Mary Steinway was poisoned less than a mile from where he would have spent the day."

Her mouth dropped open. "How dare you?"

"Your husband would have had to wait seven years for his estranged wife to be declared dead. That wouldn't have been any use to him if he wished to remarry earlier than that, would it? Once his first wife's death had been confirmed he would be free to marry again. I presume you had already met one another by that time."

Mrs Loach stood to her feet. "Your words are quite frankly the most offensive I have ever heard, Mrs Blakely! You're accusing my husband of murder!"

"At the present time I could accuse three or four people of Mary Steinway's murder. Each of them had a viable motive."

"She drank the poison at an alehouse! My husband would never set foot in an alehouse! And don't you think he would have drawn attention to himself if he had? Don't you think the police would have questioned him if he'd been present that evening?"

"You sound as though you're trying to persuade yourself of his innocence now, Mrs Loach. Have you ever asked him why he refused to attend his wife's inquest? Was it out of fear that he would incriminate himself?"

"Nonsense!"

"Are you visiting me today because you fear your husband may be responsible after all? Are you desperately trying to prove your husband's innocence out of fear that he may indeed be guilty?"

"I don't need to listen to a word more of this!" she spat as she marched toward the door. When she reached it, she spun around to face me. "You're immoral, Mrs Blakely. Immoral! It isn't right, you know, for a lady of your standing to behave in such a manner. Or that you should cast aspersions on a man who has devoted his life to doing the work of God; a man who works every single day, without pause, for the good of others. What would your husband think if he'd heard the way you spoke to me just now? He would realise what a grave mistake he'd made in marrying you, that's for sure. Call yourself a police inspector's wife? You should be ashamed of yourself. I notice there are no children in this home. That's a blessing, I must say. You're an unfit wife and would undoubtedly be an unfit mother, too!" She paused to take a breath, then gave me a nasty snarl. "This isn't the last you'll hear of this."

And with that she was gone.

Mrs Oliver stepped tentatively into the room once Mrs Loach had left. "Can I bring you some tea, Mrs Blakely?"

"Sherry, please," I replied. "An extremely large sherry."

CHAPTER 45

"That sounds rather uncalled for," said James after I had told him about Mrs Loach's visit. "And now she's made us think that she and Revd Loach have something to hide."

"She took umbrage at the fact that I'd asked Miss Havers about her husband."

"I'd say."

"Do you think Marylebone Division could be persuaded to interview them?"

"Only if there was new evidence. If it could be proven that Revd Loach was at the Salvation Army shelter the day Mary Steinway died, that may be of interest to them. They'd be even more interested if there were any witnesses who had seen him in Ratcliffe that evening, or at the alehouse itself."

"It may be difficult to find witnesses who would remember him twenty years after the event."

"It would be extremely difficult. And can we trust anyone's memory from that long ago? This is what makes an old case so hard to crack. There's a reason the police don't spend countless hours on them. And besides, if we're able to arrest Sir Octavius for Masefield's murder, we might have Mary Steinway's murderer behind bars after all."

"Where have you got to with him?"

"The men at E Division have taken statements from several witnesses who saw Mr Masefield getting into a landau."

I felt a flip of excitement in my chest. "Sir Octavius has a landau!"

"He does, but he's not the only person in London to own one, so we mustn't leap to conclusions."

"Do the descriptions of the horses match?"

"I believe they're encouraging, yes, though we mustn't forget that it would have been dark at the time."

"Oh, James, you're downplaying this whole thing. The landau has to be Sir Octavius's! He picked Mr Masefield up and then... well, he must have had someone help him carry out the attack. Not his assistant, though; he doesn't look strong enough to overpower a man. Sir Octavius must have found someone else to help silence Mr Masefield. I shouldn't think that would have been too difficult for a man like him."

"E Division are rounding up the most reliable witnesses. Once they've done that, I shall interview them further to see what they can tell us. Sir Octavius's wife has provided an alibi for him."

"That seems rather surprising, considering he's been having an affair!"

"Perhaps that wasn't surprising to her. She may have known about the affair for some time and remained committed to defending her husband, unlike the husband of Sir Octavius's mistress."

"But she risks being found guilty of perjury by providing a false alibi."

"Perhaps she's telling the truth. There's no evidence at the moment that Sir Octavius was in his landau, even if we can prove that it was his carriage people saw. He may have sent someone else out to deal with Masefield. If we can be certain that it was Sir Octavius's carriage, we can interview his coach-man... and stable boy, too, if it comes to that. It'll be inter-esting to hear their explanations for the sort of errand the landau undertook that evening if Sir Octavius remained at home."

"Has Mrs Worthers been of any further assistance?"

"She told us more about the work she carried out for Sir Octavius. He had his suspicions about who was behind the blackmail, and he really only employed her to track Masefield down and gain his trust. I never met Masefield myself. Would you consider him the type of man who might have been easily influenced by feminine charms?"

"Most certainly."

"It seems Mrs Worthers knew exactly what she was doing, in that case, and she was paid handsomely for the informa-tion. She feels responsible for what happened to Masefield now, but she couldn't possibly have known that Sir Octavius would take such drastic action. If he's responsible for Mase-field's death, that is. We can't be completely sure of anything yet."

"I'm certain he did it," I said. "I think Sir Octavius murdered John Cecil-Palmer, Mary Steinway and Robert Masefield. And he's also responsible for William Derricks's death if he forced him to confess. Being named in a divorce case should be the least of his worries. He has blood on his hands... and lots of it!"

"Can you be certain that he murdered Mary Steinway?" asked James.

"He must have done! She was there when Mr Cecil-Palmer was pushed into the water, and now the other two people who witnessed the incident are dead. He murdered

Mary because she knew what had happened and posed a risk to his political career."

"We need to find a piece of evidence that connects Sir Octavius to the White Swan alehouse twenty years ago."

"It has to have been him!"

"I think you may be right, Penny, but we need evidence. I think it's time I paid the place a visit."

CHAPTER 46

"Here it is," I said to James as we approached the White Swan alehouse the following morning.

He paused to survey the narrow, timbered facade. "Paddy's Goose is an infamous place. And there's the swan at the very top."

We glanced up at the elegant statue, soaring high above its squalid surroundings.

"Did this place get its nickname because someone thought the swan was a goose?" I wondered aloud.

"Probably. Mary Steinway lived behind this alehouse, did she not?"

"Yes." I pointed to the alleyway that led to Harris Terrace. "Just through there."

James grimaced. "A stark contrast to the family home she grew up in."

"That's why I've always been so interested in her story," I replied. "I don't think her downfall was truly of her own making. She made various unpleasant acquaintances along the way."

"She certainly seems to have done. Let's go inside."

Even though James was with me, I felt nervous about encountering Joshua Kemp again. I prayed he wouldn't be in the alehouse on this occasion.

The dingy interior was thick with tobacco smoke as we walked across the sticky floorboards of the White Swan. The hard-faced barmaid I had seen the last time stood chatting with a young man beside the bar. Her hair was elaborately curled once again and she had bright daubs of rouge on her cheeks.

The conversation paused when they spotted us, and the barmaid gave James a wary glance before smoothing down her apron and taking refuge behind the bar. I had noticed before that people of a certain criminal class immediately deduced James was a detective, even though he wore no uniform.

"'Ow can I 'elp ya?" she asked.

"I'm Detective Inspector Blakely of Scotland Yard. Is there anyone working in this establishment who would have been here twenty years ago?"

"Dunno." She looked directly at me and her eyes gave a flicker of recognition.

"Who's the landlord here?" asked James.

"Mr Dickinson."

"And how long has he been the landlord?"

"Dunno. 'Bout ten years, I'd say."

"He wasn't the landlord twenty years ago?"

"Nah."

"Do you know who might have been?"

"Nope." She strode to the other end of the bar. "Alf!" she shouted. "Alf! Someone get Alf!"

Alf eventually trudged up to the bar from a dark corner of the public house. I recognised him as the old, sallow-faced man who had been sleeping at the bar during my last visit. He gave us a puzzled glance.

"We got a detective 'ere, Alf," said the barmaid. "Says 'e wants ter know who the landlord was twenny year ago."

Alf swayed slightly as he squinted up at the beamed ceiling. I wondered for a moment whether he had heard the question or understood it, but eventually a single word escaped his lips.

"Burns," he croaked.

"Did he say *Burns?*" I asked the barmaid.

"Sounded like it."

"Do you know a Mr Burns?" I asked her.

"Yeah, but I dint think it were twenny year ago. You sure it's as long ago as that, Alf?"

"Eh?"

"Are yer sure it's twenny year ago since Burns was landlord?"

"Yeah."

She shrugged, then gave us a look that suggested we had our answer.

"Is Burns a tall man with an injured eye?" I asked.

"Yeah."

"He's the one I met at the Crescent," I said, turning to James.

"The chap at the disused train station," he responded. "I can't say I want to go to the trouble of arranging another meeting with him there." He addressed the barmaid again. "There must be records kept somewhere in this place."

"Records o' what?" She filled a tankard with beer and handed it to Alf.

"Everything, hopefully. Records of orders; people who have worked and lived in this establishment; income and outgoings. All manner of things."

"Mr an' Mrs Dickinson looks after all that stuff."

"I imagine they would. Are they here?"

"They don't like ter be bothered in the mornin's. They works late hours, yer see."

James pulled out his warrant card and showed it to her. "Can you fetch them for me, please? I'm afraid police officers are in the business of bothering people."

A short while later we found ourselves sitting with a bleary-eyed Mr Dickinson over on the far side of the alehouse. He wore an undershirt atop a pair of scruffy trousers, which had presumably been pulled on hastily when the barmaid summoned him. His wife, a large, saggy-faced lady, had dropped a number of dusty ledgers onto the table with a resounding thud. Her careless manner appeared to be a protest against being dragged from her bed at eleven o'clock in the morning.

"There's more," she snapped, before disappearing into a room at the back.

"I'm specifically looking for records that would include the tenth of June 1865," said James.

The sleepy landlord rubbed a thick hand across his face.

"They'll all be there somewhere," he responded glumly.

"That's reassuring." James took hold of some books from the pile shortly before Mrs Dickinson slammed another load on top of it.

"That's all of 'em," she said. "What is it yer lookin' for?"

"Records relating to the tenth of June 1865," repeated James.

He passed me a few books to examine. I flicked through them, realising it would take some time to decipher the faded scrawl organised into neat columns. I saw names and numbers, but didn't immediately understand what they meant.

"You're looking at 1873, Penny," said James in a manner

that left me feeling as slow-witted as Mr Dickinson looked. "Try looking at—"

"Yes, I know. June 1865. The tenth. I'll search for it as soon as I've worked out what I'm looking at here."

"Could we please have a little more light?" James asked Mrs Dickinson.

She gave an irritable huff and vanished again, reappearing with a smoky oil lamp, which she set down next to the books.

"Anythink else?" she asked. "Beer? Seein' as yer seem set on makin' yourselves comfy."

"That would be lovely, thank you," replied James. "A porter for me. Sherry for you, Penny?"

"And I'll share a beer with the hinspector too, m'dear!" chipped in the landlord.

Within a short while the drink had restored Mr Dickinson to what I imagined to be his usual self. His eyes brightened and he began to be more helpful.

"Those'll be the orders from the brewery," he said, pointing at one of the books. "Go back to the fifties, they do. Even longer'n that."

"What about the brewers' druggists?" asked James.

"Can't say we use 'em much no more."

"But they were still being used in 1865, isn't that right?"

"Oh, yeah. They was back then. There's gotta be a gen'ral ledger fer that. This one looks like a gen'ral ledger." He flicked through a particularly dusty-looking book. "Yeah, that's the one. I'll look up '65 now. What month did yer say?"

"June," replied James in an exasperated tone.

"Fraud, is it?" asked Mr Dickinson. "Someone done a bit o' fraud, 'ave they? Wouldn't put it past 'em, yer know. It's easy enough ter put the takings down as lower'n they 'as been and put a bit in yer pocket. Not a lot, mind, but a little bit

'ere an' there and no one notices. Soon adds up to a tidy sum."
He checked himself with a quick cough. "Not that I'd do any
o' that meself, Hinspector. Don't want yer gettin' the wrong
idea about me."

"I'm sure you wouldn't, Mr Dickinson. What do you
know about Mr Burns as a landlord here?"

"Jus' that."

"Just what?"

"That 'e were the landlord."

"Did you know him at all?"

"Not personal, like. 'E's a different sort o' chap to meself."

James turned to the publican's wife. "What about you Mrs
Dickinson?"

She shrugged. "Never knew 'im."

"Mr Burns was the landlord here when Mary Steinway was
poisoned," said James. "She was also known as Jane Stroud,
isn't that right?"

"Oh, so now I know why yer 'ere!" The revelation made
him sit back in his chair with a broad grin on his face.
"That's what this is all about, ain't it? That girl what was
poisoned." He held up his hands in mock innocence.
"Weren't nuffink ter do wi' me, honest. Weren't even livin'
'ere at the time. I was up Stoke Newin'ton. Missis'll tell yer
the same thing. Stoke Newin'ton was where we was livin'
then."

"Thank you, Mr Dickinson. I believe you."

"Yer do?" He lowered his hands. "Well, that's sayin'
summat. Plenty o' coppers 'ave struggled ter believe me when
I've protested my hinnocence. I blame this old face." He
pointed at his bloated features. "Ain't the face of a hinnocent,
is it? Even as a littl'un I got in trouble fer it."

"I'm sorry to hear that," replied James. "Is there a record
of the people who were working here in June 1865?"

"I'll find it for yer now, hofficer." Mr Dickinson had

become even more helpful now that James seemed to be taking him at his word.

After a little more rummaging through the books, we finally found a list of employees from June 1865. Their names were written down next to the weekly wages they had received. There were about a dozen names, and I copied them down into my notebook.

"This looks important," said the barmaid, who had sauntered over and stood watching us, hands on hips.

"They're investigatin' that girl what was poisoned," replied Mr Dickinson. "Jane Stroud, weren't it?"

"Yeah. You came in 'ere before askin' about that Molly Gardstein. Ain't that right?" This was directed at me.

"Yes, that's right."

"You wanted ter know where she was." The barmaid gave a hearty cackle.

"Yes, and I found her in the end."

The cackle turned into a gasp of surprise. The barmaid stared down at me, unblinking. "You what?"

"I found her." My tone was nonchalant, as though it had been the easiest thing in the world to do.

"Where'd she go?"

"Kent."

"The p'lice went down Kent lookin' for 'er."

"They didn't look hard enough."

"Well, 'ave they... 'as 'e," she pointed at James, "arrested 'er?"

"No, because she sadly died three years ago."

"Oh." This deflated her a little and she folded her arms. "She got away wiv it, then."

"If she did it, that is."

"Ev'ryone knows she done it!"

"We need evidence," said James. "That's why we're here. Do you have anything useful you might be able to tell us?"

The barmaid began wiping her hands on her apron. "Nope. Ain't nuffink I can tell yer abaht it." She glanced over at the bar. "Looks like Alf's needin' a refill." She headed off to serve him.

James and I took more notes from the books and eventually decided we had all the information we could glean about the White Swan from the summer of 1865.

"I think it highly commendable that you've kept all these records, Mr Dickinson," said James.

"Didn't require no effort, truth be told. Them books jus' been sittin' in a room out back. I ain't never really looked through 'em afore now."

"Well, I'm pleased they were kept, nonetheless. Our visit here today has been most useful."

"Pleased to 'ear it, Hinspector." Mr Dickinson drained his tankard. "'Ow about anuvver drink?"

CHAPTER 47

W e declined Mr Dickinson's invitation to stay any longer at the White Swan and went on our way.

As we walked along St George Street, I noticed a few people regarding James suspiciously, despite his plain clothes, but I still felt a lot safer than I had during my previous visits.

"There was quite a lot of information," I mused, "but nothing that obviously connects Sir Octavius with the alehouse the night Mary Steinway died."

"Nothing obvious at all, unfortunately. We've a lot of notes to look through, however. Something may come to light after all."

"But we need something *now*, so you can arrest him!"

"I'm hoping we'll be able to arrest him for the murder of Mr Masefield soon. That'll be a good start."

"Do you think it's a coincidence that Burns was once landlord of the White Swan? He kept company with Molly Gardstein, didn't he? Perhaps he murdered Mary Steinway and then paid Molly to run away."

"Didn't you say that he seemed fond of her?"

"He did."

"I don't see why he would pay for her to run away to Kent, in that case. Besides, Mr Nicol said the alehouse was thoroughly investigated at the time of Mary's death. I think Burns would have been considered a suspect for a while at least."

"Do you think that the original investigation into Burns would have been thorough enough?"

"It's difficult to say, isn't it? I'd have to look at the files to get an idea of that. With an established link between Robert Masefield and Mary Steinway, I have a little more authority to ask for H Division's assistance and to look through the original files now. I'll need to interview Burns, as well as anyone else who was working at the White Swan back then. Let's hope it won't be too difficult to find them. I'm pleased with the amount of information we were able to find at the alehouse. Now we can determine the staff members who were likely to have been present when Mary Steinway was poisoned."

"But it frustrates me that there was no obvious link to Sir Octavius, or to Revd Loach, for that matter," I replied. "Perhaps Mr Burns will be able to tell you whether there was an aristocrat or a reverend at the alehouse the night Mary was murdered."

"If either of them was there, I'm sure he would have been incognito so as to avoid being recognised. I'll need to obtain photographs of both men to show Burns, although expecting him to recognise their faces twenty years on may be asking too much."

"And you may not get the truth from him," I said. "If Mr Burns poisoned Mary Steinway himself, he's likely to say that either Sir Octavius or Revd Loach was in the alehouse that evening to divert any suspicion away from himself."

"I'll be careful how I phrase my questions. I'm not sure Burns is a particularly strong suspect, though."

"He told me he didn't like Jane, as he knew her. He said she didn't treat Molly well and that he called her Lady Muck."

"Not a particularly strong motive to murder her, but we can't rule him out yet. I might be able to trip him up with his own falsehoods if he's careless."

"I can't imagine him being careless. I should think he's spent a lifetime trying to run rings around the police. But if he did poison Mary, I don't know how he would have put the strychnine into her beer without her knowledge. We both heard from Mr Nicol about the practicalities of doing so. It takes a long time to dissolve and tastes horrible."

"Yes, that's what puzzles me about the poisoning. How was it achieved without rousing Mary's suspicions?"

"Mr Burns, Revd Loach and Sir Octavius," I said. "It could have been any one of them. And there's Sally Walcot to consider, too. I'm reluctant to believe that Molly Gardstein was responsible, and Mrs Garner seemed convinced of her innocence. But perhaps I'm wrong. Perhaps Molly did it after all."

"I feel as though we're getting closer to the truth, Penny. I'm sure it won't be long before we find some compelling evidence. We certainly have enough to bring Sir Octavius and Mr Burns in now."

"And as for Revd Loach, I think Mrs Loach has been defending her husband rather too vehemently," I added. "I intend to make further enquiries about them. I still think it suspicious that he refused to attend Mary Steinway's inquest."

CHAPTER 48

James headed back to Scotland Yard and I took the train home. As I travelled, I looked back through my notes on Revd Loach and reminded myself that he had been a curate at All Saint's Church in St John's Wood at the time of his marriage to Mary Steinway. I decided to visit the church in the hope of finding someone who could tell me more about him.

All Saint's Church stood on the busy Finchley Road, its tall spire rising far above the surrounding trees and rooftops. I knew that I risked incurring the wrath of Mrs Loach once again by making further enquires, but I needed to understand what sort of man Revd Loach was. *Had he been cruel, as Mrs Rendell, his former employee, had told me? Was it possible that he had murdered his estranged wife in order to remarry?*

Given the passage of time that had passed since Mary Steinway's death, I knew I would struggle to find anyone who could tell me more about the first Loach marriage, but there was still a chance.

As luck would have it, the vicar of All Saint's was present when I called. Revd Harris was a softly spoken man with gold-rimmed spectacles and greying whiskers. I introduced myself as a journalist who was reporting on the death of Revd Loach's estranged wife.

He adjusted his spectacles and pursed his lips. "A terribly sad business," he said.

"Did you know him at the time?" I asked.

"Oh no, it was just something I heard about. I was in Willesden Green in those days, but I understand he went through a rather difficult time with it all. It was most unfortunate and undeserved for such a decent man. I can't tell you any more than that, really. Our church warden is here today, and he's been attending this church for a good many years now. You can speak to him if you like."

"Thank you. If he's happy to talk to me, I would very much appreciate it."

The vicar nodded, then headed off into a chapel on the far side of the aisle.

A short while later, a rotund, balding man strolled toward me. "Mrs Blakely?" he said. "I hear you're asking about Revd Loach. You do know that he can be found at St Saviour's church in Chalk Farm, don't you?"

"Yes. I've already visited him there."

"I see. Then I'm not sure how I can help you."

I watched his face stiffen as I told him about my investigation into Mary Steinway's death. By the time I had finished my explanation, the expression on his face suggested he had no interest in helping me at all.

"You knew Revd Loach when he was married to his first wife, did you not?" I asked.

"I did, and a respectable couple they were, too. We had to keep her lunacy a secret. It was terribly trying for him."

"Did anything about their marriage strike you as unusual?"

"Nothing at all, apart from the fact that she spent some time in the lunatic asylum, of course."

"Nothing untoward happened that you recall?"

"Nothing until her lunacy took hold, and then matters swiftly took a turn for the worse. It was a tortuous time. I think someone ended up in court over a bit of stolen jewellery at one point, come to think of it."

"I recall Revd Loach mentioning that to me."

"There's really nothing more I can tell you, Mrs Blakely. I do know that Revd Loach would never have harmed a hair on his wife's head, however."

I felt sure I heard footsteps behind me as I turned into Henstridge Place, but when I turned to look I saw no one there. This was becoming a frequent experience, yet I couldn't be sure whether I was imagining it or not.

It was late by the time James returned that evening.

"We found Burns," he announced as he stepped into the front room. "He's helping H Division with their enquiries."

Tiger rubbed her head against his legs, and he stooped to stroke her.

"That's wonderful!"

"He's well known to them, of course. A little too well known, if you ask me."

"He's on friendly terms with them, you mean?"

"Quite friendly, as I understand it."

"Do you think he could be an informant?"

"I got that impression, yes."

"Which means he could be protected from punishment if he has committed a crime."

"I couldn't possibly confirm whether that actually happens or not."

"But you know that it does, James. And I know it, too." I sighed. "Perhaps the officers from H Division have a good idea who murdered Mary Steinway but decided not to charge him because he's too helpful to them."

"That's pure speculation, Penny. We can't know that for sure."

"But it might explain why the murderer was never caught."

"It might."

"Perhaps H Division persuaded Molly Gardstein to run off to Kent so that she appeared guilty."

"It's not beyond the realms of possibility."

"Do you think that's what happened?"

He shook his head. "I don't know what to think at the moment, but I hope matters will become clear sooner rather than later. There aren't many men left at H Division who happened to be working there twenty years ago. Times have changed a little since then."

"But if Burns is an informant, they won't charge him, will they?"

"I can't be certain if he's an informant; I merely suspect it."

"Then he must be."

"I'm not always right, Penny, much as I'd like to be. But there is good news. We now have enough evidence to arrest Sir Octavius for the murder of Robert Masefield. His wife has decided to amend the statement she made that provided him with an alibi for the evening of Masefield's death. It seems her conscience finally got the better of her."

"Was he away from home all evening?"

"He returned shortly before midnight, or at least, that's what she's saying now. She had previously stated that he arrived home at eight o'clock."

"Those four hours can make a big difference. More good

news! Sir Octavius counts the commissioner of Scotland Yard among his friends, though. Won't that influence proceedings?"

"No. I feel quite sure that the commissioner will be happy to see the man charged. He wouldn't allow a personal friendship to get in the way of justice."

"If Sir Octavius murdered Masefield, and it seems very likely that he did, does that mean he also murdered Mary Steinway?"

"We need to keep looking for evidence."

"It's difficult to remain patient, isn't it?" I said. "My investigations into Revd Loach this afternoon yielded nothing. I feel as though people are protecting him, but I can't understand why."

"They believe him to be a respectable man."

"Well, I think they're wrong. There must be something more I can uncover. Maybe I could find the doctor who admitted Mary Steinway to the asylum. Perhaps he could tell me something useful."

"Do you know which asylum she was admitted to?"

"No. I should have asked that. Which is the closest?"

"There's Colney Hatch and Hanwell. It could have been either of those. They admit a lot of patients, though. I believe Colney Hatch is the largest asylum in Europe."

"It'll be rather difficult to find someone who was a patient there for a few months twenty years ago, then."

"Yes, I should think it would be."

CHAPTER 49

Before I made enquiries at the lunatic asylums the following day, I realised there was something I could do closer to home. Recalling what the church warden at All Saint's had told me about the stolen jewellery during the first Loach marriage, I decided to visit St John's Wood police station.

It was a handsome gold-brick building on the corner of New Street and Lower William Street. I briefly explained who I was at the desk and was told shortly afterward that Sergeant Hilcock had agreed to see me. When he emerged from one of the offices, I saw that the sergeant had a long face, hooded brown eyes and a languorous manner about him.

"I'd like to enquire about a theft," I said. "It relates to some items of jewellery stolen from a lady named Mrs Mary Loach about twenty-two years ago."

His brow furrowed.

"I'd like to hear the details of the case," I added.

"May I ask why?"

The rather lengthy explanation I gave of my investigation

did little to persuade Sergeant Hilcock. In fact, he appeared even more puzzled by the time I had finished.

"It's not an incident I recall hearing about," he replied. "I hadn't even joined the police force twenty years ago. I'm sorry that I can't be of any help."

"My husband is Detective Inspector James Blakely of Scotland Yard," I said impetuously. I knew I wasn't supposed to use my husband's name to influence people, but my patience was wearing thin. I wanted my questions answered properly.

"I know Inspector Blakely." His brow lifted a little, which I hoped was a sign that he was about to become more helpful. "You live close by, isn't that right?"

"Yes. Just a short walk from here."

I watched as an apparent conflict of emotions played out on his face. He clearly had no wish to spend any time responding to my request, but the mention of James's name had made him feel obliged.

"It's not a matter we would usually discuss," he said. "Especially with a *journalist*."

Perhaps he had hoped this would discourage me, but I remained where I was and said nothing in response.

Sergeant Hilcock made an impatient smacking noise with his lips, as if to fill the silence. "It would take me some time to find the records," he added, "and I'm supposed to be on duty. Perhaps I could call on you and your husband with the information in a day or two?"

I thanked him and gave him my calling card.

I left the police station and walked up New Street. As I did so, a man stepped across my path and I gripped my carpet bag, worried that whoever it was might try to snatch it. He was tall and wore a frock coat with a wide-brimmed hat. I recognised his sharp features almost instantly.

"Revd Loach!" I spoke cautiously, as his face appeared stern. "What a surprise to see you here."

He took a step toward me. "It seems my wife's visit has done nothing to dissuade you."

"From what?"

"From interviewing my acquaintances and slandering my name."

"I haven't been slandering you, Reverend."

"But you're determined to rake over my past and discuss it with whomsoever you please. You're trying your hardest to make me appear guilty!"

"I'm simply trying to ascertain whether you are guilty or not."

"You have no right to do so!"

"Even if you *are* guilty? Surely a clergyman would agree that a man should be punished if he has committed murder?"

"Yes, I do agree." He took a step closer. "But I am *not* that man!" His eyes were wide and he bared his teeth.

"I heard you were cruel to Mary Steinway," I ventured.

"Who told you that nonsense?"

"Someone who would know about such things."

He gave a snort. "Well, they must be mistaken! I merely insist that you stop all this prying now. You never knew Mary. You know nothing about her."

"I've learned quite a lot about her—"

"You know nothing!" He jabbed a pointed finger at me. "I was her husband, and I knew what she was like. You have no idea what you're doing and no hope of finding the person who murdered her. Whatever reasons they had for doing so are long forgotten now.

"When she left me, I told myself I would never have anything to do with her again. That's why I refused to attend the inquest. Our marriage was difficult because her mind was broken. There was nothing I, or anyone else, could do about it. Her life ended that way because it was the only way. She never would have made a suitable mother; she never would have made it to old age. She was destined to die young because her mind wasn't normal. She was a lunatic. You have to accept that, Mrs Blakely. Accept it and then forget about it."

"Did you murder her?"

Without warning, he seized me by the throat and pushed me up against the stone wall.

"Let go!" I cried out. My eyes searched wildly for someone close by who could help, but the street was quiet. I dropped my bag and clawed at his hand, trying to pull it away, but he was too strong.

"Only if you assure me this will be the very last of it," he hissed, his face close to mine. "I want to hear you say that you will stop all this nonsense now!"

"I'll stop when I've found out who murdered Mary."

His grip tightened until I found myself struggling to breathe.

"Tell me you'll stop!" he snarled.

I couldn't say another word. I tried to slow my breathing to relieve the pressure in my neck. My ears rang, and Revd Loach's face began to swim before my eyes.

This was Mary's murderer. And now he was about to kill me, too.

I felt my knees buckle.

"What do you think you're doing?" cried a lady's voice. "Let go of her at once!"

The vicar did as he was told and I slumped onto the ground, gasping for breath.

Coughing and choking, I managed to draw air into my lungs once again. I stared down at the pavement, wary of meeting his gaze and provoking him further. He gave my bag a kick.

"I've made many mistakes in my life," he muttered, "and I'm far from perfect. But I'm no murderer."

And with those words he walked away.

"You should tell the police!" said the stout lady in a green dress as she helped me to my feet.

"Not right now," I replied. "He was just angry. It's all right, I know him."

"It's *not* all right!"

"I'd just like to go home and get some rest. I'll tell the police about it later. My husband is a police officer, in fact."

"So he is!"

I finally recognised the lady. It was Mrs Cartwright from St Peter's church.

"Mrs Blakely, isn't it? Come on, I'll help you home. Your husband will have something to say about this, I'm sure."

CHAPTER 50

"I'll have someone visit the vicarage immediately!" fumed James as he paced the front room. "The gall of the man!"

Lying on the settee with Tiger, I said nothing.

"There can be no excuse for his trying to strangle you, Penny," continued James. "No excuse at all! It makes me realise how Mary Steinway must have suffered at his hands. And perhaps the same applies to the current Mrs Loach, too. She most likely lives in constant fear of him. The man's a bully. I don't care whether he's a vicar or not, he shall answer for this!"

"It must have been Revd Loach following me all this time."

"Someone's been following you?"

"It felt that way, though I couldn't be entirely sure."

"Why didn't you mention it to me?"

"Because I thought I might be imagining it."

James shook his head. "Well you clearly weren't, and that man could have seriously injured you. I'll go down to New

Street now and ask them to bring him in. The good news I was bringing was that we've arrested Sir Octavius."

"That's excellent news!" I winced as the pain in my throat swelled following the exertion.

"Well, you'd like to think so. I'm quite certain he's behind Masefield's murder, and I thought he was responsible for Mary Steinway's, too, but I'm not so sure now, given Revd Loach's recent behaviour."

I still felt tired when I awoke the following morning.

"I've asked Mrs Oliver to look after you today, Penny," said James as he buttoned his collar onto his shirt.

"I don't need looking after."

"You need to rest."

"I feel quite all right."

"That may be so." He retrieved a blue tie from the wardrobe. "But there's no need for you to go travelling about today, is there? If you don't want to rest, at least work here at home."

I gave a gentle nod. "I've a lot of notes to look through, although I suppose there'll be nothing more for me to do if Sir Octavius decides to confess to Mary's murder now that he's been arrested."

"It would save us having to do much more work on this, wouldn't it? I can't imagine him confessing, but perhaps we'll be surprised. Sometimes people confess when they know their time's up and they don't have any fight left in them. It'll depend on how much strength he has left, and how good his lawyer is."

. . .

I worked in my writing room after breakfast, and Mrs Oliver checked on me regularly. She was clearly the sort of person who enjoyed looking after others.

"Are you sure I can't persuade you to take a little of Dr Cobbold's remedy?" she asked halfway through the morning.

I smiled as I recalled how my former landlady, Mrs Garnett, had frequently tried to foist the same medicine on me. "I shall be quite all right, thank you, Mrs Oliver." I eventually managed to persuade her that I was in no need of any assistance.

I spent the morning reading through the notes I had made over the previous four weeks. There were scribbles relating to the inquest, followed by notes from my conversations with Mary's former landlady, Mrs Walcot, and her daughter Sally; retired detective Mr Nicol; the Loaches' former servants, Mr and Mrs Rendell, Molly Gardstein's close acquaintance Mr Burns; the recently murdered former friend of Mary and Sir Octavius, Mr Masefield; Mary's former husband, Revd Loach, and his new wife Margaret; the arrested MP, Sir Octavius; private detective Mrs Worthers; and Kent-based farm owners Mrs Wiley and Mrs Garner. I looked over my notes from the various places I had visited, considering how lucky I had been to escape a mauling from Mrs Garner's dogs and a strangling attempt by Revd Loach.

Perhaps I had also been lucky that Robert Masefield had decided to carry out his blackmail campaign while I was looking into Mary's murder. He had been keen to support my investigation. I was terribly sad that he had lost his life as a result, the only consolation was that Sir Octavius had been arrested. His secrets were gradually being revealed to the world and I smiled as I imagined a cell door closing behind him. There was little doubt that he was behind Masefield's death, even if he didn't commit the murder with his own hands. *But was he also responsible for Mary's death?*

It was frustrating that we had found no evidence to connect Sir Octavius with the White Swan on the evening of Mary's poisoning. Mr Burns, on the other hand, had been landlord at the time. A bitter taste developed in my mouth as I considered him being permitted to escape unpunished for any crime he had committed just because he was a useful source of information to the police.

Mrs Oliver knocked at my door once again and I sighed in response to the interruption.

"There's a police officer here to see you, madam," she announced. "He's waiting in the hallway."

I walked downstairs to find the long-faced Sergeant Hill-cock standing beside the hallway table. He pulled a notebook from his pocket as I descended the stairs.

"Good morning, Mrs Blakely. Are you recovered from that unpleasant incident yesterday?"

"Quite recovered, thank you."

"When you're ready, I'll take down the details of the attack. But before I take your statement, I have further information relating to the theft you enquired about yesterday." He consulted his notebook. "The crime was reported to us on the eleventh of March 1864."

"And what happened, exactly?"

"Mrs Loach reported that several items of jewellery had been stolen, and that she suspected one of the servants."

"Was the jewellery ever found?"

"Yes. It had been taken by a Miss Hicks. She confessed to the crime and was imprisoned for six weeks."

"May I ask whether Revd Loach was involved in the case at all?"

"I couldn't find any mention of him, other than that he was Mrs Loach's husband at the time."

"Thank you, Sergeant."

He readied his pencil. "Now, perhaps you can tell me about the assault yesterday."

After I had given Sergeant Hillcock a full account of the assault, I returned to my writing room. I looked at the lists I'd hastily made in the flickering light of the oil lamp at the alehouse, then read through the names of all the people who had been working there at the time of Mary Steinway's death. One name jumped out at me.

Katie Hicks.

The servant who had stolen the jewellery from Mary Steinway was a Miss Hicks.

It was then that I remembered hearing the name a while back. Mr Rendell had mentioned that Katie Hicks had once been the name of the woman who was now his wife.

Mrs Rendell.

I stared at the name and tried to comprehend it. Perhaps I was mistaken. Perhaps this was a different Katie Hicks.

I recalled that Mrs Rendell had been due to start her shift as a barmaid at the Anchor the day I had visited her and her husband. *Was it possible that Mrs Rendell had worked as a barmaid all those years ago? Had she taken a job at the White Swan?*

Sergeant Hillcock said she had served six weeks in prison for the theft. With servants relying on good character references for employment, it would have been difficult for her to find work after that.

I thought back to her visit to our home, when she had taken the time to explain how unpleasant Revd Loach had been to Mary. *Was it possible that she had made him out to be as villainous as possible so that suspicion would fall on him?*

It occurred to me that I needed to tell James urgently. I found my hat and bag, then prepared myself to leave the house.

"Mr Blakely wouldn't be happy if he saw you going out, Mrs Blakely," commented Mrs Oliver. "His instructions were for you to stay here and rest."

"I don't need to rest, Mrs Oliver; I need to send him an urgent telegram."

"Why don't I go down to the post office and send it so you can stay indoors?"

"Oh, there's no need. It's only a short walk away, and I—"

"But I insist! Before he left for work this morning your husband asked me to keep a close eye on you, and I promised him I would. I won't break my promise to Mr Blakely!"

She looked so fierce that I decided there was little I could do other than to agree.

"All right," I replied. "But it must be sent immediately."

"I'll see that it is."

I retrieved my notebook from my bag, ripped out a page and scribbled down the note:

Mrs Rendell worked at the White Swan in June '65.

I passed the piece of paper to my housekeeper, who looked down at it with a frown. "Will Mr Blakely know what this means?"

"Yes."

"And it needs to be sent to Scotland Yard, I take it. Should I request a response?"

"No, Mr Blakely will be busy enough today as it is. I'll leave him to decide what he does with it."

"Very well. I shall do it right away, Mrs Blakely. You head back up to your room and rest yourself there."

I sighed again. "If you say so, Mrs Oliver."

"Up you go, please." She pointed at the staircase. "I'll just fetch my hat and shawl, and then I'll be on my way."

I went back up to my room and sat down at my writing desk. I heard the front door close and watched Mrs Oliver walk down the garden path, unlatch the gate, close it behind her and turn left toward the post office. I hoped she wouldn't stop to talk to anyone along the way and forget her errand. I knew I could trust her, but I worried the telegram might somehow fail to reach its destination. I wondered what James would do when he received it.

Mrs Oliver had almost disappeared from view, and I was about to return to my work, when another movement on the street caught my eye. A lady was crossing the road and her gaze appeared to be fixed on Mrs Oliver. As I watched, she slowed her walk and paused outside the house. She was small in stature and wore a hat over her wavy grey hair.

It was Mrs Rendell.

CHAPTER 51

M rs Rendell jumped when I pushed up the sash window, but smiled and gave a tentative wave when she recognised me.

"How can I help you, Mrs Rendell?" I asked.

"Oh." She smiled again as she desperately searched her mind for a reason to have been found standing outside our house. It was clear that I had caught her unawares. "I've thought of something else I need to tell you," she finally said.

"I'll be down in just a moment." I closed the window, my heart thudding in my chest as I descended the stairs. *What was she doing here?*

I thought of the telegram Mrs Oliver was about to send James and wondered whether he would attempt to visit Mrs Rendell at her home right away. I thought of him calling there, only to discover that she was out. If only I could tell him she was here with me now.

"Good morning, Mrs Blakely." Mrs Rendell's smile was unusually broad when I opened the door.

"You said you'd remembered something else," I said as I led the way into our front room.

I gestured for her to sit, but she remained standing. Her eyes darted around, as if she were looking for something.

"Is everything all right, Mrs Rendell?" I asked. I sensed that it hadn't been her intention to call on me at all. She hadn't wanted to be seen. *Was it Mrs Rendell who had been following me, and not Revd Loach after all? Had she feared discovery?*

"Did you mistake my housekeeper for me just now?" I asked bluntly. Mrs Oliver and I were of a similar height and build, which might have explained why Mrs Rendell had been watching her.

Something flickered across her face and her smile was briefly lost for a moment. Then she recovered herself. "Your housekeeper? No. Was she outside? I didn't see anyone out there."

This was all the confirmation I needed that she was lying.

"She left the house shortly before I saw you standing outside," I said. "It's odd, because I could have sworn that you were looking directly at her."

"I wasn't," she replied with forced cheer and a shake of her head. "I didn't see nobody out there."

The palms of my hands began to feel clammy. This conversation felt strange and unnerving. I hoped I might detain Mrs Rendell long enough for Mrs Oliver to return. Then perhaps I could ask the housekeeper to send a second telegram asking James to return home.

"Let me make us a cup of tea, at least," I said.

"Oh, there's no need for that. I shan't be long."

I felt a prickle at the back of my neck as she glanced around the room again.

This matter you wished to tell me about," I ventured. "What was it?"

"Revd Loach," she said. "He should never have been a

vicar. I didn't like to tell you this the last time I visited, but I once overheard him say that he wanted to kill his wife."

"Really?" I wasn't sure whether to believe this, but I feigned curiosity nonetheless. "To whom did he say that?"

"My husband. It was after she'd taken the baby outside in the rain one day. Revd Loach was angry at the time, so I didn't think he really meant it. But the more I've thought about it, the more I feel he might of meant it after all."

"And you've suddenly come to this conclusion twenty years later?"

She frowned in response to this comment. "It's all the work you've been doing, Mrs Blakely. That's what's made me think about it."

"But you didn't tell the police this when Mary was poisoned?"

"No. I didn't think he could've had anything to do with it! She died in the East End, didn't she? That's miles away from where he lived."

"Were you aware that Revd Loach had been visiting the East End at the time of Mary's death?"

"No, I had no idea. Was he?"

"He was volunteering at the Salvation Army shelter in Whitechapel."

"Was he now?" Her eyes widened. "That's not far from Ratcliffe, then!"

"You didn't know he had volunteered there?"

"No. I weren't working for him at the time of Mary's death."

"You had left by that time?"

"That's right."

"Do you mind if I ask why?"

"I imagine you already know the answer to that by now, Mrs Blakely. You're pretty clever at finding these things out."

"Why didn't you mention to me that you were the one who had stolen the jewellery from Mary Steinway?"

"I never stole it!" Her features twisted into an ugly scowl. "Them jewels were *mine*!"

"Yours?"

"Mrs Steinway – Mary's mother, Amelia – had promised them to me! Only she never wrote it in her will and Mary took it all."

"So you stole it back."

"I'd asked for it enough times."

"Why didn't you tell me this before?"

"I was ashamed. Why else d'you think? I served six weeks in prison for it!"

"And presumably you were unable to find work as a maid again after that?"

"That's right. No one would employ me."

"But you eventually found work as a barmaid."

She acknowledged this with a slight nod.

"Did you see Mary Steinway again after you were released from prison?"

"No, never."

"Did you know where she was?"

"I had no idea at all. Then I heard she'd left Revd Loach, and that was all I knew about it."

"How did you come to be working at the White Swan in Ratcliffe?"

All of a sudden her friendly, round face became like stone, her green eyes cold and unblinking. The sudden change in her manner unnerved me, as did her silence. I desperately listened for the sound of Mrs Oliver's key in the front door. James surely would have received the telegram by now, but no doubt he would go straight to the Rendells' home. He wouldn't think to come here.

My mouth felt dry as I stared back at the lady in front of

me. She was smaller than me and older. *Why did I feel so frightened of her?*

"Were you working at the White Swan on the tenth of June 1865?" I asked. My voice sounded tremulous. "Were you there the night that Mary Steinway was poisoned?"

Her eyes still didn't blink. Then eventually she spoke. "Amelia Steinway, the only lady who was ever good to me, died because Mary made her ill. Before she died, she told me I could have her locket and two gold rings. She promised them to me. She was too ill to write it down, but I remember as clear as day how she raised her hand and pointed to her dressing table. 'They're for you, Katie.' Them were her words. I'd been looking after Mary since she was a girl, and how did she repay me? With six weeks in a prison!"

I tried not to recoil as she spat these last words at me.

"I couldn't find work after that!" she continued. "That's why I married my husband. Can't say I cared much for him, but he was the only man I knew pretty well back then."

"How did you put the poison in Mary's drink without her noticing?" I asked.

She paused, as if deliberating over her reply. Then her face softened to a more serene expression, as if there was some relief to be found in unburdening a long-hidden secret.

"I made sure she'd already drank plenty before I done it," she said quietly. "There was a barrel I'd been tending to for a while to make sure it was all mixed in. Not easy to achieve that, you know. Spent quite a bit of time practising, I did. And when the time came, I drew her a drink from the poisoned barrel."

"But someone else might have used it!"

"They might have, but it were right at the back of the cellar. Even if they had, and someone else'd accidentally been poisoned, no one would ever have known it was me, would they?"

"But surely the police must have found the poisoned beer in the barrel? From what I heard, they searched the alehouse extensively."

"Do you think I'm stupid? I knew they'd check the barrels as soon as Mary died. Once the job was done—"

"Mary's poisoning, you mean?"

"That's right. Once it was done, the barrel I'd been tending to met with a purposeful accident. There was a leak, and I spent my time mopping up the cellar while Mary was being looked after. Then I heard she'd died."

"And Molly Gardstein?"

"Molly didn't poison her. I told Molly to leave."

"So people would think she had poisoned her friend?"

She gave a nod. "That's right. But it was her chance, you see. She'd been wanting to get away from Burns for a long time. With him distracted by what had happened at his alehouse, she had the opportunity to get out. She left right away. She didn't want no one finding out about the baby."

"Baby?"

"She was in the family way, but nobody else knew. She told me, 'cause I can be nice when I choose to be." She forced a smile, as if to demonstrate this.

"And you had threatened to tell people."

"I had to make her leave one way or another."

"Everyone thought she had poisoned Mary."

"Molly wanted out. Burns was a bully and she wanted to get away from him. I told her I could help her out, and I gave her some money."

"Where did you get the money from?"

"Lots of places. The alehouse, my husband... I even pawned a few things. I found enough to get her out of sight. And I told her never to come back or everyone would know about the baby."

"Did she have the baby?" I asked. "Did it thrive?"

She shrugged. "How should I know? I never saw her again. No one did. They all reckoned she was the murderer."

I thought about the lad named Harry who had been working at Mrs Garner's farm. *Was it possible that he was Molly's son?*

"Your husband," I said, "does he know about this?"

"No. He really has no idea..." She shook her head and laughed. "Nor's anyone... except you, Mrs Blakely."

James knows, too, I thought to myself. All I could do for the time being was keep Mrs Rendell talking.

She looked around the room again, then sighed. "So now you know everything. Mind, you knew most of it already, didn't you?"

"Won't you sit down and have a cup of tea, Mrs Rendell?" I asked her, hardly able to believe that I could ask such a polite question of a woman who had just confessed to committing a murder. I knew I had to detain her for as long as possible to ensure that she was arrested. *Perhaps I could have a quiet word with Mrs Oliver when she returned and ask her to run down to the police station.*

My behaviour was so ordinary, in fact, that Mrs Rendell felt the need to comment on it.

"You seem pretty calm, Mrs Blakely. You don't seem shocked at all."

"Oh, I'm shocked all right, Mrs Rendell. I'm shocked that anyone could so readily kill another person. But I've met people like you before; people who are consumed by the ugly notion that they're entitled to exact revenge by taking the life of another."

"I suppose you're one of those people who believes that only God is entitled to exact revenge."

"Not at all, Mrs Rendell. I believe in punishment, as determined by the law. I believe in a fair trial held before a jury. That way the jury decides what happens, just as a jury will decide what happens to you."

She smiled and shook her head. "They won't, Mrs Blakely, because you're the only one who knows what's happened. The police haven't got no evidence, so they can't prove anything. Twenty years later, there's no evidence at all. I've got away with it all this time!" She gave a sinister laugh. "I planned it all so careful, you see. No one had any idea, and they never will!"

"They'll have my word for it."

She took a step closer to me and quietly muttered, "They'll never hear about it."

CHAPTER 52

I heard Mrs Oliver's key turn in the lock. A look of alarm flashed across Mrs Rendell's face, but she kept her eyes fixed on mine.

"Mrs Blakely?" the housekeeper called out. I guessed she was calling up the stairs, expecting me to be in my room. "There was a problem with the telegram. The machine's not working at the post office!"

I felt my heart sink to my feet.

Mrs Rendell was right. I was the only person who knew what she'd done.

I needed to get out into the hallway so I could ask her to summon the police. "I'm in the front room, Mrs Oliver!" I called out. "Stay where you are, though. I need to speak with you."

I stepped past Mrs Rendell, but as I did so I realised I had made a grave mistake. I knew in an instant that I should never have turned my back on her.

I only became aware of the searing pain in my head once I was lying on the floor. I heard a loud shriek, which must have come from Mrs Oliver as she stepped into the room.

There was a shout, then a scuffle. I managed to lift my head, but the pain made my vision swim. As the struggle continued, I managed to push myself up into a sitting position. My head felt thick and my stomach nauseous, but I knew I had to help Mrs Oliver.

Both women were behind me at this point, Mrs Rendell still brandishing the poker she had snatched up from the fireplace. Her face was gripped with rage and the blows she was inflicting on Mrs Oliver were severe. The housekeeper was shielding herself with her arms but was already half slumped onto the floor.

It occurred to me that Mrs Rendell could murder the pair of us and still escape undetected. No one would ever know that she had been at the house. She could get away with murder all over again.

I launched myself at her before I was even able to stand properly, determined to bring her down to the ground. The poker came crashing down on my back as I pummelled her, but then we were both on the floor and she had lost her grip on the poker.

Her limbs kicked and flailed, and she yanked at my hair. Somehow, she got a hand up to my throat. She pushed me off her as I struggled for air. She might have been older and smaller than me, but she was certainly stronger. A gruesome grimace was fixed across her face.

I turned away, trying to pull her hand away from my throat but painfully aware that I was giving her the space she needed to get up off the floor again.

"No!" shouted Mrs Oliver, hurling herself on top of us both. Mrs Rendell couldn't fight the two of us at the same time, and she was forced to release her grip on my neck. I staggered to my feet, breathing heavily, my hair falling into my eyes.

"Get help, Mrs Blakely!" cried Mrs Oliver, who had somehow managed to sit on top of Mrs Rendell.

"Can you hold her?" I asked, worried Mrs Rendell would get the better of her as soon as I left the house.

She grabbed the poker, which had fallen nearby, and nodded in reply. "I'll try my best. Go next door; I'm sure Mrs Derwent will be at home."

Mrs Rendell tried to wrestle herself free and Mrs Oliver was almost shifted out of position.

"Quick, Mrs Blakely! Run!"

CHAPTER 53

"You've a nasty bump on your head, Mrs Blakely," said the doctor, closing his medical bag. "But, quite miraculously, you don't appear to be suffering from concussion at all. My advice would be three days' bed rest, as a precaution."

"*Three days?*" I protested.

"You must listen to the doctor, Penny," said James, giving my hand a squeeze as he sat beside me on the settee.

"And three days for Mrs Oliver, too," added the doctor.

"I shall be more than happy with that!" She smiled from her seat in the easy chair next to the fire.

"Perhaps you should take two weeks' holiday, Mrs Oliver," James said. "You saved Mrs Blakely's life, after all."

"Oh, nonsense! I only did what anyone else would have done. Thank you for your kind offer, though, sir. I shall enjoy having two weeks off."

"Three days of rest sounds like a lifetime to me," I said. "Besides, I want to see Mrs Rendell in court."

"You'll probably have to miss her initial court appearance,

Penny, but I'm sure you'll be well enough to attend the full trial."

"It's just a bump on the head; nothing more. You mustn't let me detain you from joining your colleagues at New Street station, James," I said. "I expect you'll want to deal with Mrs Rendell yourself."

"Actually, I can't say that I do. Sergeant Hillcock will be more than capable of managing her while I stay here with you. She'll need to be handed over to H Division for formal questioning about Mary Steinway's death."

"I hope she tells them what she told me."

"Yes. A confession would save everyone a good deal of time."

"She seemed rather proud of herself for getting away with her crime for so long. It wouldn't surprise me if she became quite boastful about what she did."

"And possibly relieved at finally being able to tell people," added James. "Can you imagine sitting on such a dreadful secret for so long?"

"She hid it remarkably well," I said. "I can still recall that meeting at her home when she spoke so highly of Mary, and her subsequent visit to tell me how cruel Revd Loach had been. And to think that I believed her!"

"People don't get away with such heinous crimes without being capable of great manipulation. Her every move was calculated to throw you off the scent."

"Her poor husband." I thought of Mr Rendell, who was most likely leading children around the zoo on the back of an elephant at this very moment. "He has no idea what his wife has done, or who she really is."

"Possibly not, but he's known her a very long time. Perhaps he has some inkling after all. We'll have to interview him, of course."

"And at least Sir Octavius has also been arrested. Do you

think he'll confess?"

"Not with the expensive lawyer he has assisting him at the present time. But as the threat of the gallows draws ever nearer, he may change his tune."

"And Burns," I said. "I suppose I should tell him that I found out what happened to Molly."

"I shouldn't worry about doing that."

"But I think Molly had a son, Harry. He lives with Mrs Garner. I should tell Burns about him."

"Do you think Harry will welcome that?"

I tried to imagine being told that Mr Burns was my father, it wasn't an encouraging thought. "I don't know... I shall have to give it some consideration." I gave a sigh. "I suppose I should feel happy that there have been two arrests, and that we finally found Mary Steinway's murderer." I forced a smile. "But I don't feel as content as I ought to, for some reason."

"You've suffered a severe blow to the head, Penny. You're likely to feel a little strange for a few days. That's why the doctor ordered bed rest."

"I don't think that's it," I responded. "What I feel is sadness. For Mary Steinway and for Robert Masefield. And also for William Derricks and John Cecil-Palmer. Their deaths were all avoidable. They never should have happened."

"No, they shouldn't. They were victims of two wicked people, both of whom refused to be held accountable for their actions. Despite my years of experience, I always find it quite shocking to see how much damage people like Mrs Rendell and Sir Octavius can cause."

I thought of Mary Steinway and how the death of her mother had triggered a series of tragic events. Would she have been married to someone as cruel as Revd Loach if her mother had survived? If her husband had been a kind man, would her baby have lived?

Despair, and the intemperance it had led to, had sealed

Mary's fate. What a great tragedy it was that no one had been able to save her. She had been unable to save herself: without a husband or a reputation, she had become worthless in society's eyes.

I tried to console myself with the thought that I had helped ensure she wouldn't be forgotten.

CHAPTER 54

"Now, Penelope, I need to have a word with you," said Eliza two days later as she and Francis stood in our front room. "We've just come here from Father's, and he tells us he has no intention of going back to South America just yet."

"You've seen him?"

"Of course I've seen him. I paid him a visit after you told me he was about to travel back to Amazonia. I'm sure you said he'd bought a ticket, but he said he had done nothing of the sort when I mentioned it!"

"Oh."

I noticed a smile on Francis's lips, which suggested he had an inkling of what I'd done.

"I'm not sure what happened, Penelope," continued Eliza, "but you must have got yourself muddled."

"How was he when you visited him?"

"As confused as I was!"

"But was he pleased to see you?"

"He was, actually. And..." Her eyes narrowed. "Just a moment, Penelope. Did you set this whole thing up?"

"No."

"You did!"

"I did nothing of the sort."

"But you misled me."

"Did I?"

"Yes! You misled me by saying that Father was about to leave."

"Perhaps I got muddled, as you say."

"You told me that so I would go and visit him."

"You had no intention of visiting him the last time we spoke."

"Exactly! And that's why you lied about his departure."

"I'm sure Penny didn't *lie*," interjected Francis.

"All right, it was a *fib* then!" responded Eliza. "I knew I would feel awful if I didn't see him before he left, and that's why I decided to visit him. Now you've made a fool of me, Penelope. I'm not happy about it at all!"

"Penny hasn't made a fool of you, Eliza," said Francis. "He was pleased to see you, and I think you were also pleased to see him."

Eliza sniffed and pursed her lips. Francis and I exchanged a smile.

The door opened and James stepped into the front room with Father, who was grinning broadly.

"Look who I found climbing out of a cab outside," said James.

"I'm sorry to turn up unexpectedly," said my father, "but when Eliza said she was heading over here I decided to follow her."

"This is all Penelope's fault," replied my sister. "She told me a fib so I would visit you!"

"Well done, Penny," chuckled my father. "She always was the mischievous one."

"I'd have to agree with that," said James.

"As would I," added Eliza.

"Well, I don't!" I protested.

"I'm afraid you're outnumbered, Penny," laughed James. "Will you be joining us for dinner, Eliza? Francis? Mr Green?"

My sister and father glanced warily at each other, then turned to face me.

"Yes, they will," I said brightly.

"Excellent!" said my father. "Truly excellent." His lower lip wobbled a little, then he dabbed at his eyes with his handkerchief. "Not that I deserve to sit down to dinner with my two delightful daughters and their husbands... Oh, apologies, Francis. You're not a husband yet, are you? I suppose 'suitor' would be the correct word."

"Francis is a *friend*," Eliza corrected.

"I see. And is that what he thinks, too?" asked my father.

"Of course," responded Francis with a bashful smile.

"Mr Green," said James, keen to save their blushes. "Did you happen to bring any of your coca wine with you?"

"No, I didn't."

"Thank goodness for that! I'll find us something decent to drink."

THE END

IN MEMORY OF

Graham Stanford Letts
February - April 1914

HISTORICAL NOTE

❀

During my research for this book, I encountered two spellings of Ratcliffe: one with the *e* at the end and one without. It will be obvious to you that I chose the former, but either name serves well for this ancient road with a colourful history. Its location close to the London docks made it a popular spot for sailors seeking entertainment with alcohol, opium and sex workers in plentiful supply. The highway gained notoriety in 1811 for the Ratcliffe Highway Murders when seven people were killed in two attacks on two families twelve days apart. The supposed suspect, John Williams, took his own life before standing trial and he was buried with a stake through his heart at the crossroads of Commercial Road and New Cannon Street.

If this wasn't macabre enough, Williams remains were accidentally disturbed in 1886 when a trench was being dug in the road. His skull ended up as a 'trophy' in the nearby Crown & Dolphin pub for a time. The pub still stands but the whereabouts of the skull these days are unknown. It's quite possible that John Williams wasn't the murderer at all, the author P.D. James asserts this in a book she wrote about the case, *The Maul and the Pear Tree*.

Ratcliffe Highway was also home to the famous Jamrach's exotic wildlife store which supplied animals to fairs, circuses and wealthy clients. In 1857, a tiger escaped from Jamrach's and snatched up a passing boy. Fortunately, the boy was rescued unharmed and the tiger was sold to Wombwell's circus. A statue was made to commemorate the event.

Attempts to clean up the highway's reputation in the later 19th century were partially successful and sections of it were renamed in an attempt to remove the association with the notorious highway name. The street's colourful character vanished for good when the area was badly bombed in the Blitz. Today's highway follows the same route that it always did, but most of it has been rebuilt and is unrecognisable from its 19th century days.

The White Swan pub, known as 'Paddy's Goose', was described in *Dickens's Dictionary of London 1888* as 'once the uproarious rendezvous of half the tramps and thieves of London'. By the late nineteenth century, the antics within this infamous pub were on the wane and it was lost with much of the rest of the street after WWII.

The Tower of London station, where Penny meets Burns, was built by the Metropolitan Railway in 1882 and closed two years later because a new station, built by the Metropolitan District Railway (there's a subtle difference), opened close by. This second station was called Mark Lane station and became known as Tower Hill station in the 1940s.

However, with not enough room for expansion, Tower Hill station was closed in 1967 and a new one built on the location of the original Tower of London station. When you get the tube to the Tower of London today, you're on the site of the first station which was built in 1882. It has some of London's Roman wall incorporated into its structure and there is a section of the Roman wall visible outside Tower Hill station too.

Hampstead, the home of Mary Steinway's sister, became popular in the 18th century when people went there to take the 'chalybeate' waters - the name means the water has iron in it. The area's popularity declined by the end of the 19th century as people began to favour more fashionable locations such as Tunbridge Wells in Kent. This didn't bother Hampstead though which, by then, had lots of large, fancy houses from a Victorian building spree; the area has been attracting the famous and wealthy ever since.

Well-known past residents include John Keats, John Constable, Daphne du Maurier and Sigmund Freud among many others.

Hampstead Heath is close by and well worth a visit. The earliest mention of it is in the 10th century when King Ethelred the Unready gifted one of his servants some land there.

London Zoo was founded as a 'scientific zoo' on the site it occupies today in Regent's Park, it opened to the public in 1847. By the 1870s it was entertaining its visitors with elephant and camel rides for children and monkeys dressed in costume. The only known photograph of a quagga, a sub-species of zebra, was taken at the zoo in 1864. The animal was sadly hunted to extinction by 1883. Famous animal residents at London Zoo have included Jumbo the Elephant, Guy the Gorilla and Chi Chi the Panda.

The Royal Courts of Justice, where Sir Octavius has to attend the court case, sit close to where The Strand becomes Fleet

Street. The building was built in the Victorian Gothic style in the 1870s. The reason its appearance is cathedral-like is because the architect, George Edmund Street, usually designed churches. The building has been added to over the years and is apparently one of the largest courts in Europe. The High Court and Court of Appeal sit here among others - they are all civil courts, not criminal.

Penny visits a few churches in this book: St Paul's, St Stephen's and All Saint's all existed but were lost during twentieth century rebuilding in the suburb of St John's Wood. St Saviour's Church in Chalk Farm, the church of Reverend Loach, still stands although his vicarage has been demolished.

Strychnine is obtained from the Strychnos genus of plants and is commonly used as a pesticide. It also had a medicinal use over the years and was once used by landlords to flavour watered down beer. In Brighton in the early 1870s, the 'chocolate cream killer', Christiana Edmunds, embarked on a campaign of poisoning after being rejected by her married lover. She laced chocolate creams with strychnine and placed the boxes on confectionary shop shelves and sent them to prominent people. A number of people were taken ill and, sadly, a four-year-old boy died.

The Staplehurst train accident happened in Kent on 9th June 1865. Workmen took up the track on a bridge but this was not communicated to the driver of a Dover to London train which Dickens was returning from Paris on with his mistress, Ellen Ternan, and her mother. The train derailed and some of the carriages plunged into the river. Dickens apparently did what he could to help including bringing water to trapped passengers by filling his top hat with water from the river. Forty people were injured and ten lost their lives. It's said that Dickens was deeply affected by the tragedy and that it haunted him until his death five years later.

Vin Mariani Coca wine was a popular 19th century drink created by a French chemist and made from Bordeaux wine and coca leaves. The ethanol in the wine extracted the cocaine from the leaves. It was said to boost energy and mood and was endorsed by Pope Leo XIII who appeared on its advertisements. Pemberton's French Wine Coca was the US version first produced in 1885. When some regions of the US brought in prohibition legislation, Pemberton created a non-alcoholic version: Coca-Cola.

In the 19th and early 20th centuries, many poor London families went 'hopping' - a working holiday every September to pick the hop harvest in Kent. Hop flowers are used for brewing beer. These breaks provided families with a much needed break from the cramped, polluted slums and offered fresh air and plenty of beer. Extra trains were even laid on - the 'hopping special' - to take the Londoners down to Kent. These hordes of Londoners weren't always welcome - their arrival sometimes raised tensions with the locals. But before mechanisation it was the only way to get all the hops harvested. George Orwell took a keen interest in writing about London's poor and he immersed himself with their ways of life - including hop picking in Kent in 1931. He kept a diary of his time there.

If *Murder in Ratcliffe* is the first Penny Green book you've read, then you may find the following historical background interesting. It's compiled from the historical notes published in the previous books in the series:

Women journalists in the nineteenth century were not as scarce as people may think. In fact they were numerous enough by 1898 for Arnold Bennett to write *Journalism for Women: A Practical Guide* in which he was keen to raise the standard of women's journalism:-

"The women-journalists as a body have faults... They seem to me to be traceable either to an imperfect development of the sense of order, or to a certain lack of self-control."

Eliza Linton became the first salaried female journalist in Britain when she began writing for *the Morning Chronicle* in 1851. She was a prolific writer and contributor to periodicals for many years including Charles Dickens' magazine *Household Words*. George Eliot – her real name was Mary Anne Evans - is most famous for novels such as *Middlemarch*, however she also became assistant editor of *The Westminster Review* in 1852.

In the United States Margaret Fuller became the *New York Tribune*'s first female editor in 1846. Intrepid journalist Nellie Bly worked in Mexico as a foreign correspondent for the *Pittsburgh Despatch* in the 1880s before writing for *New York World* and feigning insanity to go undercover and investigate reports of brutality at a New York asylum. Later, in 1889-90, she became a household name by setting a world record for travelling around the globe in seventy-two days.

The iconic circular Reading Room at the British Museum was in use from 1857 until 1997. During that time, it was also used as a filming location and has been referenced in many works of fiction. The Reading Room has been closed since 2014 but it's recently been announced that it will reopen and display some of the museum's permanent collections. It could be a while yet until we're able to step inside it but I'm looking forward to it!

The Museum Tavern, where Penny and James enjoy a drink, is a well-preserved Victorian pub opposite the British Museum. Although a pub was first built here in the eighteenth century much of the current pub (including its name) dates back to 1855. Celebrity drinkers here are said to have included Arthur Conan Doyle and Karl Marx.

Publishing began in Fleet Street in the 1500s and by the twentieth century the street was the hub of the British press. However, newspapers began moving away in the 1980s to bigger premises. Nowadays just a few publishers remain in Fleet Street but the many pubs and bars once frequented by journalists – including the pub Ye Olde Cheshire Cheese - are still popular with city workers.

Penny Green lives in Milton Street in Cripplegate which was one of the areas worst hit by bombing during the Blitz in the Second World War and few original streets remain. Milton Street was known as Grub Street in the eighteenth century and was famous as a home to impoverished writers at the time. The street had a long association with writers and was home to Anthony Trollope among many others. A small stretch of Milton Street remains but the 1960s Barbican development has been built over the bombed remains.

Plant hunting became an increasingly commercial enterprise as the nineteenth century progressed. Victorians were fascinated by exotic plants and, if they were wealthy enough, they had their own glasshouses built to show them off. Plant hunters were employed by Kew Gardens, companies such as Veitch Nurseries or wealthy individuals to seek out exotic specimens in places such as South America and the Himalayas. These plant hunters took great personal risks to collect their plants and some perished on their travels. The

Travels and Adventures of an Orchid Hunter by Albert Millican is worth a read. Written in 1891 it documents his journeys in Colombia and demonstrates how plant hunting became little short of pillaging. Some areas he travelled to had already lost their orchids to plant hunters and Millican himself spent several months felling 4,000 trees to collect 10,000 plants. Even after all this plundering many of the orchids didn't survive the trip across the Atlantic to Britain. Plant hunters were not always welcome: Millican had arrows fired at him as he navigated rivers, had his camp attacked one night and was eventually killed during a fight in a Colombian tavern.

My research for The Penny Green series has come from sources too numerous to list in detail, but the following books have been very useful: *A Brief History of Life in Victorian Britain* by Michael Patterson, *London in the Nineteenth Century* by Jerry White, *London in 1880* by Herbert Fry, *London a Travel Guide through Time* by Dr Matthew Green, *Women of the Press in Nineteenth-Century Britain* by Barbara Onslow, *A Very British Murder* by Lucy Worsley, *The Suspicions of Mr Whicher* by Kate Summerscale, *Journalism for Women: A Practical Guide* by Arnold Bennett, *Seventy Years a Showman* by Lord George Sanger, *Dottings of a Dosser* by Howard Goldsmid, *Travels and Adventures of an Orchid Hunter* by Albert Millican, *The Bitter Cry of Outcast London* by Andrew Mearns, *The Complete History of Jack the Ripper* by Philip Sugden, *The Necropolis Railway* by Andrew Martin, *The Diaries of Hannah Cullwick, Victorian Maidservant* edited by Liz Stanley, *Mrs Woolf & the Servants* by Alison Light, *Revelations of a Lady Detective* by William Stephens Hayward, *A is for Arsenic* by Kathryn Harkup, *In an Opium Factory* by Rudyard Kipling, *Drugging a Nation: The Story of China and the Opium Curse* by Samuel Merwin, *Confessions of an Opium Eater* by Thomas de Quincy, *The Pinkertons: The Detective Dynasty That Made History* by James D Horan,

The Napoleon of Crime by Ben Macintyre and *The Code Book: The Secret History of Codes and Code-breaking* by Simon Singh, *Dying for Victorian Medicine, English Anatomy and its Trade in the Dead Poor* by Elizabeth T. Hurren, *Tales from the Workhouse – True Tales from the Depths of Poverty* by James Greenwood, Mary Higgs and others, *Sickness and Cruelty in the Workhouse - The True Story of a Victorian Workhouse Doctor* by Joseph Rogers, *Mord Em'ly* by William Pitt Ridge, *Alice Diamond And The Forty Elephants: Britain's First Female Crime Syndicate* by Brian Macdonald, *The Maul and the Pear Tree* by P.D. James, *The Five* by Hallie Rubenhold, and *Dickens's Dictionary of London 1888*. The *British Newspaper Archive* is also an invaluable resource.

THE EGYPTIAN MYSTERY

A Penny Green Mystery Book 11

☙❦☙

"Dead men don't just walk out of hotels..." Penny faces her most baffling case yet.

A famous Egyptologist is found dead in his hotel room. Then his body vanishes. With his wife missing too, news reporter Penny is perplexed.

Can the Egyptologist really be dead? Or is it an elaborate ruse? Evidence is thin on the ground and Penny soon discovers that some people are not who they claim to be.

Desperate for answers, Penny takes the risk of confronting those close to her. In a test of her resolve, she's forced to find her own way through a maze of lies and false identities. Who can she trust? And where does the real danger lie?

Find out more:

mybook.to/penny-green-egyptian

THANK YOU

Thank you for reading this Penny Green mystery, I hope you enjoyed it!

Would you like to know when I release new books? Here are some ways to stay updated:

- Join my mailing list and receive a free short mystery: *The Belgrave Square Murder:* emilyorgan.com/the-belgrave-square-murder
- Like my Facebook page: facebook.com/ emilyorganwriter
- Follow me on Goodreads: goodreads.com/emily_organ
- Follow me on BookBub: bookbub.com/authors/emily-organ
- View my other books here: emilyorgan.com

And if you have a moment, I would be very grateful if you would leave a quick review online. Honest reviews of my books help other readers discover them too!

You can discover more about the Penny Green Series by scanning this code:

GET A FREE SHORT MYSTERY

❦

Want more of Penny Green? Sign up to my mailing list and I'll send you my short mystery *The Belgrave Square Murder*!

A wealthy businessman is found dead in Belgrave Square on a foggy November night. Was the motive robbery? Or something more personal? Penny Green tries to report on the case, but no one wants to cooperate. How can she investigate when there's so little to go on?

Visit my website for more details:
emilyorgan.com/the-belgrave-square-murder

Or scan the code on the following page:

ALSO BY EMILY ORGAN

Augusta Peel Series:

Death in Soho
Murder in the Air
The Bloomsbury Murder
The Tower Bridge Murder
Death in Westminster
Murder on the Thames
The Baker Street Murders

Churchill & Pemberley Series:

Tragedy at Piddleton Hotel
Murder in Cold Mud
Puzzle in Poppleford Wood
Trouble in the Churchyard
Wheels of Peril
The Poisoned Peer
Fiasco at the Jam Factory
Disaster at the Christmas Dinner

Christmas Calamity at the Vicarage (novella)

Writing as Martha Bond

Lottie Sprigg Travels Mystery Series:

Murder in Venice
Murder in Paris
Murder in Cairo
Murder in Monaco
Murder in Vienna

Lottie Sprigg Country House Mystery Series:

Murder in the Library
Murder in the Grotto
Murder in the Maze
Murder in the Bay